The Doctor's Reckoning

A Cyrus Darian Medical Thriller

Book 1

Arsheeya Mashaw

Ari Mashaw

AAPRESS

This is a work of fiction. Names, characters, places, and incidents are products of the authors' imagination or are used fictitiously. Any resemblance to actual events, locales, or persons, living or dead, is entirely coincidental.

Published by Double A Press

www.doubleapress.com

Paperback: ISBN: 979-8-9940910-1-2

Ebook: ISBN: 979-8-9940910-0-5

Cover design by Ian Koviak

Formatted with Vellum

1

Fall, 2010

A low groan drifted through the trees, ragged and strange.

At first, Cyrus thought it was an animal: "U-u-ck... u-u-ck." But as he lay still inside the tent, the sound sharpened into something unmistakably human. "*F-u-u-u-u-ck.*"

He jolted upright, the thin nylon tent fabric glowing with morning light. Through the half-unzipped flap, he glimpsed the trunks of gigantic Ponderosa pines gilded by the sun, their stillness at odds with the raw edge in that voice. It wasn't just someone shouting, it had weight. Pain. Panic. Years of medical training had tuned his ear to those cries. Someone needed help.

He shoved free of the sleeping bag and lurched toward the flap, still in his T-shirt and underwear. No time for pants. Grabbing his boots, he ducked out into the open, blinking at the sudden brightness. The ground bit cold against his feet as he broke into a run, hopping as he forced one boot on, chasing the sound.

His shin caught a stump hidden in the brush. Pain lanced up his leg as he tumbled hard, scraping his elbows and landing in a cloud of dust.

"Crap," he muttered, sitting up. He jammed the other boot on properly this time, cinched both laces with quick, practiced fingers, and rose to his feet.

That voice was still echoing in his head. Someone was out there, and they didn't have time to wait.

Cyrus ran down the incline, the brisk morning air of the southeastern Oregon forest rushing across his bare legs like a cold stream. Branches slapped at his arms as he tore through the underbrush, eyes locked on the direction of the sound.

About twenty yards ahead, the ground suddenly gave way to a steep five-foot drop. He skidded to a halt at the edge, swinging his arms to catch his balance just in time.

Below, in a narrow clearing, a man lay face down, his upper body draped over a thick tree branch. His limbs twitched with each attempt to move. A dark blue backpack was lying several feet beyond him, as if flung there during a fall.

"Help," the man gasped, his voice strained and breathy. ". . . this is bad. This really sucks."

Cyrus was already scrambling down the slope.

Once on more level ground, he hastily drew closer to the man, then crouched on his haunches, shaking the man's shoulder. "Hey, I'm here to help you. My name is Cyrus . . . Can you hear me?"

"D-u-u-de," the man slurred, his voice weak and distant.

Cyrus dropped to one knee. "Hold still, I want to make sure your spine is okay," he said, his voice calm but focused.

He gently cupped the man's head, keeping his neck in line. First rule: stabilize the spine until you know it's safe to move the patient.

"What's your name?"

The man groaned. "Brent . . ."

Cyrus nodded. *Alert and oriented, he knows his name. Good sign.*

"Okay, Brent, squeeze my fingers." He offered his hand and felt a shaky but coordinated grip.

Motor function intact. That's two for two.

"Can you move your toes for me?"

Brent's boots twitched.

Legs are working too. No obvious sign of spinal cord injury.

Cyrus leaned over and gently palpated the man's spine, pressing along each vertebra. Brent winced but didn't cry out.

"No sharp pain in the midline," Cyrus muttered. "Doesn't feel like a fracture."

He exhaled. "Okay, I'm going to roll you off the branch nice and easy. Stay with me."

He moved one hand to cup Brent's shoulder, slid the other beneath his hip, and carefully eased him off the heavy limb.

Brent groaned as Cyrus rolled him onto his back, but Cyrus stayed focused. The man's shirt was torn across the chest and streaked with dirt, the once-white fabric now scuffed and gray with grit. He was rail-thin, with long brown hair and a beard.

Since Brent was breathing and had a decent pulse, Cyrus did a quick secondary trauma survey of his body. No bruises or cuts on his head. He pressed gently on Brent's shoulders, probing down to the chest until he felt a crunching sensation on the right.

"Sweet mother of . . . *agh!*" Brent cried. "What the heck is wrong with you?"

Cyrus paused. Brent's breathing had just then become shallow and rapid. "I think you broke some ribs. Can you take a deep breath?"

Brent took a sharp, gasping inhale, and fell into an even faster rhythm of breathing. Cyrus placed his ear flush to Brent's right chest. No air movement. Just silence.

Absent breath sounds.

He sat back, heart pounding. Based on the short, labored breathing, the silence on auscultation, the mechanism of injury, and the broken ribs he could palpate, Cyrus calculated the grim likelihood: a collapsed lung, definitely a tension pneumothorax. A pocket of air had leaked into the space between Brent's lung and chest wall, trapped there like a balloon swelling tighter with every breath. The pressure was crushing the lung flat and pushing against his heart, leaving no room for either to work.

There was only one treatment, let that trapped air escape so the lung could expand again.

If he didn't act quickly, Brent would be dead within minutes. But instead, he froze. For a second, he didn't move.

This wasn't the plan. He'd promised himself, no more of this. But here it was anyway, and he couldn't let this man die.

He drew in a breath, held it, let it go.

Then he grabbed the edges of the torn fabric and ripped open the shirt, exposing Brent's chest. Superficial cuts and a visible depression on the right side of the chest showed where he'd impacted the branch.

Frantically, Cyrus looked around, his eyes stopping at Brent's backpack. Yanking it toward him, he dumped the contents onto the ground. First, a glass bottle hit the ground with a *clink*; a fifth of vodka. An old flannel jacket tumbled out next to it along with smelly socks and a water bottle. Cyrus shook the bag more, a porn magazine entitled *Jugs*, a Zip-top bag of granola. Finally, out fell a small syringe with clear liquid contents and an orange cap. Cyrus identified it immediately, insulin.

Diabetic, Cyrus thought, turning the syringe over in his hand.

He glanced back at Brent, and this time saw a pocketknife clamped to his belt. Without hesitating, Cyrus pounced, tugging at the knife. As he opened it, he pivoted again toward the scattered contents of the backpack.

Sweat trickled down his face, getting in his eyes. He reached his bare arm across his forehead and wiped the sweat away. Taking a deep breath, he plucked the insulin syringe from the ground. The tiny plastic cylinder was no longer than his pinky, with a small plunger protruding from the back. The orange cap protected a very small needle, like a spine from a cactus. Deftly, Cyrus used the pocketknife to cut the needle from the top of the syringe. He pushed the plunger forward to get rid of the liquid insulin, which squirted out impotently onto the ground. He removed the plunger from an empty cylinder the thickness of a pencil, now open at both ends. He pivoted back toward Brent, the open pocketknife in one hand and the cylinder in the other.

He froze again. "Damn, this wound needs to be clean."

There was no time to lose at this point; Brent's breath was coming in short, quick huffs. Cyrus pivoted away from Brent again and snatched up the bottle of vodka. With shaking hands, he opened the bottle and poured the contents onto his hands, the knife blade, and the cylinder, the crisp alcohol burning his dry skin. Finally, he poured the remaining vodka over the right side of Brent's bare chest.

Cyrus crouched over Brent, his shaking fingers holding the knife inches above Brent's skin. Cyrus took a deep breath to steady himself, and with a swift motion plunged the knife into Brent's chest between the second and third ribs. There was a crunching sound and a hiss of air like a punctured tire. Cyrus deftly pulled out the knife, inserting his finger into the hole. He probed his finger between two ribs and ripped through intercostal muscle to the warm, moist, soft tissue of Brent's lungs. With his other hand, he slid the insulin syringe into the hole while pulling his finger out, substituting the empty cylinder, which would equalize the pressure in Brent's chest.

The world paused as Cyrus watched Brent's face. Moments became years until Brent gasped, like the breath one took after swimming underwater the length of a pool.

Cyrus collapsed onto his butt; his relief first displayed as a smile then as laughter. A laugh so loud it made Brent open his eyes in alarm.

"Dude, what the hell is going on?" Brent exclaimed, his voice shaky. His eyes turned from Cyrus to his bare chest with a cylinder poking out. "What the hell just *happened*?"

Cyrus caught a faint Southern drawl in Brent's trembling voice, a lilt that stretched his incredulous question with an unexpected, drawn-out cadence.

Cyrus's laugh slowed but his smile remained. "I don't know, man, you tell me. It looks like you fell hard onto that tree limb and gave yourself several broken ribs and a tension pneumothorax."

"Tension . . . *what* now?" Brent stared at the open cylinder rising up and down with each breath, like a fishing bobber in the water.

"You had air trapped in your chest that caused your lung to collapse. I had to put a tube in to get the air out so you could breathe again." Cyrus clapped him on the leg. "I need to close the tube now. Can you take a deep breath?"

Brent breathed deep, wincing, and Cyrus put the syringe's plunger back into the open end jutting from Brent's chest.

Cyrus spoke, calm and measured, as he checked his finished work. "Alright, Brent, we're set. I'm hoping this holds until we get you to a hospital. If it doesn't, we may need to move faster than I'd like. I was already thinking about hitchhiking once we hit the road."

Brent winced, then shook his head. "No need. My truck's not far from here. Just up the trail."

He cringed as he tried to adjust his body, and Cyrus helped him sit up and rest his back against a nearby tree. The two men sat quietly for a while, the injured man panting.

The breeze stirred the tree branches above, and the birds chirped.

Brent finally spoke, his southern twang carrying. "I was just walking here, minding my own business when I heard a tree crack. It started falling right next to me, man. I was like *'Aaah!'* and started running. Next thing I know, I trip down that hill, go airborne, and fall onto that tree branch. Man, did that hurt. Then you show up."

Cyrus held out his right hand to shake. But when Brent tried to move his right hand he winced in pain.

"Oh, sorry," Cyrus said, dropping his hand to his side. "I'm Cyrus."

Brent squinted at him, as if appraising the absurd sight of the half-dressed man crouched in front of him. After a long pause, he finally broke the silence with a smirk. "Dude, why are you in your underwear?"

Cyrus smiled and shot back, "Jeez, Brent, I think what you're trying to say is 'Hey, Cyrus thanks for leaving your campsite so quickly to save my life that you didn't even have time to dress!'"

They both laughed.

Even after narrowly escaping death, Brent still managed to crack jokes. Cyrus found himself liking the guy; his relaxed demeanor and easy smile, in spite of his recent trauma, made him approachable. Cyrus took in Brent's wiry frame and sun-blotched skin. He looked like he was in his early thirties, with gray eyes and long brown hair, unevenly parted down the middle, that fell to his shoulders and framed his face. A thick, curly beard, gave him a rugged appearance. Despite his rustic look, Brent's expression was open and inviting, with a curiosity in his eyes that made Cyrus feel at ease.

Cyrus got up and inspected Brent's wound to ensure the impromptu chest tube remained in place. "We're going to have to get definitive treatment for this at a hospital. Do you think you could walk?"

"I don't know, man, can you help me up?" Brent grunted as he attempted to stand.

Cyrus was short, only five-foot-five, so even with Brent's arm slung over his shoulders, he had to stretch to keep him upright. They staggered together toward where the backpack had landed.

Cyrus steadied Brent until he found his balance, then let go and stuffed Brent's scattered belongings back into the old blue backpack.

Then he draped the red-and-black flannel jacket over Brent's shoulders.

"Sorry I had to tear your shirt," he murmured.

Brent gave a weak nod.

Cyrus shouldered Brent's pack himself. "It'll be a while before we get you to a hospital," he said. "My campsite's up that hill. I need to grab my things, but I don't want to leave you alone with that chest tube."

Brent managed a crooked grin. "Up a hill with busted ribs and a giant plastic cylinder hanging out of my chest? Sure, why not? I've always wanted to try extreme hiking."

Huffing with each step, Brent pointed behind them and remarked, "Think REI carries this model of chest tube? Might make a killing." He paused to catch his breath. "So, what are you, some kind of doctor yourself?"

"I used to be," Cyrus replied tersely.

Brent frowned. "What do you mean used to be?"

"It's a long story, Brent, let's just say my path veered." Then Cyrus changed the subject. "What were you doing out here anyway?"

"Dude, I've been out on a vision quest, man," Brent's gray eyes widened with excitement. "It's where you go out on your own in nature and spend time alone fasting, so you can get some insight into what life is about. Sounds awesome, right? But I only got as far as getting a new-mow-thora-thingy, or whatever the crap you called it."

Cyrus chuckled, and they continued their slow progress to his campsite. At the peak of the incline, Brent collapsed onto a log to rest, breathing heavily. As he rested, Cyrus looked down at himself, remembering he didn't have any pants on. Smiling, chagrined, Cyrus jogged the rest of the way to his camp to locate the missing pants, tucked safely in his backpack, and slid them on.

Fully clothed, Cyrus went back to check on Brent. Unfortunately, things seemed to be getting worse. His chest was heaving harder now, his face pale and slick with sweat. Worry spiked deep within Cyrus's chest; he crouched beside him and pressed his ear against the right side of Brent's upper back, listening intently.

The faint, crackling rasp of breath was even weaker than before. Cyrus pulled back, his brow furrowed. "Your breath sounds are decreasing," he said grimly. "The pneumothorax must be getting worse. The tube I put in needs a one-way valve to work right."

Without waiting for a response, he sprinted to his backpack and dropped to his knees, tearing through it in frantic handfuls. He yanked out his multi-tool knife, set it aside, and kept digging. Finally, his fingers closed around a roll of duct tape. He snatched it out but cursed under his breath.

No plastic gloves.

He glanced over his shoulder at Brent. "We need something like a latex glove, or even a condom. I hope we can make it to your truck with time to drive and get some at a store."

Brent, despite his exhaustion, managed a weak grin. He reached into the back pocket of his jeans and pulled out a battered wallet.

"Dude, I have a condom in here." He flipped it out and handed it to Cyrus. "Be prepared, that's what I always say."

Cyrus let out a shaky breath of relief, snatched the condom, and grabbed the duct tape and his multi-tool knife. Without wasting another second, he set to work.

Cyrus removed the plunger from the syringe and as he worked, he explained quickly, more to keep himself calm than anything else. "The key to the valve is the condom. Once it's unraveled and the tip is cut off." He sliced the end cleanly with the tiny scissors from his multi-tool knife, "you tape it to the end of the tube. It'll act like a one-way valve, letting air escape from your chest cavity but not letting any back in."

He moved with practiced urgency, wrapping duct tape around the cylinder in Brent's chest, making sure each layer was sealed and airtight. When he finished, he stepped back for a moment, inspecting his work with a quick nod of satisfaction.

"Okay," he said, straightening. "Take a few deep breaths for me."

Brent inhaled, and the latex tube fluttered and pulsed with each breath, a thin stream of air hissing out under pressure.

Cyrus bent low again, pressing his ear to Brent's back. After a few long moments, he breathed out a sigh of relief. "That's better. Lung sounds are improving. But the tube's not secured, hopefully it doesn't get pulled out."

Cyrus got to his feet and hastily packed up his campsite, shoving supplies into his backpack with rough efficiency. He hoisted his backpack onto his back with a practiced motion, the familiar weight settling comfortably against his shoulders. He wrapped Brent's dirty blue pack around his front, securing it snugly against his chest, creating a cocoon of gear. The two then navigated the terrain back toward the creek bed; the dual packs forcing Cyrus to sway faintly with each step.

They walked again down the slope to where Cyrus first found Brent, the forest thick around them, and Brent spoke up. "If we follow that dried creek bed for about a mile or so, we'll find the logging road I drove up here on. Then you get to meet Mystique!"

Cyrus turned with a quizzical look. "Mystique? Who the heck is that?"

"My old beater of a truck, man," Brent replied, as if it were an obvious choice to name a vehicle.

Cyrus continued walking but let out an exaggerated sigh, rolling his eyes dramatically as a smirk tugged at the corners of his mouth. He was amused despite himself.

The morning wore on, the heat building as they hiked, sweat trickling down their brows and bodies. The trail wound upward and narrowed before finally opening onto a dirt road, an old logging road, sun-bleached and half reclaimed by time. Grass and weeds crept up through the center and along the edges, where the soil hadn't been compacted by the faded memory of old tires.

Brent let out a relieved but shaky cheer. "Thank Baby Jeebus. We're out of water, and I'm gonna collapse, dude. I can't wait to get in Mystique. I think I left more water with her."

Around a bend, Cyrus spotted what he could only assume was "Mystique." An old white Toyota pickup truck sat crooked on the dirt road, its once-bright paint dulled and coated in a layer of grime. Small scrapes marked the corners, worn into the body by years of hard use. The tires, though worn, still looked tough enough for rough roads.

Relief washed over Cyrus as he tossed the packs into the truck bed, each landing with a satisfying *thud.*

When he turned back, Brent was rummaging through the passenger-side foot well. He gave a cry of delight and pulled out a large jug of water.

Cyrus stood back as Brent drank greedily, tilting the container high, the water spilling down over his mouth and splashing onto his cheeks. He pondered the water-stained face of a man who'd nearly died.

He hadn't meant to get involved. Hadn't meant to care.

He reached into his back pocket and pulled out a creased photograph, its edges softened from folding and unfolding. In it, he stood beside a young woman with long dark hair and warm brown eyes, her arm looped through his. Two children, a boy maybe six and a grinning toddler girl, laughing at something just out of frame. Cyrus barely recognized the man in the center, late thirties, olive skin sunlit against a clean white shirt, short black hair neatly combed, a thin nose, smooth jaw, and eyes that still looked forward with something like hope.

The background of the photo was the county fair. His mind drifted to the time when the picture was taken. A warm dusk, the Ferris wheel turning, Freddie counting bulbs, Samira tugging at his sleeve and waving a sticky prize ribbon she'd won at a game booth.

He leaned toward Juliette. "Don't look now, Juliette, but Ms. Sours is headed our way. Brace for a full town bulletin." Ms. Sours reached them smiling at Juliette, "Dr. Stone, thank you for the home visit for my mother today. It settled her right down." Then she turned to Cyrus. "Oh, hi, Dr. Darian, sorry to interrupt your family time."

"Oh, you're not interrupting, Ms. Sours," he said, "you just saved me from losing again at the ring toss." Ms. Sours laughed. Juliette laughed. Freddie declared that four fish would make a school, and Samira clapped with sticky hands. For a moment everything felt simple and bright.

Brent coughed, and muttered thanks, and the world returned. Sadness rose, sharp in Cyrus's chest. He wiped a tear away with the back of his hand. Then the familiar weight settled on his shoulders.

What if he dies anyway?

He exhaled slowly, already doing the math in his head, signs to watch for, timelines, what he'd do if Brent crashed again.

He had walked away from that world. But maybe that world wasn't done with him.

2

Cyrus gripped the wheel as "Mystique" jostled along the logging road, the forest blurring past in flickers of sun and shadow. The scent of pine filled the cab, but all he could focus on was the rasp of Brent's breathing beside him.

The makeshift chest tube jutted from Brent's right side, taped in place but far from secure. The flannel jacket Cyrus had thrown over him earlier hung open, the fabric pushed aside to clear the tube, leaving it starkly visible against his pale, sweat-slicked chest. Every bump in the road made him flinch, his face tightening in pain. Cyrus kept glancing at the tubing, half-expecting it to shake loose with the next jolt.

Brent took a long drink of water from his bottle and glanced over.

"So," he asked, voice ragged, "how'd a guy like you end up out here anyway?"

Cyrus hesitated; his eyes fixed on the road ahead. "I've been hiking west from Colorado," he said carefully, the words measured. "When I started in Colorado, I just picked a direction," he continued, "I remember feeling like west was far enough from where I started."

Brent tilted his head. "Yeah, but, what made you decide to just hike out in the first place?"

Cyrus sighed long and heavy, eyes fixed on the road ahead. "Sometimes walking away is the only choice you've got," he said at last, the words quiet but firm. After a beat, he added, "Maybe after we get your pneumothorax checked out, I can explain."

Brent studied him for a moment, the smile fading a bit. Then, with a nod and a shift in tone, he asked, "So how long you been out here? Like, actually living in the wild?"

"I didn't keep track of time exactly . . . probably about four months and eight days or so."

Brent winced as the truck jolted, pressing a hand gently to his side. "Jeebus, man," he said through clenched teeth, forcing a crooked grin, "what if you *had* kept track of time exactly? You're weird, dude."

Cyrus chuckled, keeping his eyes on the road. "What about you? Where are you from?"

Brent lit up despite the pained crease in his brow. "Cullman, Alabama, home of the Bearcats, baby!" He winced as the truck jostled. His breathing hitched, a faint wheeze escaping through gritted teeth. "God, this road is not chest-tube friendly," he muttered, half-laughing, half-groaning.

Brent shifted in his seat, taking shallow breaths but still grinning. "Anyway, after I got sick of working for the city, I drove this beast west, hung a Ralph in Winnemucca, ended up in Lakeview. Diabetes flared up, landed me in the hospital out here. Wild, man, middle of nowhere, and they still had insulin."

He didn't wait for a response. His hand pressed lightly to his ribs, and he winced as he adjusted in the seat, but the grin never quite left his face.

"After I got out, I worked at a gas station. Did you know in Oregon you can't pump your own gas? Blew my mind. I became a 'gas jockey.'" He added air quotes with a grin. "Which is just a fancy way of saying I stood around chatting up tourists while I filled their tanks."

Cyrus opened his mouth, but Brent steamrolled ahead.

"One day I was eating lunch at The Eagle's Nest, you been? Decent burgers, and I met this dude named Danny. Super cool guy. He tells me about this commune he lives in, but not like full-on, drum-circle, hippie kind of place. More like a co-op. Everybody works, shares food, grows stuff together. Danny ends up inviting me to live with them when he hears what I'd been up to."

"So, you live in a commune? Do you like it there?"

Brent coughed, shifting with a grimace. "The commune's been good to me," he said, voice thinner now. "It's quiet. Real people. No one cares what job you had or didn't have. We grow what we can, fix what breaks, help each other out like a real family." He paused, wincing. "Still gotta pay off the land, though, nothing's free, not even out there."

Cyrus nodded absently and tightened his grip on the wheel, flicking his eyes between the road and the tube protruding from Brent's chest, watching for any sign it was slipping or blocked.

Brent drummed his fingers on the passenger door, then glanced sideways at Cyrus. "Listen, can I ask you a question? You clearly know about medical stuff, with this tube thingy in my chest and all. I've been having this weird tingling in my feet."

"Both feet?"

"Yeah, both."

"For how long?"

"A couple weeks. Comes and goes."

Cyrus nodded slowly. "Well, you've got diabetes, but neuropathy usually develops over years, not weeks. Could be something else."

Brent shrugged, satisfied enough. "Eh, probably just slept funny. It'll go away. But I've also been super nauseated lately. Like, all last week. And thirsty. Like, ridiculously thirsty."

Cyrus looked over, more serious now. "You having diarrhea? Watery stools?"

Brent recoiled. "Ew, dude! No, gross. Definitely not."

"Fevers?"

"Nope."

Cyrus kept his eyes on the road, frowning. "Hard to say. But we're heading to a hospital, they'll help you figure it out."

With Brent's directions, he drove them into the town of Lakeview and to the small hospital. Cyrus pulled into the parking lot, the tires letting out a quiet screech as he rolled to a stop in front of the Emergency Department. The engine sighed and fell silent, leaving the soft rumble of an ambulance idling nearby to fill the air. A few other vehicles were parked nearby, and the distant sound of an approaching siren added a layer of urgency to the quiet scene.

Cyrus opened the truck door. "Alright, Brent, you think you can make it to the ED on your own feet?"

Brent winced as he used his right hand to open the door. "Dude, all that bouncing around made me so sore and tight. This sucks."

"Wait here, then," Cyrus said over his shoulder as he jogged to the ED entrance.

A moment later, Cyrus came back pushing a wheelchair rattling along in front of him to find Brent waiting for him at the side of the truck. Without missing a beat, he helped Brent into the chair and headed for the entrance. Cyrus wheeled Brent through the sliding glass doors and up to the registration desk. The woman behind the counter, mid-fifties with frosted hair and clunky glasses, didn't look up as they approached.

Brent cleared his throat. "Name's Brent Carlson. I need to be seen by a doctor."

At that, she glanced up, and her expression shifted. Recognition flickered in her eyes, followed quickly by something more skeptical.

"Oh," she said. "You've been here before, for diabetes, right?" She narrowed her eyes. "Aren't you one of those folks from that weird cult up near Klamath Falls?"

Brent let out a sharp breath. "Look, Betty," he squinted at her name tag, "it's not a freaking cult."

Betty blinked, caught off guard. She straightened a stack of papers on her clipboard and changed tack. "Okay then, Brent. What brings you in today? Diabetes flaring up again?"

To explain, Brent yanked open his flannel jacket as if he were Superman, revealing the cylinder jutting from his chest. A condom rim taped over the end fluttered faintly with each breath.

Betty's eyes widened at the sight, but the surprise vanished as quickly as it came. Her fingers flew over the keyboard, entering information with practiced efficiency. When finished, she looked up, sighed, and rolled her eyes, already weary of the situation, judging by her half-hearted tone. "They'll call you in a minute, Brent. You can wait in the lobby."

Cyrus guided Brent toward a corner of the room to wait. He could tell Brent was irritated.

"It's so damn frustrating," Brent muttered, his gaze distant as if still processing the interaction. "People in this town don't get it. Couple years back, we put up a sign, *Reckoning Grove: All share the work, all share the wealth.* Just meant we look out for each other, right? But the local paper snapped a photo, ran it front page, and called us some kind of communist cult. Ever since then, folks treat us like we're brainwashed or dangerous. They don't see the good we're trying to do, just that headline."

Cyrus looked ahead at Betty typing at her computer, trying to find the right words. He understood Brent's frustration. "I get it," Cyrus said, his voice quiet but sincere. "I can't count how many shops or diners I've been where the whole place goes silent when I walk in. People staring at me like I'm a terrorist or something. Because of how I look, or . . . I don't even know."

He paused, and Brent's expression softened, and for the first time since the confrontation with Betty, he didn't look quite so angry. "Yeah," Brent murmured. "Guess we've got more in common than I thought."

A moment later, the forceful voice of a man came from behind the registration desk. "What the heck is going on, Brent?"

Quick footsteps, the hollow clip-clop of clogs, echoed toward them. A doctor rounded the corner, green scrubs showing beneath a crisp white lab coat that stood out against the drab hallway. He looked to be in his sixties, with silver hair, a clean-shaven face, and storm-gray eyes set deep above a slightly crooked nose. His brown clogs gleamed under the fluorescent lights as they struck briskly against the floor, each step carrying a practiced purpose. Without slowing his pace or stopping to speak, he reached Brent's side, expertly parting his flannel jacket with practiced hands, exposing Brent's injury in the middle of the busy lobby.

"What in God's name is going on here?" the doctor exclaimed.

"Doc, it's a new-mow-thor-a-jiggy. My new friend Cyrus fixed it," Brent said with the air of a boy proud to show off his new toy.

The doctor looked over at Cyrus, his eyes widening in disbelief, sheer horror etched across his face. His brow furrowed deeply, and his mouth hung open as he struggled to process what he was witnessing.

He turned toward Cyrus, his expression unreadable. "I'm Doctor Bronson. Are you ready to explain this, son?" he asked, his voice edged with condescending irritation.

Cyrus remained calm; he'd dealt with irritable, pretentious doctors before. "He had a tension pneumothorax after falling onto a tree limb in the woods. I did what I could to save his life."

Dr. Bronson straightened, shooting another hard look at Cyrus. "You're telling me you improvised this in the middle of nowhere?"

Cyrus held his ground, feeling the familiar weight of scrutiny. He knew that look, the one doctors gave others when they assumed they knew better. He'd worn that coat once too, and he'd been questioned enough times to know how to respond.

"I found him lying on the ground, half-conscious, on top of the branch he'd fallen onto," Cyrus said evenly. "He had obvious rib fractures, I could palpate the instability, and he had flail chest."

Brent snorted from the wheelchair, wincing. "Flail chest? Man, that sounds like I was having a seizure or something. Y'all gotta work on your branding."

Cyrus allowed a faint smirk before continuing. "After that, I listened to his lungs. Breath sounds were clear on the left, but completely absent on the right. I determined a tension pneumothorax."

Dr. Bronson raised a hand, cutting him off sharply. "Which is exactly why you should have gotten him here *immediately,*" he said, his voice tight.

"I wanted to," Cyrus said, keeping his tone steady. "But he became unresponsive and tachypneic. I didn't have a choice."

Dr. Bronson's jaw tightened, but when he said nothing, Cyrus went on.

"I made an incision between the ribs and inserted a plastic tube. I had to improvise a way that created a one-way valve so air could escape but not re-enter."

He didn't mention that the latex valve came from a condom. Some details, he figured, were better left unsaid.

"After that, Brent stabilized. No signs of respiratory distress since then. We hiked to his truck and came straight here."

Dr. Bronson looked back at Brent's wound and the improvised chest tube, this time studying it in detail. At first, he had struggled to grasp its purpose, but after hearing Cyrus's explanation, the ingenuity clearly piqued his interest. As he continued to study it, realization spread across his face, his eyes lighting up with understanding. The brilliance of the device clicked into place, and he stepped back to look at Cyrus, as though genuinely impressed. That moment of admiration evaporated quickly, though, as the older doctor's mind raced toward dealing with the next steps.

Dr. Bronson walked toward the entrance to the ED. "We've got work to do, boys." He called over his shoulder at Cyrus, "You, bring Brent into Bay 1."

Betty pushed the button at her desk, and the entrance doors opened like curtains drawn back on a stage. As they walked through, they entered a small chamber with only three patient rooms. Although tiny, the emergency department looked well put together, with modern equipment, its walls painted a calming shade of pale blue that offered a sense of reassurance, and a design no different from any big-city ED, but smaller. In one corner, a sign read "Bay 1," and under it stood a narrow bed, medical supplies neatly organized on shelves, and a small sink. The faint beeping of monitors and the murmur of staff created a backdrop of urgency, while the scent of antiseptic lingered in the air.

Cyrus pushed Brent's squeaky wheelchair toward Bay 1 and then helped him onto the exam bed. A nurse methodically inserted an IV and placed adhesive electrodes on his chest to monitor his electrical cardiac activity, via telemetry monitoring, then left them to wait.

Not long after, Brent was wheeled off to radiology for a chest X-ray and then brought back to the exam room. Surrounded by the sterile order of the hospital, the two outdoorsmen sat like weathered stones, each lost in his own thoughts. The rhythmic beep of the monitor echoed quietly, Brent's heartbeats were steady, but when Cyrus glanced at the telemetry screen, he noticed an occasional irregularity. A beat that came too early, followed by normal electrical activity. *PVCs,* he thought. *Usually benign. Probably just Brent's body reacting to the day's trauma and stress.*

Then, a hurricane of energy, Dr. Bronson entered, his presence filling the room with authority and purpose.

"Brent, the pneumothorax is gone according to the chest X-ray, but you do have a couple of broken ribs. I'm going to take that damn contraption out of your chest now, and then we'll see if I need to put in another chest tube and keep you in the hospital or just keep it out."

"Keep anything out of me, Doc." Brent raised his hands to ward off the doctor. "I don't want to come back here or stay here."

Dr. Bronson crossed his arms and gave Brent a pointed look. "Listen, just because we don't clearly see a pneumothorax on the X-ray doesn't mean there isn't one. It could be small enough to miss, or solved for the moment, but it could still expand again, if that happens, it's serious." He paused, his gaze shifting briefly, sharply, toward Cyrus. "Especially considering the chest tube placed in the field might not have been done . . . exactly by the book."

Brent shifted uncomfortably but shook his head. "I feel fine. I get it, Doc. I understand the risks. But I'm not letting anyone shove another tube in me unless it's absolutely necessary."

Dr. Bronson eyed him a moment. "We'll see." He turned away from Brent and called, "Sandy, get Bay 1 ready for a procedure," and then moved out of sight around a curtain.

Cyrus sat quietly, but his eyes drifted again to the telemetry monitor above Brent's bed. The rhythm still carried a steady beat, but now the premature spikes were more frequent, clusters of PVCs flickering across the screen.

That's not normal, he thought, unease tightening in his chest. *Even with the strain from the pneumothorax, he shouldn't be having this many.*

A moment later, Dr. Bronson returned briskly, setting down a tray of supplies with practiced efficiency. He snapped on a fresh pair of sterile gloves, then worked in silence, methodically sterilizing the skin around the improvised chest tube, the cool sting of the antiseptic making Brent flinch.

As Cyrus watched, he found his thoughts drifting. Medicine had its specialties, cardiologists, dermatologists, nephrologists, but it was the rural generalists he respected most. Doctors like Dr. Bronson didn't have the luxury of handing things off. Cyrus himself had been a rural doctor. When he had practiced in a small Virginia town, he'd juggled it all, taking calls in the ED overnight, rounding on patients before clinic, squeezing in home visits during lunch, managing procedures in the afternoon, and swinging by the nursing home before heading to his own home. It was exhausting, often thankless, but it had taught him to be resourceful. To be present.

His thoughts faded as Dr. Bronson picked up a pair of surgical forceps, clamped the tube with a practiced click, and without warning, gave a sharp, decisive tug.

Brent jolted, sucking in a breath, then muttered through gritted teeth, "Geez, Doc, buy me dinner first next time."

Dr. Bronson didn't even glance up, already pinching the wound Cyrus had created closed and stitching it with brisk, tidy movements. The suture thread tugged through Brent's skin with small, quick pulls, each one making Brent's fingers curl around the edge of the bed. After finishing, he leaned back, peeling off his gloves with a snap and tossing them onto the tray.

During this procedure, Cyrus stood in the corner with his arms crossed, monitoring Dr. Bronson's work. He pretended indifference to a colleague's expertise, but his eager curiosity betrayed a genuine interest and respect.

Dr. Bronson asked, "So are you some kind of doctor?"

"Something like that," Cyrus replied, trying to hide his admiration for the clean, efficient way Dr. Bronson handled the procedure.

Dr. Bronson gave a short, humorless laugh. "You're either a doctor or you're not. There's no such thing as 'something like' a doctor."

Cyrus held his gaze for a moment before answering. "I used to be," he said quietly. "A lot's changed since then."

Dr. Bronson shook his head, a faint note of disapproval threading through his voice. "You must be from a different generation. Where I come from, being a doctor isn't just a job, it's a calling. Doesn't matter what sacrifices you have to make, if you know how to save a life, you don't run away from that."

Cyrus didn't respond. His mind drifted back to a different time, back to when everything still felt possible.

He and Juliette were third-year medical students together then, full of nervous excitement, finally working in the hospital for their clinical rotations. He could still picture them sitting at the old kitchen table in Juliette's childhood home, talking over each other as they tried to explain to her father, an old-school physician, how exhilarating it felt to finally be part of the hospital world.

Juliette's father smiled in that patient, amused way of his. "When I was a resident," he said, setting down his coffee cup, "I was on call every other night. That meant I didn't sleep every other night."

Cyrus and Juliette fell quiet, hanging onto his words.

"There was a three-month stretch where I was so dog-tired," her father continued, "that one night, after getting home, your mother put a plate of spaghetti in front of me . . . and I fell asleep right into it. Face first."

Juliette laughed, the sudden, bright crow of amusement she made when she was genuinely delighted. He looked across the table at her, wide-eyed, both of them caught somewhere between awe and disbelief at the sheer endurance it took to live that life.

Brent's casual drawl interrupted Cyrus's thoughts. "Doc, as you can tell, I ran out of my insulin, and I don't really want to come back here with that high blood sugar thing you admitted me for a few months ago. Any way you could get me some more free samples?"

Dr. Bronson gave him a long, steady look, less like a physician and more like a concerned father. "Brent, some of your labs are off. Your blood sugars are alarmingly high. You're not in diabetic ketoacidosis yet, but you're heading in that direction."

Brent opened his mouth to respond, but the doctor raised a hand gently.

"And combined with the pneumothorax, I'm not comfortable sending you home. I'd like to keep you here overnight for observation. Just to be safe."

Brent shook his head vehemently. "No way, Jose. I'm not staying here, Doc. I'll come back if I need to."

Dr. Bronson snorted out a sharp breath through his nose and rubbed his temples with both hands, the gesture tight and controlled. "You're not understanding the big picture, Brent," he said. "This isn't just about how you *feel* right now. You're teetering on the edge of a serious metabolic crisis."

Still feeling a responsibility to help, and thinking of Brent now as a friend, Cyrus stepped forward to bridge the tension. "Brent, I think he's right. I've been watching the monitor, you've had several PVCs, which are irregular beats of your heart. It could be your body reacting to stress or dehydration, but I wonder if your electrolytes are off."

He turned to Dr. Bronson. "Have the labs come back yet?"

Instead of showing appreciation, Dr. Bronson's expression hardened. "I don't need some pseudo-doctor quitter second-guessing my decisions," he snapped, glaring at Cyrus. "I've got this."

He turned back to Brent. "If you're not smart enough to take care of yourself and listen to a doctor who actually stayed in the profession, then fine. You'll have to sign the paperwork to leave *Against Medical Advice.*"

With that Dr. Bronson turned on his heels and left as quickly as he had entered. Cyrus and Brent stared slack-jawed at each other. Cyrus marveled at how insecure and defensive Dr. Bronson got with such slight pushback from a patient. Cyrus had seen it before, Dr. Bronson was the type of paternalistic doctor who didn't appreciate shared decision-making.

Twenty minutes later, Brent's nurse came in and set two small pill bottles and a paper bag filled with insulin vials on his lap as he sat on the bed. "Well, you sure did manage to piss off Dr. Bronson," she said with a half-smile. "But, honestly, that isn't hard."

Then she handed Brent a single sheet of paper, the heading in bold: *Leaving Hospital Against Medical Advice.* It was filled with dense legal jargon, warnings about risks and liabilities, and a signature line at the bottom waiting for Brent's name. Cyrus recognized the form immediately; he'd seen it countless times during his years in practice. It was a hospital's way of documenting that a patient was refusing recommended care, essentially signing away the hospital's legal responsibility if things went wrong.

Cyrus leaned forward. "Brent, don't do this. I know you've had a rough time in hospitals, but this, this is serious. You could go into full-blown DKA overnight. Or worse."

Brent looked away, his jaw clenched. "I've been in hospitals before. I know what it's like. It's traumatic, man. I'd rather die than be here."

Cyrus stared at him for a long moment, then stood. "Okay... fine. I'm going to grab a wheelchair from the registration area," he said quietly to the nurse. "I'll be right back."

Cyrus pushed through the doors of the ED and went back into the lobby. The air felt cooler here, quieter. He made his way down a side hall where a row of wheelchairs sat neatly parked, metal frames catching the overhead light. Choosing one, he tugged it free, the wheels squealing faintly against the tiles, and started back.

His mind wandered. Once Brent was home, maybe he could find another trail, something farther out, quieter. But then he thought about the way Brent had insisted on leaving against medical advice, those PVCs flickering across the telemetry monitor still etched in Cyrus's mind. How long would Brent manage on his own? What would happen once Cyrus left him?

A voice crackled over the intercom, cutting the thought short, "Code Blue. Emergency Room, Bay One."

Cyrus froze.

And that's when everything changed.

3

Staff were converging on the emergency department from every direction, nurses, techs, even a few physicians, all moving with practiced urgency. Cyrus didn't ask questions. He simply fell in behind someone in green scrubs and followed them through the open ED door, his pulse ticking upward.

It's him, he thought. *It has to be Brent.*

He hadn't liked the look of those PVCs, isolated at first, but then coming in clusters. Something had shifted. Something had gone wrong.

As he turned the corner, he was met by a chaotic sea of bodies clustered around Bay 1. He could just make out Brent's legs through the swarm of movement, his body supine on the gurney, a nurse straddling the bed, rhythmically pressing down on his chest.

"Stop compressions, let me see what his rhythm is!" Dr. Bronson's voice cut through the clamor, sharp and commanding.

There was a brief pause. Then: "V-tach. That's a shockable rhythm, get the pads!"

Cyrus didn't need to ask what was happening. He'd been here before, too many times. Brent's heart had lost its ability to beat in any way that could sustain life. Now, they had entered the algorithm to treat cardiac arrest, a high-stakes protocol where every second matters. Compressions. Defibrillation. Medications. The goal: force the heart to remember how to beat again.

He stepped closer, helpless for the moment, watching the chaos. People often imagined a *code blue* as something almost beautiful, a well-rehearsed choreography where each role clicked into place, the paddles came out, a jolt of electricity worked some miracle, and the patient sat up, gasping, brought back from the brink. But Cyrus knew better. He had been in too many of these rooms, seen too many bodies go limp under the weight of all that effort.

In truth, only about twenty percent of patients survived a code. Most never opened their eyes again. For many, this was simply how the end began, under bright lights, surrounded by strangers, with someone counting compressions and another calling out medications in a voice too steady to match the urgency in the room.

"Everyone clear!" Dr. Bronson shouted.

There was a pause, a whine of charging paddles, then the flat *thump* of electricity discharged into Brent's chest.

"God damn it," Dr. Bronson snapped. "Start compressions again."

"Should I push the epi?" a nurse asked.

"Yes, Nancy," Dr. Bronson barked. "Hurry the fuck up!"

And so it continued. For the next thirty minutes, the code unfolded in brutal, repetitive rhythm, six full cycles of chest compressions, medication pushes, and electric shocks. Each cycle began with a sliver of hope and ended with the same crushing disappointment.

After the last round, there was a pause. "Alright. Fuck," Dr. Bronson muttered. "Stop compressions."

The words yanked Cyrus backward in time. Another room, another body on a bed, the smell of sweat and antiseptic heavy in the air. He remembered staring at the woman's lifeless chest, the flat line across the monitor, until a colleague's hand settled gently on his shoulder. *She's gone. Cyrus, you have to call it.* The weight of that moment pressed down on him again, suffocating, the voice echoing as if from inside his skull.

Then, suddenly, the present snapped back into focus, Brent's still body on the gurney, Dr. Bronson's voice, the room frozen in grim stillness. Cyrus's breath hitched. His chest tightened. Air wouldn't come fast enough, and he felt himself suffocating. His hands began to tremble, his pulse pounding so hard he could feel it in his throat. The walls of the ED seemed to lean in, narrowing, pressing closer.

He staggered a step, catching himself against the wall, legs unsteady. He was having an anxiety attack. If he didn't leave now, he knew he would crumple to the floor. His breaths came quick and shallow, ragged, as if his body were clawing for oxygen.

He pushed past the staff, through the double doors, ignoring the stares as he barreled through the lobby. People turned, eyes following him, but he couldn't stop. Not until the doors hissed open and he stumbled into the sunlight.

Outside, the parking lot was blinding, the sudden quiet disorienting after the storm inside. Cyrus collapsed onto the curb, hunched forward, clutching his stomach as he gasped for air. He sat like that, breathing, shaking, rocking, for what felt like hours, until the rhythm of his chest finally began to slow.

The quiet pressed in, broken only by the occasional hum of a passing car. The ordinary world kept moving, indifferent to what had just unfolded inside.

He stayed on the curb, elbows on his knees, head in his hands. His body felt hollowed out, as if the last of him had been scooped clean by invisible hands. The adrenaline was gone. All that remained was exhaustion, and a deep, gnawing ache he couldn't quite name.

It had been a long time since he'd let himself think about that other code, the one he still carried like a scar. His failure. The memory clawed at him, but he shoved it back into the dark corner where he kept such things. Forget. Move on. Survive.

For a while he just sat there, staring at the pavement, letting the heat of the sun soak into his shoulders. His thoughts circled, then wandered, piecing together the strange path that had led him to this curb outside a rural hospital. Eventually, inevitably, his mind settled on Brent.

Brent had been crude, irreverent, irritating at times, but funny. Even at his sickest, he'd cracked jokes, thrown out one-liners like grenades. Cyrus had felt a strange pull toward him, a sense of duty, sure, but something more personal too. He'd wanted Brent to make it. Needed him to.

Why did this happen? he wondered, staring at the cement beneath him. Brent had been relatively young. Fit. Even with the pneumothorax and the sky-high blood sugars, this outcome didn't make sense.

And then those PVCs on the telemetry monitor had bothered him. Something wasn't right. It was like his heart was warning them, and no one listened.

Footsteps approached. Cyrus looked up and behind to see Dr. Bronson walking toward him, his shoulders sagging, his face gray with fatigue. Dr. Bronson stood there, without a word, his gaze fixed somewhere far off. For a moment, the two of them simply stared into the distance together, Cyrus hunched on the curb, Dr. Bronson standing just behind.

Then Dr. Bronson spoke, his voice low. "It'll be okay," he said, as if talking to a son rather than a colleague. "This happens. People die."

Without a word, Cyrus pushed himself up from the curb. Dr. Bronson stepped aside, letting him pass, and together they moved toward a bench tucked beside the emergency department entrance. They sat down without a word, the weight of what had just happened lingering between them like a third presence.

Finally, Cyrus spoke. "I know people die," he said. "But this doesn't add up. Brent was young and otherwise healthy. Even with a resolved pneumothorax, or if this was something like a hyperosmolar hyperglycemic state, he shouldn't have coded like that."

Dr. Bronson's eyes narrowed faintly, his posture stiffening. "You're overthinking this son, his electrolytes were fine, thyroid levels were fine." He said sharply. "Paralysis by analysis. You're digging around for answers that aren't there."

Cyrus didn't back down. "It just seemed off. The PVCs were way too frequent to be coincidence. I appreciate that Brent's electrolytes were normal but before I brought him in here, he was describing acute onset neuropathy bilaterally as well as nausea and thirst, no fevers or diarrhea. Don't you think that was consistent with something like botulism? or some other etiology?"

Dr. Bronson cut in, his tone flat but edged with long experience. "Jesus, son . . . sometimes people die. You do your best, and then you move on."

The quiet returned, heavier this time. Cyrus sat still, his thoughts spinning as the clinical detachment in Dr. Bronson's words echoed in his mind.

Dr. Bronson clenched his jaw and looked over at Cyrus, the stern edge returning to his face. "Listen," he said, "I didn't come here to discuss Brent's medical situation."

He rubbed a hand over his face and sat back on the bench, staring out across the empty parking lot. "I need to notify next of kin and figure out what to do with the body. Problem is, Brent didn't have any next of kin listed. He considered the folks out at that commune his family."

Cyrus looked over, surprised. "The one he says he lived at?"

Dr. Bronson nodded. "Yeah. They call it Reckoning Grove. It's basically a cult, far as I can tell. No phones, no landlines, some of them carry cells, but they're always off. They don't exactly make it easy to help them. It's like they want to stay stuck in the 1800s."

He looked at Cyrus, eyes tired but expectant. "Could you go out there? Tell them what happened. Ask what they want to do with the body. Somebody has to take Brent's truck back there anyway."

Cyrus blinked. "I don't know . . . I just met him. I don't even know where it is."

Dr. Bronson frowned, the annoyance flashing back into his voice. "Yeah, well, it's like a patient, once you start taking care of them you need to finish things up, and notifying his friends is how you can do that." Dr. Bronson paused and pointed behind him. "Betty over at registration can give you directions."

He stood up without another word and walked off, leaving Cyrus alone in the stillness once again.

Cyrus sat there for a long moment, staring at the open blue sky of the southeast Oregon high desert. *How the hell did I get pulled into this?* he thought. *I never should have become involved.*

He let his shoulders sag, then leaned back onto the bench. The least Cyrus could do was make sure Brent's friends knew what happened. It was the right thing to do. Then, maybe, he could finally disappear into the wilderness again, like he wanted to.

Besides, Dr. Bronson was right—he had Brent's truck, *Mystique.* He figured Brent would've wanted it returned to the commune, not left abandoned in some hospital parking lot like an afterthought. Returning it felt like a way to close the loop.

And yet . . . something deeper and more significant gnawed at him.

He thought about how people at the hospital, even Dr. Bronson, talked about the commune, like it was some backwoods cult. Like the people out there didn't count the same as the townsfolk. Maybe that's why no one was asking more questions. Maybe that's why the hospital wasn't treating Brent's death the way they would if he'd lived in town.

Something was suspicious about how Brent had died; the puzzle pieces didn't fit. GI symptoms, fatigue, the neurologic changes . . . normal electrolytes, and even normal TSH as Dr. Bronson had said.

Cyrus frowned. The list of possibilities was longer than his arm: complications of diabetes, other endocrine diseases, vitamin deficiencies tied to poor nutrition at the commune, lead poisoning, porphyria, Guillain-Barré syndrome, a foodborne illness or infection like botulism. Each one flashed through his mind in quick succession, none settling cleanly into place.

What unsettled him most was the larger implication, if this was an infection, a nutritional deficiency, or even lead exposure, Brent might not be the only one. Others at the commune could be at risk too.

Cyrus didn't get the sense that Dr. Bronson was prejudiced against the commune members, but he clearly didn't think something was amiss. So, if no one else was going to look into it, maybe he had to. Maybe if he could find others at the commune with early symptoms, he could bring it to the attention of the health department, stop this before anyone else died.

That was the part he didn't want to admit, the part he thought he'd buried. He'd walked away from medicine, from being the one people turned to. But the instinct to help, to fix what was broken, hadn't left him. Not really. And now it was tugging at him again, just when he thought he'd escaped it.

Cyrus stood slowly, feeling the ache in his legs, in his chest. Dr. Bronson's words in his head. *Sometimes people die.*

But sometimes, they shouldn't.

4

Mystique rumbled west along Highway 140 past the Drews Reservoir before turning off onto a series of dusty backroads. Eventually, it reached the gravel drive that led to the commune. Its tires crunched over the small rocks and pebbles, leaving a trail of billowing dust behind it. As it neared a house, Cyrus brought the truck to a creaking stop. He put the truck in park and turned off the engine; metal softly clicked and popped, a slow exhale as the heat dissipated.

In front of the truck, the gravel driveway tapered off, its rough stones thinning into the soft edge of a wide, grassy patch that stretched out for perhaps three hundred feet before a white farmhouse. A few wildflowers grew haphazardly near the steps, while the house itself watched over the quiet scene, still and timeless against the wide-open sky.

On the portion of the grassy patch near the drive, three figures were working to raise a wooden sign. With a solid thunk, Cyrus shut the truck door and walked toward them. Two men were standing on either side of the sign, their hands gripping the smooth edges of the broad, white-painted board.

The sign was mounted on two thick wooden posts that extended downward into the earth. One man stood using a sledgehammer to drive the posts deeper into the ground, each strike sending a dull, rhythmic thud through the air. The other held the sign steady.

Meanwhile, a thin, brown-haired woman, probably in her mid-twenties, stood quietly, holding a level against the edge of the sign. She wore a faded blue skirt and over it a loose white shirt rolled at the sleeves, her posture focused but calm.

As the three stepped back to check their progress, the bright white sign stood out boldly against the green grass and wide blue sky. Cyrus read it to himself.

RECKONING GROVE: PREPARATION, SUSTAINABLE EARTH STEWARDSHIP, AUTONOMY, COOPERATION

Noticing Cyrus, the woman set down her level and approached him. As she came closer, Cyrus could see her features more clearly. Brown hair cascaded over her shoulders in soft waves, catching the sunlight and framing her face. Her features were striking in an understated way, strong, dark eyebrows arched as though drawn with a careful hand, giving shape and intention to her expression. But it was her eyes that held him: warm brown, steady and unguarded, with the depth and softness of rich earth after rain.

She reached out a hand. "I'm Dana," she said, her voice calm but curious.

Cyrus shook her hand. "I'm Cyrus."

Dana's eyes dropped to the truck parked behind him. "Why are you driving Mystique?" she asked, her brow furrowing. "Where's Brent?"

Cyrus felt the weight of the moment press against his chest. He had delivered bad news more times than he cared to remember, but this, this wasn't the setting for it. Open field, wide sky, nowhere to sit, nowhere to soften the edges.

He glanced around, hoping for a bench, a porch step, anything, but there was nothing but grass and dirt.

"I need to speak to whoever's in charge of your commune," he said finally.

Dana tilted her head slightly. "Reckoning Grove is a leaderless organization," she said. "We make decisions by vote. If you've got something to say, you can say it to me."

Cyrus hesitated, then drew a slow, steadying breath.

"I found Brent this morning in the woods. He'd fallen and suffered a collapsed lung, a pneumothorax it's called. I managed to stabilize him and took him to Lakeview Hospital." He paused, eyes meeting hers. "They started treating him. But he had a complication . . . and he . . . he died."

Dana's face drained of color. Her mouth opened slightly, but no sound came out. She stared at Cyrus like she hadn't fully registered the words, her expression frozen somewhere between disbelief and grief.

Cyrus looked past Dana and saw the two men who'd been working on the sign walking toward him.

The first was massive, easily more than a foot taller than Cyrus, with a thick frame wrapped in well-worn denim overalls over a faded T-shirt. His strong, clean-shaven features suggested Eastern European roots. He looked to be in his late thirties, and despite his size, there was a calmness to the way he moved. His warm, thoughtful eyes studied Cyrus, but he scratched absently at the right side of his neck. Cyrus could see a red, blotchy rash, or perhaps a birthmark, stretched from his cheek down to his collarbone.

The other man was shorter and stockier, with a completely bald head that gleamed faintly in the late sun. A light brown beard covered the lower half of his face, and when he sneered, uneven, yellowed teeth showed through. His rounded belly pressed against a dirty white T-shirt with the faded lettering *Creedence Clearwater Revival*, and his jeans were frayed and stained at the hem.

Dana seemed to break from her trance. She blinked, startled by their approach, then quickly turned her head, her voice quiet and distracted. "That's Vlad," she said, nodding toward the larger man. "And that's Grady."

She tried to offer Cyrus something like a polite smile, but it faltered, unable to disguise the shock still etched into her face.

Cyrus nodded at the two men. "Hey. I'm Cyrus."

The big man was the first to speak. "Like Dana said, I'm Vladimir." He brought his huge hand down from scratching his neck and extending it to shake Cyrus's. The mighty paw dwarfed Cyrus's slender hand. "Call me Vlad." He withdrew his hulking hand. "What's this you were saying about Brent?"

Cyrus glanced at the other man, expecting, perhaps, that he'd offer a hand too, but Grady just stood there, gripping the handle of the sledgehammer he'd been using earlier, his expression unreadable.

Cyrus cleared his throat and gave them the short version, sticking to the facts. He'd been backpacking in the Fremont-Winema National Forest when he found Brent with a pneumothorax. With his medical training, he stabilized him and gotten him to the hospital, but Brent died there from complications.

"I'm really sorry," he said as he finished.

There was a long pause.

Grady finally stepped forward, sneering. "Okay, so you're telling me that some rando like you just shows up in my good friend's truck and says he's dead? And we're supposed to believe that you didn't have something to do with it?"

Cyrus opened his mouth to respond, but Grady didn't give him the chance.

"So, where you from anyway?"

Cyrus offered a mild, almost disarming smile. He knew that question, knew the weight behind it. Most people didn't mean his last address, they meant his skin, his face, his difference. He liked to play it out anyway.

"I came out here from Colorado."

Grady gave a short snort. "Naw. Where you really from?"

Cyrus kept his smile in place. He'd forced the man to show his hand. "Oh, my parents are Persian, but I was born and raised in Indiana."

"India?" Grady's voice sharpened with sudden intensity.

"No," Cyrus said evenly. "Indiana. The state. Midwest. Of the United States."

Cyrus raised his hands as if to surrender, his voice steady but low. "Look, I know this seems weird, and I get that it's a lot to take in. But I didn't come here to stir things up, the hospital asked me to come by here and . . . I guess I just wanted to close the loop."

He glanced at each of them, then back to Grady. "I really liked Brent. He seemed like such an awesome guy. Funny, sharp, kind. I only knew him for a day, but . . . I felt it. I just thought you all deserved to know. I can see how much he meant to you, and I'm sorry this is how you had to hear it."

Grady narrowed his eyes; his expression caught somewhere between a smirk and a scowl. "You know, outsiders are always looking to take advantage of folks around here. I'm getting sick of it. And now you come along, expecting us to trust some random stranger saying he's a doctor with news like that?" He gave a sharp shake of his head. "Hard to swallow, Little Man."

Dana's head snapped toward him, her eyes wide. "Grady, what the hell?"

Vlad's expression darkened. He stepped forward, placing himself between Grady and Cyrus. "Shut it," he said firmly. "Come on, we've got to finish the sign."

For a moment, no one moved. Then Grady's jaw tightened, his voice snapping, "Fine, sorry I got upset," he muttered, though his eyes narrowed on Cyrus. "But it just seems fishy, you showing up here, and telling us Brent just died."

As Grady stalked off, Vlad turned back to Cyrus, his voice apologetic. "I'm really sorry for that. Grady's . . . a hothead. Always has been. He cared a lot about Brent, and this is just how he deals with bad news, badly."

Cyrus gave a small nod, the tension still heavy in his chest.

Dana stepped closer, her voice softer now. "I'm sorry, too. I liked Brent . . . a lot. I think I was just stunned. I didn't know what to say."

She turned to Vlad. "Go finish the sign. I'll show Cyrus around."

Dana motioned for him to follow, and they began walking slowly past the sign. Beyond it stretched a wide grass field, soft and untamed, the blades shifting gently in the afternoon breeze. About a hundred yards ahead, nestled next to a stand of aspen trees, stood the farmhouse with its white paint and wraparound porch.

"I really am sorry about Grady," Dana said, glancing over at Cyrus as they walked. "He's wary about outsiders, people tend to give our commune a bad rap, and he thinks visitors mean us harm."

"It's okay," Cyrus said. "I understand. He must've been really close to Brent."

Dana nodded, the wind tugging gently at the fabric of her dress.

As they walked closer to the farmhouse, his thoughts raced. He didn't believe for a second that Grady's outburst was just about grief. He'd seen men like that before, men who used anger like armor, who threw words like punches. There was something else behind Grady's eyes, something calculating. He wasn't just mourning a friend. He was a bully.

He knew better than to show a bully any sign they'd gotten under his skin; that was giving them the win, and it only encouraged them to push harder.

No, for someone unimposing, like he was, he had to use his mind. The trick was to stay light, to laugh it off, to make it seem like whatever jab came next barely registered. If Grady threw another punch, even a verbal one, Cyrus would be ready, with a joke, a shrug, something that took the sting out of the air before it could settle.

Dana pointed at the house. "About fifteen years ago, the guy who started Reckoning Grove got a loan from the bank for the land and to build this."

From across the wide grassy yard Cyrus studied the main house. White-painted and sturdy, it stood with a quiet confidence. A dark red door drew the eye at the center, and a porch wrapped along the front and one side, a wooden swing swaying faintly at one end. Sunlight caught the windows and scattered soft gold across the yard, giving the place a sense of welcome and weight.

They crossed the wide stretch of grass toward the main house, Dana walking a little ahead, hands swinging at her sides.

"We've got twenty-one people living here," she said, then faltered. "Oh. I guess . . . twenty." Her eyes flicked down, and Cyrus didn't need her to finish; she'd just remembered Brent was gone.

She cleared her throat and kept going. "Altogether the land's about eight hundred and fifty acres, but most of us stay right here, in this central spot. That's the main house." She nodded toward the three-story structure. "Most of us live inside, some have their own rooms, some share."

Cyrus followed her gaze past the house, to where an old RV sagged in the grass. "That thing's been here forever. Somebody abandoned it years ago, and Brent claimed it. Said he liked having his own space."

Her hand lifted, pointing off to the right of the house. "That's our garden and compost piles. They provide us with most of what we need to eat, and we can vegetables to get through the winter. For anything we can't grow ourselves, we have a van the whole commune shares to make trips into town for supplies."

Beyond the garden, the land dipped toward a stand of trees. "If you go even farther, you'll find our spring. Filtered straight through the earth." She glanced toward the farmhouse. "About a year ago, we put in a pump and plumbing so the water comes straight up to the house. The spring feeds itself, what we use matches what flows in naturally, so it balances out. Doesn't run dry."

As they walked along, the grass felt soft underfoot. "We don't have much power out here off grid, but we scraped together enough to install solar panels. They keep the water pump going, run the lights, and power the refrigerator in the farmhouse. Beyond that, we make do."

She gestured out across the property. "Past this point, we don't really use the land much. It's shaped like a long rectangle; we're on one end of it here. A ways past the spring and the solar panels there's a creek, and beyond that, more of our acreage. But it's a long walk, so most of us don't go out that far unless there's a reason."

By then they had reached the porch steps. The house loomed above them, the swing at one end rocking softly in the breeze.

As they stepped onto the wooden porch, the boards creaked underfoot. The porch, painted a muted gray, showed subtle signs of wear, areas where the color had softened from sun bleaching and treading feet. Dana swung open the dark red door, its hinges protesting as it moved. The entire scene exuded a sense of rustic charm, a welcoming entry to a space that felt both lived-in and loved.

They stepped into a spacious foyer, soft natural light pouring through tall windows and pooling across the floor. To the left, a broad wooden staircase rose upward, its dark banister polished smooth by countless hands. Handwoven rugs in earthy patterns softened the hardwood beneath their feet, while a few woven hangings and framed photos along the wall: faces gathered on the lawn, families posed on the porch, moments of community frozen in time.

"This is where most of us live," Dana said, her voice carrying lightly under the tall ceiling. "And where we all come together for meals."

She led him past the staircase into a wide room beyond. Several long wooden tables filled the space, each ringed by a collection of mismatched chairs. Sunlight streamed through tall windows, casting golden rectangles across the tabletops. Here the walls were livelier, brightened with painted landscapes and more handmade crafts, artwork layered in the same way conversations must have filled the room over the years.

"I'll give you the grand tour later," Dana added, turning back to him with a small smile. "But I wanted to show you this, so you know where to come for dinner."

Cyrus lifted a hand. "Oh, sorry for the confusion. I only came to let you know about Brent. I was hoping to ask a few questions, then I'll get out of your way."

Dana studied him for a moment, her expression softening. "Well, the least we can do is send you off with a good home-cooked meal."

With that, she continued past the staircase and led him down a short hallway toward the back of the house to a screen door. They stepped outside to a large backyard looking out on a beautiful view of the rugged mountains of the Oregon high desert. The sun outlined the edge of their silhouettes in light orange. Below the hills, a glistening silver ribbon wound its way through the landscape, shimmering in the dying light. The expansive yard and the stunning backdrop radiated tranquility.

This terrain differed from the places where Cyrus had been hiking in Colorado or even Idaho, which were part of the Great Basin region. A different kind of beauty dominated the landscape on the east side of the Cascades, raw and untamed, and it made him feel small yet oddly at peace. The high desert held a quiet power, its starkness offering solitude different from the dense forests he had explored.

Cyrus's gaze landed again on the small RV parked just beyond the back yard. He saw now that it leaned slightly to one side on a set of cement bricks that acted as supports where the tires used to be. Its once-beige paint had faded and was adorned with rust-colored streaks. Weeds and wildflowers had crept up around its base, half-swallowing the frame in a tangle of green and gold.

"That's the RV I mentioned earlier," Dana said. "It was donated to Reckoning Grove when the previous owner left. Brent claimed it not long after."

She hesitated, then went on. "Look, I know you've got plans to leave," she said. "But you seem like a good person, and I really appreciate you coming all the way out here, telling us about Brent, bringing Mystique, and...well, dealing with Grady." A faint smile tugged at her mouth.

She nodded toward the RV, sitting weathered but upright. "Occasionally people are curious about our commune, so we developed an open-door policy here at Reckoning Grove. Folks can stay for two weeks, no questions asked. After that, the whole commune takes a vote, a majority decides if someone can stick around. I'm not saying you'd want that. But you look tired, like maybe you could use a place to catch your breath."

Her gaze softened. "Think about it. Rest, quiet, no pressure."

Cyrus nodded slowly, feeling a surge of gratitude for her offer. "Thanks, Dana, that is so nice, let me think about it before dinner." Then Cyrus glanced back toward the truck and added, "but for now I left our backpacks, mine and Brent's, in the back of Mystique."

"Don't worry," Dana said. "Someone will fetch them shortly."

She gestured toward the RV. "Listen, I know it's weird, but take a rest in Brent's RV for a little bit. Then, come by the house around eight. I'll be baking my famous bread to go with dinner."

At that, Cyrus's stomach gave a loud, undeniable growl. He let out a breath and gave a tired smile. "I guess I'll be there."

5

Cyrus swung open the door of the old RV, and the whole structure creaked as he stepped inside.

Within, the space was tight but functional. To the left, a twin-size mattress was wedged against the wall. In front of it sat a cluttered table piled with clothes, papers, and something that might've once been a plate of food.

Cyrus set the plate in the sink of the small kitchenette, then settled on the mattress and quickly fell into a light doze. An hour later he was awake again, sitting on the narrow bed, elbows on his knees, staring up at the stained ceiling where old water damage had bloomed into faint rust-colored blotches. The hum of insects drifted in through the screen window, blending with the distant creak of wind in the trees.

He'd come here to tell the people at Reckoning Grove about Brent and to deliver Mystique, but he also wanted to learn more about Brent's mysterious symptoms: the nausea, neurologic symptoms, the thirst. Maybe at the dinner gathering, someone would say something, mention some detail that would make this all click into place. He told himself it had to be something simple, an infection moving through a tight camp. Maybe a bad batch of stew. A few careful questions at dinner could sort it out. Who was sick first? What they ate? Any fevers, rashes, or diarrhea? If the answers lined up, he could warn them to call the county health office, shut the kitchen for a day, get samples pulled. Then he could leave after dinner, with the right people alerted and the problem already shrinking in his mind.

A knock interrupted his thoughts.

He got up and swung open the RV door. Vlad stood there, the giant of a man Cyrus had first met with Dana and Grady. The late light catching in his hair and casting long shadows across the yard. He held both backpacks, Cyrus's and Brent's, as if they weighed nothing.

"Brought your stuff," Vlad said. "And . . . sorry again. For how Grady acted."

"No problem," Cyrus said, taking the bags. "I've seen worse."

He tucked the backpacks into the narrow strip of space between the mattress and the small cabinet near the back wall and returned to the doorway.

Vlad gave a nod toward the house. "It's time for dinner. Come on, I'll show you the way."

They walked together near the garden as the light faded into a warm, dusky gold.

"You know," Vlad said, a grin spreading across his face, "I've got to tell you this story about Brent." He leaned in. "So one day, Brent decided he could take me in a wrestling match. He thought he could beat me if I had my hands and legs tied."

Cyrus raised an eyebrow, intrigued. "And?"

Vlad chuckled. "I was tied up, right? But that didn't stop me. I still flipped him over in, like, five seconds. That man, he never learned."

Cyrus laughed, the sound more genuine than he expected. The image of Brent, so confident and sure, being defeated by a tied-up

Vlad, was too good to pass up. There was something about Vlad, his blunt honesty, his easy humor, that made Cyrus trust him.

He hesitated, then asked casually, "Hey . . . have you noticed anyone at the commune with nausea lately? Or like, vague numbness, hands, feet, that kind of thing?"

Vlad tilted his head, eyes drifting past Cyrus toward the porch light. "No," he said after a beat. "Can't say I have." He scratched at his neck. "Brent was always on about the food, though. Hovered over the kitchen. The canning, especially. Checking seals, making people reboil batches, talking about low-acid vegetables needing longer times. Said one bad jar could make folks real sick."

Cyrus nodded.

"Maybe someone at dinner will know more," Vlad said, stepping to the back door and pulling it open for him. "After you."

As they entered the house, a wave of warm, inviting air rushed out, carrying with it the mouthwatering scent of onions and herbs mixed with the savory fragrance of fresh broth. The delicious aroma lingered, beckoning them farther inside, promising a satisfying, home-cooked meal.

In the dining area, the mood was subdued. Voices murmured softly around the table, broken occasionally by the clink of silverware and the scrape of chairs on the old wood floor. No one was laughing. Cyrus could feel it in the silence between words, in the way people spoke gently, as if mindful not to break something fragile.

They must already know about Brent.

The gentle conversations quieted even more as they entered, and everyone's eyes rested on Cyrus. He felt the pressure of a spotlight on opening night. His eyes met Grady's. Grady stared at him with unmistakable ill humor. But as Cyrus glanced around the room, he saw mostly open faces, curious, maybe, but not unfriendly. The overall feeling was one of cautious acceptance. Cyrus saw young people in their twenties and others that ranged all the way up into their sixties. He counted twenty people in all.

It would've been twenty-one with Brent, he thought, the number catching in his chest like a breath held too long.

Vlad spoke up, his voice calm but carrying. "This is Cyrus, the one who brought us the news. He helped Brent when no one else could. We'd like to show him what acceptance and cooperation look like here at Reckoning Grove."

The suspense in the room slowly eased. A couple of people greeted him with, "Hey, Cyrus," and conversations that been hesitant grew louder and more relaxed.

Vlad gave Cyrus a small nod, then gestured toward a table near the far wall. "Go on, sit with Dana," he said quietly. "You'll be in good company."

Cyrus made his way over, offering a tentative smile as he pulled out a chair. Dana looked up and smiled warmly, an unspoken reassurance that cut through the tension tightening his chest. He exhaled, relieved, and slid into the seat between her and an older man with a handlebar mustache.

She turned and gestured around the table. "This is Charlie," she said, nodding to the man beside Cyrus. Charlie gave a slight lift of his chin in greeting. "Mags," she added, motioning to a woman across from them. She looked to be around Dana's age with freckles on her cheeks. She responded with a friendly wave. "And that's Danny," she said, pointing to the young man beside Mags, early twenties, lean, and sharp-eyed, who gave an easy-going nod. Cyrus briefly recalled Brent describing a man named Danny who had convinced him to stay at the commune.

"Everyone, this is Cyrus."

Cyrus folded his hands on the empty tabletop, the low murmur of conversation starting to build again. Dinner hadn't been served yet, but at least for now, he didn't feel like an outsider.

As Cyrus took in the room, a man walked in from what must be the kitchen, struggling with a large, steaming pot of stew. Thick tendrils of steam rose from the pot. The man's glasses fogged from the heat, and his thinning hair glistened with a sheen of sweat from the effort. He wore a worn pair of jeans and a button-down shirt, its sleeves rolled up to his elbows as he carefully navigated the space. Vlad stood to help, taking hold of both handles of the heavy pot and nudging aside the smaller man. As if the pot were no heavier than a leaf, Vlad carried it toward the table, the steam rising around them in swirling clouds.

Dana insisted that Cyrus sit while she fetched two generous bowls of stew. She returned a moment later, setting one in front of him along with a thick slice of freshly baked bread.

Cyrus glanced around and saw others dipping bread into their bowls, smiling and sharing quiet stories. He lifted a spoonful, gently blew on it, and took a taste. The flavor burst on his tongue, earthy, hearty, perfectly seasoned. Each ingredient sang in harmony, the spices complex but balanced. A trace of garlic and thyme lingered on the finish.

As Cyrus ate, he appreciated the quiet clinking of forks and spoons filling the space. Conversation remained low, respectful, until Danny, seated at the far side of the table, set down his glass and leaned forward.

"You know," he said, glancing around, "I was just thinking about the first time I met Brent. It was at the Eagle's Nest, place was half-empty, middle of the afternoon. He was sitting at the bar eating onion rings like it was a five-course meal."

A few people looked up, curious.

Danny chuckled. "He told me he'd been driving west from Alabama, and when he got to Nevada, he 'hung a Ralph.' " He made air quotes with his fingers." Somehow ended up in Lakeview. I had no clue what 'Ralph' meant, so I asked him."

He shifted in his seat, putting on an exaggerated southern-drawl impression. "Dude! You know, a right. Instead of right, you say Ralph!"

A couple of chuckles rose from the table.

"So then I ask him, 'Okay, so what's a left?' And without missing a beat he goes, 'A Louie.' Like I should've known that since birth."

People started smiling now, a few with forks frozen halfway to their mouths.

"And then I ask him, 'Alright, smart guy, what do you call a U-turn?'" Danny leaned back, laughing now. "And he goes, 'Oh, that's *flipping a bitch,* obviously.' Like it was in a damn dictionary."

Laughter broke out around the table, not loud, not wild, but full and warm. The kind of laughter that had been waiting quietly for permission to exist again. Cyrus couldn't help but smile, the tension in his shoulders easing just a little.

Dana smiled, still laughing softly. "Brent had the weirdest way of describing things. Remember how he talked about weather, like it was some battlefield report? 'Storm front moving in like a squadron of bombers,' or something like that."

Next to Cyrus, Charlie perked up. Cyrus noticed the ends of his meticulously groomed handlebar mustache twitching slightly as he smiled. His long graying hair was pulled back into a neat ponytail, and despite looking well into his sixties, his sharp blue eyes sparkled with a mix of mischief and conviction, like he was on the verge of revealing something big.

Charlie leaned in. "All jokes aside, Brent was on to something. You know there's a reason for all this climate change, right?" he said, lowering his voice a notch. He turned to Cyrus like he was about to let him in on something important. "Ever hear of HAARP? Bad weather is not just bad luck . . . they're messing with the whole system."

"Uh, no, I'm not sure I have," Cyrus said hesitantly.

Charlie sat back again. "I don't blame you. It's 2010 and people still don't realize how the U.S. government hides things in plain sight. So, HAARP stands for High-frequency Active Auroral Research Program. It's a research project in Alaska with the stated purpose to 'study the properties of the ionosphere to help civilian defense purposes,' but you know that ain't the real truth. HAARP is actually manufacturing chemicals to manipulate the weather and climate.

You know how everyone keeps talking about global warming? Climate change?"

Charlie didn't bother letting Cyrus respond to his rhetorical question. "In reality, when you look up at airplanes in the sky, you're seeing chem trails. You're seeing the chemicals HAARP has been manufacturing and loading onto those planes. That's what's causing global warming."

Cyrus had never spent time speaking with a conspiracy theorist before. He did have a friend from high school who believed the earth was flat, but he'd done whatever he could to avoid conversations with the guy so as not to cause friction. Charlie on the other hand sounded as if he genuinely cared about Cyrus's well-being. His body language was open, conveying a willingness to help and a desire for Cyrus to grasp the gravity of the situation.

Charlie added, "Brother, it's all the government's plan to restart civilization. They know we're falling apart. That's why I moved here. To get ready for when things go to hell."

Dana leaned forward, her voice warm. "Charlie, give him a minute to settle in before you introduce him to the shadow government." She gave Charlie a quick smile and a gentle nudge with her elbow, then turned back to Cyrus. "Tell us, what were you up to when you found Brent?"

Cyrus shifted by a fraction, weighing his words. "I hiked here from Colorado. Took me a while. I'd stop along the way, pick up odd jobs to make some cash for food and supplies."

Dana tilted her head, studying him across the table. "Why'd you decide to hike all the way from Colorado?"

Cyrus hesitated, his fingers brushing the edge of his plate. "Sometimes life piles on more than you can handle. Walking seemed like the only thing I could manage." He gave a faint, apologetic smile. "Where are you from, Dana?"

"Actually, I grew up not too far from this area on a ranch with my parents and brother." She paused, then added more softly, "After high school, I went to college in Corvallis. My plan was to move back to the ranch when I was done, but my parents died in a car wreck, and when I tried to move back to help with it . . . ." Dana searched for the right words. "Things didn't quite work out between my brother and me, so I bummed around and worked a bit. But I missed having a family, and I moved in with this new family here a few years ago. Haven't really looked back."

Dana's words struck a chord in Cyrus. He wasn't sure why, but the idea of finding a new kind of family resonated with something deep in him. He, too, felt unmoored, adrift, without a real home.

He stared down at his bowl, gently stirring the last few bites of stew without appetite, her story echoing in his mind.

Around the room, the mood remained subdued. Voices were low, the clink of silverware steady but restrained. Still, there was something grounding in the way people sat together, the quiet understanding that threaded between them. This wasn't some wacky cult like he'd heard others describe it. These were good people, he thought, Dana with her calm presence, Charlie with his wild theories and kind eyes.

Cyrus set his spoon down. "Can I ask you all something?" he said quietly. "Something's been bothering me about Brent's symptoms before he died. He mentioned some nausea, weakness . . . and this weird tingling in his legs."

Charlie looked up, brow furrowed. Dana leaned forward, concerned. Danny paused mid-bite.

"You guys haven't seen anyone else around here with symptoms like that, have you? Nausea, leg numbness, anything odd?"

They each glanced at one another, thinking.

Dana finally shook her head. "No . . . not that I've heard."

Charlie added, "Not unless someone's keeping it to themselves."

Danny grunted, pushing his bowl away. "I've been working with most folks all week, nothing like that."

Cyrus gave a small nod, lips pressed together. Disappointed maybe, but not ready to let it go. "Thanks for the info, guys. I didn't mean to pry, but I guess I can't stop thinking like a doc."

The others didn't seem offended. They simply went back to their meals, finishing up dinner and turning their attention to neighbors in easy conversation.

Cyrus sat a moment longer, staring at the remains of his stew. It had been good, better than he'd expected, but the satisfaction of the meal did little to settle the knot in his chest. *This just isn't working,* he thought. He had imagined walking in, finding others with the same symptoms Brent had, reporting it to the health department, and being done with it. But after asking around, no one seemed to know anything. Either Brent was the only one, or the illness was limited to just a few.

Either way, pressing harder wasn't the answer. Cyrus resolved that he'd stop peppering these people with questions and instead keep his eyes open, watching and waiting for what might surface.

He rose, gathered his dishes, and carried them to the sink in the kitchen before wandering back out to the dining room, where Dana and Charlie were deep in conversation. Dana's eyes lit when she saw him, and she reached out a hand.

She grasped him gently by the arm. "Let me show you something cool." As she led him out of the house, her touch was light but confident, guiding him with ease as they stepped off the porch and into the cool night air. Carrying a small lantern, she led him around the side of the house, her pace unhurried, like she'd done this a hundred times before. Her hair smelled fresh and earthy, with a hint of lavender. The faint glow of the house faded behind them, replaced by the darkening sky and the quiet hum of crickets in the distance.

As they approached a small clearing, Dana gestured ahead to a circle of stones, where the faint remains of charred wood and ash sat in the center. "Pretty much every night after dinner we have a bonfire here," she said softly, her voice tinged with affection.

She paused for a moment, then added, "Except tonight will be different. Brent's gone . . . and since we don't have a leader here, we'll talk as a group, figure out together how we want to honor him. That's how we do things at Reckoning Grove. Everyone gets a voice."

The night sky unfolded in a vast, velvety canvas, sprinkled with countless stars that shimmered like diamonds against the deep indigo backdrop.

As Cyrus drew closer to the circle of stones, other people appeared in the dark. Grady's distinct voice pierced the gloom, speaking to others settling nearby.

"I can just picture Little Man trying to roast a marshmallow," Grady said, chuckling to himself. "Bet he'd burn it to a crisp, then try to tell us that's how the experts do it."

He laughed loudly, some others joining in, unable to hold back their chuckles. "Guess we'll have to teach him how real campers handle a fire."

Dana's grip on Cyrus's arm faltered, then dropped entirely. She didn't say anything, just stared straight ahead, her jaw tight, the warmth between them suddenly gone.

Cyrus stood beside her, the chill of the night settling deeper into his skin.

6

Cyrus stepped closer to the group of people, tension coiling in his chest. As he'd determined earlier when first meeting Grady, he had to look unbothered in order to defuse the situation quickly or he would lose favor with the whole group.

With a nervous but determined smile, he raised his hand, catching Grady's attention. "You're right, Grady." He kept his voice steady but light. "Last time I made s'mores, the fire department showed up. True story."

A ripple of laughter spread through the group, the sharp edge of

Grady's jab softening. Cyrus let the moment hang just long enough, then leaned toward Dana, pitching his voice loud enough for the others to catch. "Seriously, better keep me away from the matches. One spark and I'll have the whole forest applying for disaster relief."

That earned another round of chuckles, even a few genuine laughs. Cyrus grinned, turning the energy back toward Dana as if nothing had rattled him. Her shoulders, once stiff, loosened, and the corners of her mouth lifted in a smile she didn't bother to hide. When she looked at him this time, there was something new in her expression, a quiet appreciation, maybe even respect, as the tightness she'd been holding finally eased..

Minutes later, the flickering flames illuminated the faces of those gathered nearby. The tense situation from earlier was forgotten, leaving a cozy atmosphere filled with light conversation. Shadows flickered on the ground, intertwining with the soft light of the fire, while the smell of burning wood mingled with the cold night air.

After circling the group, Cyrus sat on the ground next to another man he recalled seeing at dinner earlier. The man was dressed in an old button-down shirt with a faded checked pattern, the fabric softened by frequent washing. His glasses caught the light of the fire and his gray-brown hair was combed back but showed signs of thinning. He sat quietly, with his knees up and arms wrapped around them, his posture relaxed.

"Mind if I sit here?" Cyrus asked.

"Sure. You're the guy who tried to help Brent, right? The doc? I'm Gus Modrall." Then added, "nice comeback to Grady. He's such a bully sometimes, always testing people."

He shook Gus's hand. "Thanks Gus, nice to meet you. I'm Cyrus."

They sat quietly for a while watching the fire blaze and crackle, reading the flames like a deep poem.

After a while, Cyrus asked, "Can I ask you how long you've lived here?"

"Certainly. I've been here about nine years now. I got here about a year after the founder of Reckoning Grove died. His name was Kevin Daugherty."

Cyrus noticed how precise and measured Gus was when he spoke.

"Wow, so the commune kept going after he died, huh?"

"Yeah, he was interesting. He was sure some sort of global event would bring down society, so he bought all this land." Gus turned his head as if watching a car driving across the expanse, "about eight hundred fifty acres. He got a loan for the land and to build that house and started recruiting people to join his vision for this intentional community. As people started coming, it slowly became a commune where they bought into his vision and shared everything. Including that damn loan."

"Sounds like that bugs you."

"Yeah, well, I used to be a lawyer. I used to be a partner in this business litigation firm. When I came here, I wasn't into that whole doomsday prepper thing, I just wanted to get away from the rat race and start my life over again. I was drawn to the self-sufficiency of the people here. I suppose since I was so good at suing companies for big money, they felt I was good with numbers, so they made me the accountant and job coordinator here."

"Okay, that's pretty cool."

"The irony of it is that now that I'm in charge of accounting and Reckoning Grove's money, I have to deal with the bank and that damn loan. I'm back in the rat race anyway!" Gus tossed a twig into the fire. "It's annoying."

"Sorry, I wish it wasn't like that for you." Cyrus said.

"Ah, sorry to gripe so much. I love it here. I love the people and what we're accomplishing. We're self-sufficient, and if we could get that loan paid off, we could last forever."

Cyrus frowned. "How in the world do you guys even make any money to pay off the loan now?"

Gus leaned back, his expression thoughtful as he explained. "Reckoning Grove gets by you know. We sell vegetables at the farmers' market in the summer, and a few of us pick up work in town, carpentry, odd jobs, that kind of thing. We rent out part of the land for grazing, which helps cover the loan. And years back, one of our members left but still believed in what we're doing. She left us some money, and we've stretched it carefully ever since. Everything we bring in goes into a shared pot, just enough to keep the place running and cover what we can't grow ourselves." He gave a small nod, as if reassuring himself of the idea. "It's weird; every once in a while, someone will try to buy the land or make us leave, but we keep getting by."

They both stared into the flames again, listening to the crackles and pops and relishing the peacefulness of the night.

Something struck Cyrus about what Gus said. "Wait, people try to kick you out? Even buy the land?"

"Yeah," Gus said with a short laugh. "People come around all the time trying to get us off this land. Neighbors gripe that our compost piles stink up the place or claim we're hurting their property values. The city hassles us about zoning and permits, always looking for a way to say we don't belong. Then you get the salesmen, slick types in suits, talking about big, beautiful subdivisions and country estates. And once," he added, shaking his head, "an ultra-religious church tried to buy us out. Their preacher came in spouting fire and brimstone, said this land was meant to be holy ground and we were desecrating it. Told us we'd be doing God's will if we sold. He didn't get far with that pitch."

Gus paused, scratching at his chin as if something had just clicked. "Oh, James, another guy who lives here. He used to be part of that church." His brows knit as he searched for the name. "What was it called again? Ah, right . . . Church of the Sovereign Covenant."

He poked at the fire, eyes reflecting the glow. "Always someone trying to tell us what to do. But nothing ever sticks. We vote, we hold our ground, and we're still here. Truth is, I think we're stronger for it. I love this place."

After a while, an older black man stood up and cleared his throat.

He waited a moment for everyone's attention then spoke, his voice steady but somber. "The purpose of this gathering tonight is to discuss plans for Brent's funeral ceremony. We want to honor him in a way that respects his wishes and reflects how much he meant to all of us." He paused, scanning the faces in the firelight. "Does anyone have any initial thoughts?"

A few moments passed before Danny, the man from Cyrus's table who had recruited Brent, raised his hand from the back of the circle.

"Thanks, Calvin," he said. "I had a conversation with Brent about a year ago, after he'd gotten out of the hospital one time for his diabetes issues. We ended up talking about death." He looked down briefly, almost apologetically. "At the time, I felt a little weird discussing something so heavy, but Brent didn't seem to mind. He told me when his time came, he wanted to be cremated. He said he wanted his ashes spread here, on the grounds of Reckoning Grove, near where Kevin was buried."

A quiet murmur spread through the group as Danny finished speaking. Many nodded in agreement, clearly moved by the idea of laying Brent to rest in a place he'd loved.

Calvin took a deep breath and nodded thoughtfully. "Thank you, Danny. That's a beautiful way to honor Brent's memory. We'll need to figure out the details, but it sounds like a good place to start."

Grady cleared his throat, glancing around the circle. "I can call the funeral home in town and arrange the cremation. I've got a cousin that works there," he added, his tone resolute. "But I'll need help from Gus to cover the costs from our commune funds."

Gus, still sitting next to Cyrus, nodded. "That shouldn't be a problem," he replied. "We'll figure it out."

There was a quiet appreciation from the group and a few murmured words of agreement. It was clear everyone wanted to make this process as seamless as possible, honoring Brent's wishes without hesitation.

The rest of the conversation revolved around the logistics and timing of the ceremony. Uncertainty about when Brent's ashes would be ready meant they couldn't finalize the details yet. Instead, they agreed to wait until Grady heard back from the funeral home then regroup to make further plans.

As the group began to scatter, Cyrus remained seated, letting the fire's warmth settle into his limbs. Beside him, Gus sat quietly, hands clasped around a tin cup, his clean-shaven face ruddy in the firelight.

After a moment, Gus leaned in slightly. "I heard you've been asking around. About what made Brent sick."

Cyrus straightened, the flicker of the fire mirrored in his eyes. "Some of his symptoms didn't add up."

Gus rubbed his ear. "Couple weeks back, Brent told me he thought mice had gotten into our underground cellar. Found droppings near the oats, maybe the lentils too. He got pretty worked up about it, started eating less, said the oatmeal tasted off."

Cyrus turned to him. "Did anyone else get sick?"

"Not that I heard," Gus said. "But Brent seemed spooked. Kept saying we needed to clean things up better. That we were asking for trouble."

Cyrus looked back toward the farmhouse, his mind already moving. Mice could mean contamination, sure, but so could careless waste disposal. Bad runoff. Poor composting. He'd seen it before—nitrates leaching into gardens. Maybe it wasn't the food itself, but where it was grown. Or what was seeping into it.

He stood slowly, brushing off his pants. "Thanks, Gus."

"Sure thing," Gus said, tipping his cup toward the fire.

As Cyrus turned toward the shadows beyond the porch, his gaze lingered on the garden. The moonlight silvered the rows in a faint outline, while the bonfire behind him threw a restless orange glow across the edges, making the plants seem to shift and stir in the night. Maybe Brent had been paranoid, his nerves stretched thin by pain and worry. No one Cyrus had spoken with exhibited nausea, numbness, or anything that fit. It could have been a one off, a bad day that turned worse, and not a pattern waiting to repeat.

He let his shoulders drop. He had done what he could, he had saved Brent's life on the mountain, and for tonight that would have to be enough. He would sleep, he would get up early, thank Dana, and be on the road by first light, back to the quiet of the off-grid miles where no one expected anything from him. The thought felt almost gentle as he walked back towards the RV.

7

Cyrus woke to the pale gray light of morning filtering through the cracked blinds of the RV. For a moment he lay still, disoriented, the quiet pressing in around him. Then it all came back, Brent's death, the dinner, the firelight flickering on solemn faces.

He sat up slowly, the metal bed frame groaning beneath him, and rubbed the sleep from his eyes. The air inside the RV was cool and still carried the faint scent of old fabric and damp wood.

Pulling on his jacket, he stepped outside into the crisp morning air. The ground was slick from dew, and a few birds called from somewhere in the trees.

Inside, the house smelled of fresh coffee and eggs cooking. In the dining area, a couple of people were already seated at one of the tables. One was Charlie, the goofy conspiracy theorist, deep in conversation with the man who had served the stew the night before. He had short brown hair, a receding hairline, and wore round, wire-framed glasses that made him look thoughtful. He held a can of Diet Coke, condensation beading in the light.

Cyrus couldn't tell what they were talking about, but he caught stray words as he passed. "Tide line." "Canned beans." "Throw away." The phrases tugged at him. Juliette used to can in their kitchen, and the tide line always made her tense. A tide line was the ring of residue that formed inside a jar when the process didn't go right. It meant air and food had mixed during cooling, a sign that microbes could survive and an oxygen poor-pocket could form where toxins or infection might grow, even if the lid still looked sealed.

He remembered what Vlad had said the evening before about Brent hovering over the canning, checking seals, making people reboil batches.

As Cyrus walked closer, the two men looked up at him. The second man's face lit up as soon as he spotted Cyrus. Standing and pushing his round glasses up with a quick motion, he gave a small, friendly chuckle. "Glad to meet you in person, Cyrus," he said, his tone warm and welcoming. "I've already heard so much about you, and we haven't even met yet!"

He stepped closer, his expression softening with genuine gratitude. "Thanks for trying to save Brent. We all really loved that guy." He shook Cyrus's hand to show his appreciation. "I'm James Rubin." He let go and stepped back.

The three men didn't talk for an awkward moment.

Cyrus said, "Guys, any way I can get myself some coffee?"

"I can't live without my cup of Joe either." Charlie punched at Cyrus's shoulder with a grin. "Let me get you a cup. Do you want anything in it?"

"I'd love a little milk or cream in it, but don't sweat it, I can get it," Cyrus added quickly.

Before he finished, Charlie was heading over to the table where coffee was brewing.

James arched his head back to finish his Diet Coke. Afterward, he took a breath and said, "Every morning we usually grab some breakfast before we start doing the chores that we were assigned."

Charlie returned, handing Cyrus his coffee. "Thanks!" Cyrus smiled.

James continued, "Charlie and I drew the short straw today.

We're cleaning all the composting toilets, but you know what they say . . . a dirty job, but someone's gotta do it."

Cyrus thought of how they had given him a bed for the night and a hot, generous dinner without hesitation. They had welcomed him in and asked for nothing.

Helping James and Charlie felt like a simple way to say thank you, something useful, without politics or posturing. He could pitch in for a few hours, keep his head down, and be on his way by afternoon.

"I'd love to help you guys," Cyrus said.

"That's awesome," James said with a grateful smile. "Well, take your time and finish up your coffee and meet us at the composting toilets out to the side of the house."

Cyrus watched as Charlie and James walked out together. He took a sip from his mug, but instead of lingering on the taste, his eyes roamed the dining hall. The night before, he'd been too stressed by all the new faces and conversations to notice much about the room, but now he let himself take it in. The space was large enough for five heavy wooden tables, each surrounded by a hodgepodge of mismatched chairs, straight-backed kitchen seats, sagging armchairs, even a stool or two. The walls carried an almost hippie charm: faded tapestries with sunbursts and mandalas, hand-painted signs with half-peeled slogans, and shelves cluttered with mismatched pottery. Woven rugs, worn thin in the middle, brightened the scuffed wooden floorboards. The place felt cobbled together but lived-in, the kind of room where people had gathered for years, sharing meals and stories long before he arrived.

Cyrus met James and Charlie ten minutes later. The outhouse was a large wooden structure made from aged cedar planks and standing on a gentle incline, perched on a slope of packed dirt and weathered stones. The exterior looked well-kept, with a simple tin roof that glistened under the sunlight. A small set of sturdy steps led up to the entrance, which was divided into three separate doors, each leading to its own small room.

Charlie's raised voice reached Cyrus first. "You gotta start with cleaning the toilets, man; it won't work the other way around."

James threw his hands in the air with disgust. "I'm agreeing with you. I don't understand why you keep arguing with me."

As the two heard Cyrus approach, they both looked relieved to stop their argument.

"Glad you're helping us, Cyrus," James said. "We were just discussing how to start."

Charlie chimed in, stroking his handlebar mustache as if he were a professor. "Cyrus, you're going to appreciate poop more than you ever have before, my man. We are part of the ecosystem, and this compost toilet gets the ball rolling, so to speak. Let me show you how this baby works."

Charlie walked up the incline and stepped into one of the three cubicles, encouraging Cyrus to follow. "Breathe it in, baby . . . what do you smell?"

Anxious, Cyrus started to realize this was probably more than he'd anticipated having to do when he volunteered. But as he neared the space, he didn't smell the unpleasant tang of the typical outhouses. Instead, there was merely a damp wooden smell.

"You see," Charlie said with an excitement one would never expect over such a subject, "after you make your deposit, you put a small shovel of sawdust over it in the hole." He pointed at a bucket filled with sawdust and the handle of child's shovel sticking out. "The sawdust doesn't just help with the smell; it's also a carbon source for the microbes." He continued to describe the process by leading Cyrus back outside, down the incline to the back of the outhouse. The three toilets' cubicles sat above large wheelie bins with their lids open. They looked exactly like the kind of bins Cyrus used to put his recycling in.

Charlie tipped the bin onto its two wheels and rolled it out from under the back of the outhouse. Inside was what Cyrus expected to see . . . poop intermixed with wood chips and toilet paper. Underneath, a water valve stuck out and was attached to a water hose.

"What is that for?" Cyrus asked, pointing to the water hose.

James said, "Oh that's the liquid diverter. It's one of the reasons it doesn't smell that bad. The bottom of the bin has a big filter; pee gets filtered through it and diverted to the irrigation fitting, flowing out the hose into that reed bed." James pointed about ten feet away at a muddy bed full of tall, green stalks, their feathery tops rustling together in the wind.

"Cyrus, you never realize the value of a urine diverter until you've seen it in use. Urine diversion is the key to preventing odors," Charlie said smiling with a look of a wise mentor.

"More than I think I ever wanted to know." Cyrus smiled.

James smiled too. "Well, let's get cleaning, and I'll show you how we make compost."

The three used the cleaning supplies James brought from the house. In each of the three rooms they swept the floor, disinfected the toilet seats, and then resupplied toilet paper and filled up the sawdust bucket. When they were done, Cyrus had a sense of accomplishment, but they weren't through yet.

"Alright, this is the best part, Cyrus," Charlie said proudly. "Let's move that poop."

"I think you're getting way too excited about this, Charlie." James smirked.

It was easier than Cyrus feared. They unscrewed the hoses from the bins and tilted each bin onto its wheels to roll it toward the garden. The three men pulled the wheelie bins in a caravan. The rhythmic motion of the bins over the uneven ground mirrored their movements, the plastic containers trailing behind like obedient beasts of burden.

Near the large garden, wooden pallets formed into makeshift crates enclosed several mounds of material, holding the heaps in and preventing them from spilling over the edges.

They helped each other shovel the contents of each wheelie bin into the large containers and then covered them with extra garden debris like old grass clippings and weeds. Charlie explained that each pile was in different stages of decomposition. If the temperature reached high enough the process could take a couple of months, but if not, it could take as long as two years before it turned into usable compost.

As Charlie explained, he leaned in, his eyes lighting up with enthusiasm as he launched into a detailed breakdown, gesturing with his hands to illustrate each point.

After a while, Cyrus's attention drifted past Charlie and James out to the high desert stretching endlessly beyond them.

The rugged landscape of Eastern Oregon unfolded in soft shades of gold and rust. Stiff, weathered green sagebrush stood rooted and unmoving, while patches of rabbit brush, their own foliage tinged a similar muted green, swayed gently in the breeze. At the tips, clusters of golden blooms caught the light like tiny flames flickering against the earth-toned backdrop. His eyes lingered on the distant mountain range, striking against the clear blue sky. The peaks stood resolute, bathed in the desert sun's warm, otherworldly light. A scene of such quiet beauty made the drone of the explanation fade into background noise, leaving him lost in the vastness of the land.

Cyrus adopted a look of attentiveness, nodding at the right pauses. When Charlie was finally finished, Cyrus thanked him but turned their attention to the view.

"This sure is beautiful. How far out does your commune's land go?" Cyrus asked.

"It goes past the foothills you see out to the west beyond that river." James pointed toward the winding river and foothills in the distance, his finger tracing the gentle rise of the land.

"Yeah, if you go out that way, you'll see an old mine from the 1800s. Pretty cool," said Charlie. "You know, I was hiking out near there a couple years ago and saw some people poking around the old mine site. It's on our land, you know. I'm convinced they were checking out the mine for something. I could see with my binoculars they had equipment and shovels and stuff. I bet they were planting monitoring equipment because of us."

James let out an exasperated sigh. "Charlie, we love you, man, but you have to stop with all the conspiracy bullshit. Oregon had a mining boom back in the 1850s, when they mined for gold and other minerals. It's part of Oregon history. Every once in a while you'll see some overzealous eco-tourist who wants to explore things, not knowing it's our land, and strays onto the property to learn about our illustrious history."

A tense quietness about him hinted that Charlie had been chided for his beliefs in the past. His face grew stern; lips closed in a line. "Yeah, well, I've been here eight years and never saw anyone there before or since."

"Let's lay off of the weird theories," James said in an annoyed tone.

Cyrus wiped his hands on a rag, the sharp scent of bleach still clinging to the air. A moment ago, the mood had been light, three guys joking around, cleaning up like it was summer camp. But now the air felt heavier.

After working with James and Charlie, Cyrus decided everything seemed . . . well-maintained. Tidy, even. Nothing that supported the theory Gus had planted in his head the night before.

Still, not all of it had been a waste.

Cyrus glanced between the two men.

At first, he had thought James was one of the friendlier ones, easygoing, with a good sense of humor, and over breakfast Cyrus had heard him mention tide lines, which made him sound practical and careful. But the way he snapped just now, the edge in his voice when Charlie brought up the old mine, it felt off. Too defensive. Too harsh.

That was more than annoyance, Cyrus thought. That was a shutdown, and it sounded like someone hiding something. The shift came so fast it left him unsettled. Maybe there was something more complicated with James. Maybe even something darker. Either way, he needed to keep his eyes open.

"Come on," James said suddenly, breaking through Cyrus's thoughts. "Let's get some lunch."

8

As the three entered the dining room, Cyrus took a breath, nervous he'd have another confrontation with Grady. But it was past lunchtime, and there were only a couple other people lingering. One of the two was Vlad. He was eating with a hearty appetite, his muscular arms flexing with every movement as he scooped up large bites from a round bowl. His jaw worked steadily, focused on his food, but every few moments, he paused to scratch at his neck, where Cyrus had seen the skin rash the day before. The scratching was quick and distracted, as if Vlad barely noticed it anymore. As he dug in for another bite, Cyrus caught a clearer view of his hands, patches of rash on his palms. That gave Cyrus pause. The blotchy discoloration wasn't just redness, some areas looked unnaturally dark, the skin raised and rough, as if it had been scraped or calloused without reason.

Yesterday, in passing, Cyrus had assumed it was a birthmark. But now, seeing it closer he realized it wasn't.

It was something else. Something rare.

James and Charlie sat with Vlad, engaged in conversation. Cyrus stood there awkwardly unsure of what to do.

At a nearby table, he spotted a man sitting alone. Cyrus recognized him immediately, the one who had spoken first at the bonfire the night before. Calvin.

He was a large, solidly built man with dark skin, wearing a pair of well-worn overalls. His frame filled the chair easily, arms thick with muscle, and he projected a quiet kind of strength. Strands of white threaded through his close-cropped hair and beard, and Cyrus guessed he was in his mid-sixties. He sat, chewing slowly, his shoulders rounding as leaned over his plate, and there was something unhurried in the way he worked through his lunch.

Betting on the warm comfort he felt from the man, Cyrus walked toward him.

Calvin looked up from his meal and smiled. "You're the guy who tried to help Brent, huh?"

Cyrus nodded. "Well, yeah, I tried"

He nodded back, then hooked his foot around one of the empty chairs next to him and slid it out with a soft scrape on the floor. His gesture was casual but clear, an unspoken invitation for Cyrus to sit.

"I'm Cyrus."

"Yeah, I know. I'm Calvin Ellingson."

As Cyrus sat, he let out a sigh. "Nice to meet you, Calvin. So, what do you all have for lunch?"

"There's leftovers from last night, or we have stuff for sandwiches. We have homemade bread—Dana makes it—and we raise chickens, so you could make a chicken sandwich."

Cyrus's stomach growled at the memory of the stew from the night before. He got up to ladle a large helping of stew in an empty bowl and quickly returned to the table.

The two men sat eating quietly for a while before Cyrus asked, "So have you lived here long?"

Without looking up from his food, Calvin replied, "My wife and I were the first to move here when Kevin started Reckoning Grove."

Cyrus recalled the night before when Gus described Reckoning Grove's beginnings and the founder's death.

Calvin continued, "My wife is white, and as you can see, I'm not. We lived in Klamath Falls at the time. K-Falls is a couple hours from here. I don't know if you did much studying about the history of Oregon, but it started as a white-only state. In fact, there was a ton of racist language in the Oregon constitution until about eight years ago."

Cyrus's eyes grew wide. "Are you kidding me? Where am I?"

Calvin continued without missing a beat, "Bunch of cities in Oregon were called sundown towns, which meant if you're black, don't let the sun go down on you in our town. Well K-Falls was one of those back in the day. Even though there wasn't any more segregation, there were enough people reminding Cindy and me that we got sick of it. We wanted to start over again, and that's about when we met Kevin. Kevin had all these crazy ideas about starting a perfect community, and Cindy and I bought into it. We've been here since."

"How many years is that?" Cyrus asked.

"Oh, man, gotta be . . . Wow, sixteen years. Damn, time flies when you get older, huh?" he said with a distant look in his eyes.

"You know, my dad has a saying," Cyrus said with a smile. "Life is like a toilet paper roll."

Calvin's far-off look instantly faded, and he looked back at Cyrus. His posture shifted faintly, curiosity and interest sparking in his expression.

Cyrus continued, "When you're young, time goes slow, like the beginning of the full toilet paper roll. Then when you get older, time flies by quick, the way the roll spins by like a flash."

"Your dad's something else," Calvin replied, and they both laughed.

Then Calvin pushed his plate a few inches away. "Haven't been feeling up to eating lately," he said quietly. "Just feeling sick all the time."

Cyrus's smile faded. As Calvin spoke, he noticed something odd, faint, reddish patches along the man's palms. Subtle, but unusual.

Almost exactly like he'd seen on Vlad. And paired with nausea or loss of appetite? That set off quiet alarm bells in his head.

But the nausea! His pulse quickened. This was the first person he'd met with symptoms that matched Brent's.

Before he could ask more, Calvin stood up, his expression shifting.

"I want to show you the garden where Cindy and I were working this morning," he said, his tone inviting.

Cyrus hesitated for half a second, then rose to follow. "Sure," he said, managing a smile. He'd ask more once they got there; whatever was going on, this may be the break he needed.

The two men walked out past the outhouses, the scent of earth and fresh air mingling around them. The garden sprawled across nearly an acre, long runs of tidy beds in straight, well-kept rows. Cyrus was struck by the sheer size of it, then reminded himself it had to be this large, enough to feed twenty people year-round and still leave a surplus for the farmers' market in summer. Ever the doctor, his gaze shifted to Calvin's stride, recalling Brent's mention of numbness in his feet. He watched for a hitch or drag, but Calvin's steps landed even and sure.

In the middle of the garden, amidst the sprawling greenery, was a petite woman in her sixties, her white hair pulled back with two small clips, but as they approached Cyrus noticed patches where her hair seemed thin or missing. Cyrus couldn't help but notice it. Despite her age, she had a youthful manner—her movements were lithe, and she bent low with a trowel in her hands, working the soil with practiced ease. She wore a faded pink T-shirt and a pair of dirty jeans, the kind of honest dirt that could only be earned from hours spent working outdoors.

When she noticed them approaching, she stood up from her task, wiping her hands on her pants. A quick, friendly smile crossed her face. "You must be Cyrus." They shook hands, and Cyrus was surprised by her firm and strong grip, a sign of someone accustomed to hard work.

"I'm sorry I didn't get a chance to meet you earlier at breakfast," she said, her voice laced with an apologetic tone. "I've been feeling nauseated the last few days, no appetite. But I'm glad you're here."

Cyrus's eyes sharpened. Another one.

That made two people, Calvin and now Cindy, with the same vague but troubling symptoms Brent had described. Nausea. Appetite loss.

Cindy walked a few steps ahead, her rubber boots pressing softly into the garden path as she waved a gloved hand toward the rows of vegetables. "These are our fall staples," she said. "Kale's doing great this year, see how the leaves catch the light like that? Like they're proud of themselves."

Cyrus smiled as he took it in, the ruffled green leaves fluttering in the breeze, a patch of pumpkins nestled nearby, their round orange bodies glowing gently in the afternoon sun. Thick vines curled like lazy question marks across the soil.

"Those pumpkins'll be ready soon," Cindy went on. "We've got carrots and potatoes farther down, too. This time of year, the ground just gives and gives."

The scent of earth and crushed leaves hung in the air, rich and clean.

Cindy bent forward to check a row of beets, brushing a bit of soil from the base of one with practiced fingers. "My doctor, Doc Bronson, tells me I'm supposed to cut way back on salt and fluids," she said casually, straightening up with a small grunt. "Congestive heart failure. But I swear, eating all this good food from the garden's helped more than any pill they've given me."

Cyrus eyebrows rose; he knew Dr. Bronson. "You're drinking a lot of fluids?"

She nodded, pulling off one glove and wiping her brow. "Yeah, lately I've been so nauseated, water's the only thing that settles me. I know I'm not supposed to, but when your stomach's churning, you do what works, right?"

Cyrus hesitated, a flicker of concern tightening in his chest. He glanced at Cindy, studying her for a moment, her pale skin, the subtle weariness behind her eyes.

"I don't want to alarm you," he said carefully, "but the fact that you're both feeling nauseated worries me. When I first met Brent . . . he had similar symptoms. Nausea, no appetite. Some weakness. It might be nothing, but I have to ask, when did it start?"

Calvin frowned, glancing at Cindy.

"A couple weeks ago?" she offered, and Calvin nodded in agreement.

Cyrus continued, "Have you been eating the same foods? Drinking the same water?"

They both gave him a strange look.

"Well, yeah," Calvin said. "We all eat from the same kitchen, same food as everyone else."

Cyrus nodded slowly, but the unease in his chest didn't fade. Something didn't add up, but he was getting closer.

He watched Calvin and Cindy move through the garden, their quiet coordination and care offering a glimpse of a life rooted in purpose. For a brief moment, he imagined what it might feel like to stay, to belong to something so grounded.

But the image didn't hold. His mind drifted back to the rash on Calvin's palms and Vlad's rash. Then the nausea, suffered by both Calvin and Cindy. He recalled the differential he had pieced together after Brent's death and turned it over again. Last night he had told himself it was only Brent, that he would spend the night and slip out in the morning. But now there were others with symptoms, and that changed everything.

Perhaps it was botulism overlaid with something else, a viral infection like hand, foot, mouth disease caused by coxsackievirus. And though the commune's diet seemed balanced, he knew several rashes could point toward nutritional deficiencies—niacin, zinc, riboflavin. All of those could account for the skin findings.

Cyrus folded his arms, eyes narrowing as the wind moved through the trees. He had planned to leave, but this felt different now. Maybe he should stay one more day and try to fit the pieces together.

He walked back toward Brent's old RV. From a distance he saw something on the door, a pale square trembling in the breeze. As he drew closer, he saw a note taped above the handle.

YOU'RE LOOKING FOR THINGS THAT AREN'T THERE.

YOUR QUESTIONS ARE CAUSING ANXIETY.

PLEASE LEAVE WITHIN 36 HOURS.

He stood very still. So, there was something here. Someone wanted him to stop looking.

For a moment he thought he should go. Pack up, keep moving, let Reckoning Grove handle its own problems. Then Brent's face rose up in his mind, the gray stillness after the last breath. Cindy's nausea. Calvin's rash. He had been a doctor once. Whatever else had fallen away, that part of him still urged him on.

He glanced around the quiet yard and felt the hair lift on his arms. He would be careful. He would keep his head down. But he would stay, at least one more day, and try to fit the pieces together.

9

The next morning, Cyrus sat at a wooden table in the dining room, a coffee cup warming his hands. Across from him, Dana settled into a seat, her long brown hair cascading over her shoulders, framing her face softly. She wore a simple cotton shirt and jeans that perfectly matched the relaxed vibe of Reckoning Grove.

Around them the room hummed with low conversation, dishes clinking, chairs shifting, but Cyrus could tell by the way Dana folded her hands and leaned in that this wasn't just small talk.

He mirrored her posture, setting his cup down.

"I stayed out by the fire a little longer last night after you left," she said quietly, her voice calm but purposeful. "There's something I think you should know."

Cyrus's brow furrowed. "Everything alright?"

Dana hesitated, her gaze drifting across the room. She didn't look nervous, just thoughtful. Concerned.

She took a breath, brushing a strand of hair behind her ear. "I'm not sure yet. But something doesn't feel right."

Dana glanced around once more, then leaned in a little closer, her voice quiet. "I wanted to tell you something before you heard it from someone else. Grady's been saying things, about you."

She paused, choosing her words carefully. "He's telling people you might be some kind of sleeper agent. That you're here to set up . . . a militia camp with bad intentions."

Cyrus blinked.

Dana's expression was steady, but there was a hint of frustration in her eyes. "He's bringing up this old story, something that happened years ago out in southeast Oregon, where a group of Muslim men were training for some kind of terrorist attack, but got stopped before they could do anything. He's twisting it to make people nervous about you. I thought you should know."

Cyrus sighed. "Jesus, Dana, there's always something, huh?"

He leaned back in his chair, rubbing a hand over his face. The plan had been simple, stay a few days, keep his head down, and move on. But now, thanks to Grady, everything felt twisted up. It was maddening, how one bully with a big mouth could stir so much trouble when all Cyrus wanted was to lend a hand and then disappear.

For a while, he'd tried to shrug off the whispers, even joke his way past the sharp edges of gossip. But the tactic was wearing thin. If Grady kept this up, brushing it aside wasn't going to cut it. Next time, Cyrus thought, he might have to deal with the man directly, put an end to it before the rumors grew into something worse.

Dana eased into her chair, the wood creaking softly beneath her. She leaned an elbow on the table, her smile lingering as if replaying what Cyrus had just said. "So," she asked, tilting her head toward him, "other than Grady, what do you think of Reckoning Grove so far? And more importantly, what's next for you?"

Cyrus wrapped his hands around his mug, nodding slowly. "First off, thanks for letting me stay, Dana. I really love this place so far, the spirit of it, the people." His voice dropped, thoughtful. "But there's something bothering me about Brent's death. I can't shake the worry that it wasn't just bad luck. If there's something here causing infections, I'd like to stay a couple more days, look into it. And," he glanced around at the mismatched chairs, the warm clutter of the dining hall "I'd love to pitch in with chores, too. It only feels right to repay the generosity you all have shown."

He didn't mention the note on the RV door. No point scaring Dana yet, and he wasn't sure what to make of it until he knew more.

Dana's expression softened, the smile giving way to something closer to gratitude. "Thank you, Cyrus. If you think something's wrong, it would be good for all of us if you helped with your expertise. We could use that kind of watchfulness here. Like I said, our rule is anyone can stay for up to two weeks before we vote." She hesitated, then let a playful note creep back into her voice. "And since you're offering, I'm cooking dinner tonight. If you really want to help, you can come find me in the kitchen."

He gave a small, reluctant smile. "Alright. That sounds fun."

She stood and picked up her plate, pausing before turning toward the kitchen. "I'll be down in the kitchen this afternoon getting things ready," she said over her shoulder. "Meet me there around three, we'll get started on dinner prep. I gotta go, but maybe, while we cook you could tell me more about your concerns."

With that she walked off to rinse her plate and put it away.

Cyrus finished his breakfast, toast and eggs, then spent the morning wandering the grounds of Reckoning Grove. As he walked toward the far end of the commune, past the garden, a glimmer in the distance drew his eye. Moving closer, he saw the source, a large, still body of water shimmering under the midday sun.

When he reached the edge, Cyrus paused in quiet awe. The pool was no larger than thirty feet across, a near-perfect circle of crystal water. Its surface gleamed like polished glass, so clear he could see the bed of rounded stones and pale sand shifting beneath the gentle flow. A soft burble rose from where the underground pressure forced the spring up, feeding the basin in a steady, endless trickle. Cyrus recalled reading about Artesian springs, the water, forced upward under pressure, had already passed through layers of sand and stone, leaving it naturally filtered before it reached the surface.

To his left, a squat metal pump sat at the edge, its low, steady hum vibrating faintly through the ground as it drew water toward the farmhouse. The sound blended with birdsong and the rustle of leaves, a mechanical heartbeat tethered to the earth's veins.

When Cyrus rose, his eyes caught the glint of dark glass in the field beyond. Several rows of solar panels tilted toward the sun, just as Dana had described when he first arrived. Together, sun and spring sustained this place, off the grid, fragile yet complete, as though the land itself had decided to shelter the people who called it home.

He turned and started wandering back toward the main cluster of buildings. The farmhouse came into view, its pale paint catching the afternoon sun. Just beside it, half-concealed by a patch of tall grass, was a wooden door at an angle: cellar access.

Cyrus froze when he spotted the cellar doors tucked into the slope beside the farmhouse. His heart kicked against his ribs. This had to be it, the cellar Gus mentioned at the bonfire, the very one Brent had been talking about before he died.

He reached for the handle, the metal cold against his palm, and pulled. The hinges groaned as the doors swung open. A breath of cooler air drifted up, damp and tinged with earth. Cyrus drew in a steadying breath and started down the narrow, creaking steps.

The light behind him fell into a dusty beam and thinned as he reached the packed earth floor. He let his eyes adjust. Bins of potatoes and squash sat under the stairs. Shelves ran along the wall, heavy with jars. Soups, jams, tomatoes, green beans. Some labels were tidy. Others were scraps of old tape, edges lifting, ink gone faint.

He moved closer. Several jars had times written under the date, but the timing looked wrong for safe canning here. At this elevation they should have used a pressure canner or added more time and acid. These notes were short, like a quick water bath, and a couple labels didn't match the batch count on the log.

He picked a quart of green beans that looked off. The liquid was a little cloudy, a faint ring clung below the shoulder. He studied the label. The handwriting had that small crossbar on the 7, the way some people write it, and the letters matched, too. It was the same hand as the note on the RV door yesterday. His heart kicked hard. He was onto something.

Cyrus tucked the jar carefully into his jacket. The local health department could test for botulinum toxin. If he was right, this could explain everything.

An hour and a half later, Mystique rumbled down Crater Lake Parkway into Klamath Falls, Oregon. The early-afternoon sun lay flat and brilliant over the town, casting sharp shadows across wide streets. Cyrus steered off the main drag and onto Vandenburg Avenue. To his left, tidy suburban storefronts and modest homes, similar to any mid-sized American city, stretched in neat blocks: clean facades, lawns trimmed, signs for cafés and hardware stores.

But all around, the setting betrayed something more raw and majestic. The city lay at about 4,000 feet elevation, perched in the high desert basin east of the Cascade Range. The air was dry; the vegetation sparse but vivid, clumps of sagebrush, light green juniper, distant ridges etched with the yellow and red brown color of ochre and russet soils. Beyond the outskirts, low rolling hills rose gradually, holding the threat and promise of wilderness.

It felt almost contradictory, this ordinary town life, swinging in the cradle of stark, wide-open terrain. Suburban strip malls and neat pavement, all framed by wild high desert land, blue skies that seemed endless, and mountains that loomed out of nowhere. Cyrus fingered the jar in his lap, certain the health department would see it for what it was, a threat that could sicken an entire community if left unchecked.

He'd been all over the country these past few years, big cities, back roads, nowhere towns, but something about Klamath Falls gave him pause. Maybe it was the way the dry high desert air met the cool, pine-scented breeze. Maybe it was the space, how everything here felt spread out, untethered.

Back east, in Corlen, Virginia, where Cyrus had been a small-town doctor, rural life had been different. Tighter. Even the most remote places had a back road that led to somewhere familiar. Here, though, fifteen thousand people lived in a town that felt like it was floating in the middle of nowhere. The nearest big town was two hours out. A big city like Portland? Five.

He didn't mind. There was something honest and self-sufficient about it. And he hoped that honesty extended to the people at the health department.

He pulled into a small lot and parked in front of a squat, beige building: Klamath County Public Health. The sign out front was sun-bleached and leaning slightly, but the front doors were clean and well maintained.

Cyrus killed the engine and sat for a moment, staring at the entrance. Then he grabbed the jar he'd brought and stepped out. As he walked toward the doors, he felt a flicker of an emotion he hadn't felt in a long time—purpose. He felt like he could fix something . . . finally.

He pulled the left-hand door open and headed toward the front desk. Inside, the lobby smelled faintly of disinfectant and aging carpet. The woman behind the desk glanced up from her computer with a practiced smile.

"Can I help you?"

"Yes," Cyrus said. He held up the sealed jar of vegetables. "I need to talk to someone, about a possible pathogen in a nearby community."

The receptionist blinked but nodded and handed him a clipboard. "Fill this out, please. Someone will be with you shortly."

Cyrus sat in the waiting area, the jar resting on the floor beside him. The minutes ticked by, slow and quiet. He watched the second hand on a faded wall clock drag its way around the face twice before a door opened.

A man in his mid-forties came out, glancing around the room. He had graying dark hair, thick eyebrows, and wore a navy polo tucked neatly into khaki pants. An ID badge swung gently from a neck lanyard as he moved.

"Cyrus?" the man asked.

Cyrus stood. "Yeah."

The man extended a hand. "Justin Reed. I'm the environmental health administrator."

They shook hands, and Justin gestured down the hall. "Come on back. Let's talk."

He led Cyrus into a small, cluttered office. Papers were stacked on every flat surface, and a worn map of Klamath County was pinned to the far wall. A coffee mug sat precariously on top of a half-empty printer tray.

Justin dropped into his chair and motioned for Cyrus to sit across from him. "Alright," he said. "What's going on?"

Cyrus leaned forward, resting the canned food on the edge of Justin's desk. "I'm a physician, visiting from out of town. I'm staying at a place nearby, a commune. People there are showing strange symptoms: fatigue, nausea, and what looks like acute neuropathy. I think there's a chance we're looking at an outbreak of *Clostridium botulinum*."

Justin raised an eyebrow, his expression still neutral.

"I brought this," Cyrus continued, holding up the glass mason jar. "They can their food themselves. I was hoping you could have it tested."

But at the mention of "commune," something shifted. Justin's posture stiffened imperceptibly.

"Wait," he said, eyes narrowing. "You're not talking about Reckoning Grove, are you?"

Cyrus nodded. "Yeah. That's the place."

Justin let out a long, exasperated breath and leaned back in his chair, arms crossed. Whatever curiosity or concern had been in his face a moment ago vanished.

"Okay, look. I don't have time for all you folks from *that place* coming in here with some new theory every month. Poisonings, infections, government trackers, heard it all. Like I told the last guy: unless you've got symptoms worth worrying about, we're not chasing shadows."

Cyrus stared at him. There was something in the way Justin said *that place*. It wasn't just dismissal, it was disdain. The same kind of thinly veiled antagonism he'd sensed back in Lakeview, that quiet prejudice against anyone from Reckoning Grove. Maybe Brent's frustration hadn't been paranoia after all. Maybe the people in town really did see the commune as a nuisance, or worse. And Justin's reaction seemed like proof.

"What am I supposed to do, then?"

"You need a licensed medical provider to report it."

"I *am* a doctor," Cyrus said sharply. "And I *am* reporting it."

Cyrus paused. He understood this was an important moment; he had to convince this man to follow up. "Listen, I understand your hesitation, these symptoms are mild. Classically botulism is a rapidly progressive, severe neuroparalytic illness. But sometimes presentations can be mild with low-level toxin exposure. What I'm worried about is that if we don't catch things sooner something much more dire will happen. In fact, one of the people who lived there just died a couple days ago."

"Fine, Dr. Cyrus," Justin replied dryly, taking the jar from him and placing it on his cluttered desk. "I'll be sure to investigate it. Right after I finish my stack of paperwork, field two outbreaks of flu, and figure out where our lab samples from last week disappeared to."

Cyrus gritted his teeth. "Who came in here before me? You said someone else from the commune was here?"

Justin shrugged. "I don't know. Some guy. I don't keep names when I toss out bad leads."

Cyrus stood, frustrated.

"Thanks for your time," he muttered, already halfway out the door.

The sun was beginning to dip toward the horizon as he stepped back into the fading afternoon light. He glanced at the time, recalling that he'd promised Dana he'd help with dinner.

Cyrus jogged back to the truck, fired up the engine, and turned back toward the open road. He drove with one hand on the wheel, the other tapping restlessly against his thigh, his mind racing. The health department's brush-off gnawed at him, not just the indifference, but the casual contempt. Was that what people really thought of Reckoning Grove? Some far-out cult? Was that bias going to keep people from getting help? From being believed?

And then there was the other thing, "some guy" who'd come in before him, asking questions.

Someone else was poking around. But who?

And why?

10

Cyrus entered the dining room, his shirt damp with sweat, barely making it in time.

At the same moment, Dana walked in cradling a bowl piled high with red tomatoes. She paused when she saw him, her eyes narrowing slightly.

"You okay?" she asked. "You look like you just sprinted up the hill."

Cyrus wiped his brow with the back of his hand, trying to steady his breath. "Just taking a little . . . extended tour of the commune," he said with a weak smile.

Dana tilted her head, clearly unconvinced. "Uh-huh."

She studied him for a moment longer, then let it go with a shrug, turning back to sort the tomatoes. "Well, we've got work to do. Can you get the door to the kitchen?"

Cyrus pushed open the door and stood to the side so Dana could pass.

"I was thinking we'd make hamburger soup, salad, and bread. I brought in the last of our late fall tomatoes, and Charlie had to go into town yesterday to pick up supplies like ground beef."

Dana stopped talking as she set down the tomatoes on the counter. "I usually make two batches, one for vegetarians and the other with meat. And of course, my special fresh baked bread." She cupped her hands around an imaginary loaf of bread.

"Sounds delicious," Cyrus said. "I'm hungry already." He glanced at the counter, fresh squash, onions, a bundle of herbs, a sack of rice. No jars. Relief slid through him. He'd tell Dana about the canning soon, but not yet; better to wait for the health department call than scare her on a hunch.

They began by cutting up the fresh tomatoes, carrots, and onions.

As he prepped the ingredients, Cyrus snuck a taste of a tomato from the garden. The explosion of flavor was immediate and overwhelming. The bright and fresh sweetness was a sharp contrast to the bland, mealy tomatoes he used to buy at the grocery store. He closed his eyes, savoring the moment, the natural sweetness lingering long after he swallowed. This was what a tomato was meant to be, vibrant and alive, with layers of flavor that told the story of the earth it had come from.

They put half the prepped ingredients with ground beef into one pot and half with the vegetable protein in another. As the ground beef sautéed at the bottom of the pan, the aroma filled the kitchen, rich and inviting, the meat's savory scent mingling with the tang of caramelizing onions. They then poured in vegetable stock and turned the heat down to a simmer. With a gentle flourish, Dana added garden fresh oregano, basil, thyme, and ground pepper. The delicate, herbal fragrance mingled beautifully with the hearty scents already simmering, adding a subtle complexity to the dish.

As the soup simmered, Dana started on the bread. She began by combining water, yeast and sugar.

"I usually make about four or five loaves— enough for dinner and lunch the next day. But first you have to wait for the yeast to activate. When the yeast starts feeding on the sugar, it makes carbon dioxide," she said as she mixed. "Watch for the bubbles."

Cyrus knew this but didn't want to interrupt. He enjoyed watching her gentle, patient hands and their rhythmic motion.

"The secret's in using extra sugar and yeast. Extra sugar excites the yeast to make it fluffy and sweet."

When the yeast was ready, Dana mixed in flour and salt.

She kneaded the dough, the warm kitchen light illuminating her focused expression. A few specks of flour dusted her cheek, and a loose strand of brown hair had fallen over it, framing her face. She moved with a confident rhythm, her hands working the dough into a smooth, elastic ball, her brow furrowed in concentration.

The striking scene transported Cyrus to another time and another kitchen.

A kitchen alive with the sounds of laughter and the soft hum of activity. Cyrus sat at the table, leaning back in his chair, watching Juliette roll dough on the floured countertop. The late afternoon sunlight streamed through the windows, casting a warm glow on the scene.

On the counter beside her sat their two children, Freddie and Samira, both perched precariously like little birds, giggling and wriggling with excitement. Every few moments, Juliette would pinch off a small piece of dough and hand it to them, their tiny hands grabbing it eagerly. They popped the dough into their mouths, their faces lighting up with delight.

"More, Mommy! More!" their youngest, Samira, pleaded, bits of raw dough still clinging to her lips.

"Alright, alright," Juliette said laughing, her voice carrying the kind of joy that made the whole room feel brighter. She tore off another piece and handed it over.

Cyrus couldn't help but grin. There was something mesmerizing about the way Juliette worked, the rhythm of her hands and arms as she kneaded the dough, the light bounce of her breasts . . . her hair tied back but with a few stray strands escaping to frame her face.

He got up and walked over to her, drawn by the magnetic pull of her energy.

"Don't think I'm giving you a full piece," she teased, glancing at him from the corner of her eye. "You're as bad as the kids."

"I'll take what I can get," he said with a smirk.

Juliette broke off the tiniest piece of dough and, with a playful smile, lifted it to his lips. He opened his mouth, letting her place it on his tongue, then chewed slowly, savoring the soft, yeasty sweetness. "Not bad," he said, nodding approvingly.

She rolled her eyes. "It's not done yet."

Cyrus chuckled, leaning closer. She had a smudge of flour on her cheek under her left eye. Without thinking, he reached out, brushing it away with his thumb.

"There," he said softly.

She glanced up at him, her smile softening. Before either of them could say a word, he leaned forward and kissed her.

The kiss was brief, tender, and familiar, a moment of quiet connection amid the chaos of life.

Cyrus's attention slipped back to Dana as she pounded the last of the dough on the counter. She shaped the dough into a loaf and looked up. "We need to let these sit for a while in a warm place so they can rise."

They turned their attention to the salad. Cyrus tore the lettuce into bite-sized pieces while Dana diced ripe tomatoes, cucumbers, and bell peppers, their colors bright and vibrant against the cutting board. As she whisked together olive oil, vinegar, salt, and pepper for a simple dressing, the fragrant mixture came together beautifully.

They tossed the lettuce and vegetables in a large bowl, creating an inviting salad that perfectly complemented their meal.

By then enough time had passed that the dough had risen.

Dana moved toward a counter. "You have to score the bread to help it expand more and keep it from cracking." She opened a cabinet and came out with a tiny razor blade.

Cyrus frowned, confused.

"Most bakers use a bread lame, but it's cheaper to buy a bunch of razor blades like we keep here." Dana approached the loaves of bread with the sharp blade and expertly scored the surfaces with clean, diagonal slashes.

Cyrus couldn't help but admire her precision. "You're really good at that."

She looked up and smiled warmly. "Thanks. My mother taught me," she replied, her voice softening at the mention of her family.

"Were you close with your family?" Cyrus asked, leaning against the counter.

Dana nodded, her expression turning wistful. "Very. My family was everything to me. I even went to college so I could do a good job when I came back to work on their ranch. It was the plan my whole life."

Cyrus hesitated but asked gently, "What happened?"

Dana paused, her hand resting on the edge of the counter. "In my senior year of college, my brother called me one evening out of nowhere and told me there had been a terrible car accident. My parents . . . they were gone. Just like that. He said they died instantly." Her voice wavered, but she steadied herself. "I kept asking him for details, but he was evasive. Wouldn't tell me much beyond the basics. It didn't sit right with me, but I was so shocked at the time, I didn't push harder."

Cyrus frowned, sensing more. "What happened to the ranch?"

Dana's face darkened. "That's the strangest part. I tried to move back and help my brother with the ranch, but he wouldn't let me.

Said I had ruined everything, and I didn't belong there anymore. It didn't make sense. We used to be so close, like a team. He wouldn't even let me go through their things. It was like the life I thought I'd return to just . . . vanished overnight." Her voice cracked, and she shook her head as if trying to shake off the weight of the memory.

Cyrus stepped closer, placing a gentle hand on her shoulder. "Dana, I'm so sorry that happened to you. That's . . . awful. That isn't something you deserved."

Dana looked at him, her eyes glistening. She placed her hand over his, squeezing it lightly. "Thank you, Cyrus," she said, her voice steady but full of gratitude. "It means a lot to hear that."

They held each other's gaze for a moment, her hand still resting lightly over his. For an instant, the world around them narrowed to the two of them. But then the sound of voices and footsteps echoed from the entrance to the dining area. Dana pulled her hand back, and they both turned away, shifting their focus back to the work at hand.

Dana reached for the knife again, hesitated, then said quietly, "Do you have family, Cyrus? Anyone waiting for you somewhere?"

He didn't answer right away. The chopping slowed. When he finally spoke, his voice was clipped, almost too neutral. "Not anymore."

Dana looked over, her brow creasing. "I'm sorry. I didn't mean to,"

"It's fine," he said quickly, cutting her off. He picked up another potato and sliced into it harder than necessary. "Let's just finish up with dinner."

Dana nodded and said nothing more. She gave the soup a gentle stir, then replaced the lid. They moved in quiet sync, each tending to small tasks, the moment slipping easily back into the rhythm of the evening, unspoken understanding, nothing forced, no questionable topic broached.

The warm, savory smell of hamburger soup filled the air, mingling with the sharp tang of fresh bread. It wrapped around the room like a comforting blanket as the members of Reckoning Grove trickled into the dining hall, their chatter light and cheerful after a long day's work.

Cyrus and Dana moved between the tables, setting out bowls and baskets of bread, the energy around them easy and expectant, the kind of simple pleasure that made everything, for a moment, feel right.

People found their seats, laughing, jostling, ready to dig in. The dining room filled with the sounds of clinking silverware and the low murmur of conversation as dishes were passed hand to hand.

A moment later, the floorboards creaked near the entrance, and Vlad stepped into the room. He moved with his usual slow, heavy gait, broad shoulders hunched, eyes scanning for an open spot. Without a word, he made his way to an empty seat near the far end of the room, settling in beside a few commune members Cyrus hadn't met yet. They gave him small nods of acknowledgment, shifting to make room as he grabbed a bowl and started ladling soup onto it.

Out of habit, Cyrus looked for the rash on Vlad's neck, the one he had seen the other day, but now, the skin was swollen, the redness creeping further across his neck. Vlad's hand hovered near it, itching to scratch, but he winced at the pain and stopped. With an uncomfortable look he tried to take a bite of food, but his face twisted in discomfort. He grimaced and set the spoon aside with a frustrated huff.

Without thinking, Cyrus got up and moved to sit next to Vlad. He wanted to evaluate his neck.

Vlad glowered at him. "I'm fine."

Cyrus pressed his lips together, hurt. "I just wanted to look at your neck. It looks infected."

"Fuck, last thing I need. I'll tough it out."

Cyrus wasn't convinced. "I think you need to go see a doctor. That looks angry."

Vlad didn't look at Cyrus, instead staring forward with an irritated scowl. After a brief pause, he stood, leaving the bowl of soup untouched, and stomped out of the room.

Cyrus made his way back to the table and sat down beside Dana with a quiet sigh. “If that abscess keeps growing, he could stop breathing,” he murmured. He rubbed at his temple, the worry gnawing at him. “Vlad seems like the kind who tries to tough everything out, but infections don’t play by those rules.”

11

Enough morning light slipped through the RV blinds to awaken Cyrus. He pulled on his boots, a clean shirt and underwear then opened the door and set his weight on the first step.

The metal shrieked and dropped out from under him. He pitched forward, scraped a palm on the metal door frame, then slammed shoulder and hip into the dirt. For a second all he could hear was the ringing in his ears.

He rolled to a knee and looked back. The bracket of the triple stair hung crooked, screws backed out, one sheared clean. Not an accident.

A note was taped above the door handle.

TIME IS UP.

LEAVE FIRST THING TOMORROW MORNING.

He scanned the yard, slow and careful. Nothing moved.

If someone wanted him gone, he must be close to finding the truth. He brushed the dust from his hands and headed for the house. He would tell Dana they needed to stop using canned food, then he could leave for good.

As Cyrus crossed the dining room to get coffee, he spotted Dana sitting at a table with Charlie. Charlie leaned in slightly, murmuring something to her with a crooked grin, causing her to let out a light, easy laugh. He also saw Grady in conversation with James at another table. Their gazes flicked briefly toward him before returning to their conversation. Grady's stare pierced him from behind as he poured the warm dark coffee into his mug.

With his cup cradled in his hands, Cyrus eased in next to Dana and Charlie. As he did, Charlie subtly scooted a few feet away. He had been more standoffish since Grady started spreading rumors about Cyrus trying to set up a terrorist camp. Nevertheless, Dana smiled with a warm welcoming look, inviting Cyrus to settle.

"Well, what are you all up to today?" Cyrus asked.

Charlie grunted as if not interested in answering. An annoyed look in her eyes, Dana nudged Charlie's side with her elbow as if to say, "Be nice."

She answered Cyrus's question. "Well, I have the day off. I was thinking of taking a hike down to the old mine. I've actually never been there since I moved here."

The idea intrigued Cyrus. "I'd love to come, would you mind?"

The topic of the mine lightened Charlie's mood. "That's where I saw those people poking around, the ones I told you two about. Fuckin' James thinks I'm making stuff up, but I'm sure something was fishy about that."

"Well, I'm going as a tourist," Dana said. "I'm not doing any soil testing or looking for gold."

"Fuck it. I'm supposed to work in the garden today, but I'm going too," Charlie said, the pull of adventure too much for him to deny.

Cyrus decided this was the moment to bring up the canned food. He opened his mouth but froze as Grady's voice cut through the room.

"Hey, Little Man," he said loudly, his fork scraping against his plate. "When you gonna start training us for the big jihad? I need to know if I gotta bring my own AK or if that's part of the starter kit."

Cyrus's heart skipped a beat, and whatever he had been about to say slipped from his mind as he instinctively shifted his focus, turning toward Grady.

"Something bothering you, Little Man?" Grady taunted, a smirk on his lips.

Although every instinct urged Cyrus to avoid a confrontation, he couldn't back down. He had avoided Grady enough these last few days, and his weakness caused others at Reckoning Grove to distrust him, either because they believed Grady or because they also thought Cyrus weak. As he processed Grady's taunt, a wave of anxiety washed over Cyrus. He had to stand up to Grady, but the prospect of confrontation made his throat dry and his legs itch to run.

He took a deep breath. "Grady, I don't understand what your problem is with me. I feel like I have a lot of respect for you and what you've done for the community here." Despite his attempt to sound confident, the words came out with a quiver.

A smile grew on Grady's face, the smile of a bully who knows he's gotten under his prey's skin. He stood with a menacing crack of his knuckles.

James also stood and attempted to stop Grady, putting his hand on the angry man's shoulder. "Grady, please," he said.

Grady merely brushed James's hand from his shoulder and took a step around the table toward Cyrus.

Things were escalating, and there was nothing Cyrus could do or say about it. He began to rise but was too late. Grady closed the distance between them so that as Cyrus stood and turned, his thighs pressed against the table, throwing him off balance. He leaned slightly back and looked up at Grady. Grady towered over him.

Cyrus had always been shorter than most of the men he interacted with, and when the other person meant to harm him, he became that much more vulnerable.

Grady had squared up at Cyrus in a fighting stance, fists clenched, a smile on his face as the table pushed at the back of Cyrus's legs. From the corner of his eye, he saw that the others in the room stared at this spectacle like deer caught in headlights, bracing themselves for the inevitable clash between the two men.

Cyrus felt like crying. He was definitely not a fighter. He had attempted to take self-defense classes a number of times in his life but never followed through. Grady's warm, fetid breath feathered his face.

Suddenly, Gus rushed into the room, eyes wide with panic. "I need help!" he shouted, breathless and frantic. The urgency in his voice shattered the tense atmosphere, cutting through the strained moment between Grady and Cyrus like a bolt of lightning.

Cyrus's heart raced for a different reason now, the fear he felt moments ago replaced by alarm. Grady's expression altered from smug confidence to surprise, his brow furrowing as he turned toward the newcomer. The heavy tension in the air dissipated, replaced by confusion and concern as everyone's focus shifted to the urgent plea for assistance.

The lawyer Cyrus had met the first night at the bonfire wore a mask of sheer panic. His breathing was rapid, his chest heaving with each frantic gasp. "Something's wrong with Vlad. He's not talking anymore, and I don't think he can breathe. Please, someone's gotta help!"

Without thinking, Cyrus slid past Grady and strode to Gus. He faced Gus directly, his expression a mix of urgency and determination. With both hands, he gripped the lawyer by the shoulders, his fingers tightening to convey the weight of his request. "Gus, I need you to tell me where."

Gus's eyes sharpened, a look of clarity breaking through his fear. "Vlad's my roommate. He's upstairs." He pointed upward with a shaking finger.

Following where Gus had pointed, Cyrus ran up the stairs, the others hurrying behind. Cyrus recalled the rash and swelling on Vlad's neck in previous days. Heart pounding, he reached the top of the stairs and approached the door Gus indicated at the end of the dimly lit hallway. Taking a deep breath to steady himself, he pushed the door open and stepped inside, his attention immediately going to the large figure sprawled, helpless, across the bed.

Cyrus rushed to his side. Vlad's chest rose and fell in shallow, labored breaths, and beads of sweat glistened on his shaved head. Cyrus needed to act quickly.

He focused on Vlad's neck, on the swelling on the right side, the skin stretched tight and shiny. Surrounding the area, a deep redness fanned out, contrasting sharply with the pale, swollen flesh. The tightness gave the impression of immense pressure building beneath the surface, creating a grotesque bulge threatening to explode at any moment. Vlad's windpipe had been engulfed by the swelling as if a thick vine were constricting it, tightening with every breath.

As he evaluated what to do, footsteps approached. He turned to see several others entering the room—Dana, Charlie, Gus, and James — their faces constricted with horror. Grady appeared from behind them, cutting through the group with determination. He then pushed past Cyrus, moving forward as if he knew exactly what needed to be done. His movements were decisive and assertive, exuding confidence as he focused on Vlad, ready to take charge of the situation.

As he stepped in closer, the sight of Vlad's swollen neck and labored breathing caused his bravado to falter, and horror washed over his face. For a brief moment, uncertainty gripped him, and the severity of the situation sank in.

After a deep, steadying breath, Grady's demeanor shifted once more. His look of fear faded, replaced by a newfound determination. "I know what to do," he declared, his voice regaining its assertive edge. "He needs a tracheotomy; I saw it in a movie one time. Someone find me a pen. I've got a knife right here. I gotta stick the knife in his throat where the Adam's apple is, and then put the tube of the pen through the hole."

"Grady, stop!" Cyrus blurted out, as he tried to regain control. "I'm a doctor, you will absolutely kill him if you try that. There are key arteries there, and blood will squirt into his lungs, and he will die. We need to optimize Vlad's airway, first off."

Grady's jaw tightened, his hands still hovering near Vlad's throat. "Optimize his airway?" he snapped, eyes flashing. "That's fancy talk for doing nothing while he chokes to death. You think I don't see what's happening? He can't breathe!"

Cyrus stepped closer. "I know what I'm talking about. If you cut him now, you'll kill him faster."

Grady's voice rose, sharp with anger. "I never trusted you. From the first damn day, I knew something was off. You stroll in here with your stories about being a doctor, well, I don't buy it. You're an outsider, and outsiders mean harm to us." He jabbed a finger toward Cyrus's chest. "Vlad is my friend. If I don't do something, he dies. I'm not letting you stand here and watch him suffocate while you spout your big words."

"Grady," Cyrus pleaded.

"No!" Grady cut him off, practically shaking now. "You're not a doctor. You're a fraud. And I'll be damned if I let you decide whether he lives or dies."

Ignoring Grady, Cyrus grabbed Dana's hand and led her to Vlad. "Here, let me show you," he said, guiding her gently but firmly. He positioned himself beside Vlad, demonstrating how to tilt his head back properly in "sniffing position."

With one hand, he cupped Vlad's chin, applying enough pressure to lift it gently while using his other hand to support the back of his head. "It's not going to fix anything, but I'm hoping this will help open the airway enough," he explained, his voice steady despite the chaos around them.

Once he felt satisfied, he stood up. "Keep him like that. I'll be right back, buy me some time, and don't let Grady kill him," Cyrus shouted as he turned and ran down the hallway.

Grady yelled, "He's an idiot, where's the fucking pen?"

Although Cyrus bounded down the stairs two at a time, it still felt like a race against time, every step driven by urgency. With every frantic step, a gnawing anxiety crept into his mind. He couldn't shake the fear that Grady, in his overzealous determination, would kill Vlad. Cyrus knew exactly where he was going, but it seemed so far away. The path ahead stretched endlessly, each stride requiring more effort than the last, as if time itself conspired against him, dragging him down when all he wanted was to break free and reach his goal.

Finally, Cyrus burst into the kitchen, his breath coming in quick, sharp gasps. He sprinted to the spot where he and Dana had made bread the night before, the familiar scent of yeast and flour still lingering in the air. With urgency fueling his movements, he yanked open the pantry door, his heart racing as he searched for the razor blades used to score the dough.

The shelves were lined with jars and boxes, but Cyrus's focus narrowed as he spotted the pile of blades tucked away in the corner, gleaming in the dim light. He grabbed one, his hands steady despite the chaos swirling in his mind. Time was of the essence, and every second counted.

Cyrus spotted the stove where a gas burner was hissing softly beneath a pot of boiling water. Without hesitation, he moved the pot to the side, the steam rising in a rush as he cleared the space.

His gaze landed on a pair of tongs hanging next to the stove, and he snatched them up. He used the tongs to grasp the razor blade, holding it carefully over the gas flames for a count of thirty seconds. The heat flickered beneath it, and the metal glinted ominously in the light.

Once the blade was glowing hot, Cyrus held it steady with the tongs, the heat pulsing through the metal. He hesitated—he should wipe Vlad's skin with alcohol first. Rubbing alcohol, anything. But he had no idea where it would be, and there was no time to search.

Screw it, he thought. If I save him, he's getting antibiotics anyway.

He turned and sprinted up the stairs and down the hall, the hot blade clamped in the tongs, adrenaline propelling him forward. Reaching Vlad's room, he found a crowd of people standing in the doorway, their expressions a mix of concern and confusion. Without hesitation, Cyrus pushed past them, adrenaline coursing through him.

"Get out! Give him space!" he yelled, his voice cutting through the murmurs and drawing their attention.

Cyrus entered the room holding the tongs next to him like a warrior brandishing a sword. Dana still held Vlad's head in her hands, her eyes wide with fear as she looked up at Grady standing over them, a menacing figure, one hand gripping a pen while the other brandished a knife, poised dangerously above Vlad's neck, ready to strike.

"Grady, stop!" Cyrus shouted, his voice laced with urgency, but Grady didn't seem to hear him, locked in his own twisted focus.

Without a second thought, Cyrus pushed forward, then hip-checked Grady aside. The blade was no longer hot. Cyrus grasped the razor blade in his fingers and dropped the tongs on the floor with a *clank*. He crouched over Vlad. There was no time. Vlad was barely breathing and was turning blue. Behind Cyrus, Grady gave an angry growl.

Cyrus firmly inserted the sharp blade into the taut skin of Vlad's neck with surgical precision. At first, a thin trickle of blood seeped out, bright and thick against the pallor of his skin. But then, without warning, a massive spurt of thick, foul-smelling pus erupted from the wound, gushing forth with such force it shot past Cyrus like sludge pouring out from a broken sewer pipe.

The viscous, putrid fluid sprayed violently, hitting Grady squarely in the face as he tried to shove Cyrus aside again. The sudden eruption sent him stumbling back, eyes wide with disbelief and horror as the rancid liquid splattered across his cheek, and into his open mouth.

A collective shriek of disgust erupted from the onlookers, a chorus of gagging and startled yelps as several turned away, hands over mouths. The air grew thick with a noxious odor, sharp and sickly, but Cyrus didn't flinch. He remained locked in; this was a crucial moment, one that could mean the difference between life and death for Vlad.

Satisfied with the depth and size of the incision, Cyrus placed the blade on the floor next to Vlad. With both hands, he pressed firmly on the swollen abscess at Vlad's neck, using his fingers to gently but decisively milk the thick, putrid pus from the wound. Each push released more of the foul-smelling fluid, and the tension in Vlad's body began to ease as the pressure on his throat subsided. Cyrus focused intently, determined to clear the blockage and relieve the man's suffering, even as the noxious odor filled the air around them.

Finally, less and less pus came out of the incision site. The oppressive weight on Vlad's windpipe ceased. Slowly, Vlad's chest rose and fell as he gasped for air, his breaths initially shallow and hesitant. But then, with a surge of strength, he drew in a deep breath, filling his lungs with precious air.

Cyrus watched intently as Vlad's eyes fluttered open, revealing a flicker of awareness amidst the confusion. Relief washed over Cyrus as Vlad started to breathe easily again, the tension in the room shifting from panic to hope.

After realizing Vlad was going to be okay, the rest of the world slowly came into focus for Cyrus. He looked up into Dana's amazed face, her mouth open in incredulity.

In the background, Grady retched, trying to spit up the bits of pus that had flown into his open mouth. "Water! I need water!" he shouted between retches.

Cyrus stood slowly. He looked around the room trying to locate something to clean the mess with but couldn't find anything. With a calm, business-like voice, he said, "Does anyone have a first-aid kit? We'll need to put a bandage over the incision site."

His focus changed from wound care to the people around him. The room was still full of people with more heads poking in from outside the door. Everyone's eyes were wide in disbelief.

Then he felt a hand on his shoulder.

He looked up.

James stood next to him, eyes wide, his voice low with disbelief. "How did you know?"

"Vlad developed a cellulitis from scratching at that rash on his neck," Cyrus explained. "That eventually consolidated into an abscess as well, right next to his trachea. It got so large it was starting to close off his airway."

He paused a moment, letting the seriousness of the moment settle in.

"A tracheotomy wouldn't have fixed it," he continued. "The real problem was the abscess. It had to be incised and drained to relieve the pressure so Vlad could breathe again."

Cheers filled the air, and Vlad's roommate Gus grabbed Cyrus by the shoulder. "Cyrus!" was all he could say.

Someone handed Cyrus a first-aid kit the size of a school lunch box, faded white with a red cross on the front. Cyrus knelt beside Vlad to bandage the open site.

"I don't think he needs an ambulance, but someone should take Vlad to the hospital. Oh, and when you get there, tell Dr. Bronson I said hi."

Dana gazed at Cyrus in awe. "Holy crap, Cyrus, that was amazing! You saved Vlad's life."

He gave a small, tired smile. "Thanks," he said, his voice quiet.

Dana smiled back, then was pulled away by someone calling her name. Cyrus watched her go, a rush of warmth creeping into his cheeks. He wasn't used to this kind of attention, and part of him felt embarrassed by the praise.

As the buzz of voices carried on around him, he turned his gaze to the ground, his thoughts racing.

He'd ignored them. Vlad and Calvin's rashes.

He'd locked onto the idea of botulism, nausea, neuropathy, fatigue, and let that frame everything else. But botulism didn't cause a rash. Especially not like that one.

He clenched his jaw, shame prickling under his skin. He'd been so determined to find an answer that he'd ignored the clues that didn't fit. And now it burned in his memory like a warning flare.

Cyrus let out a slow, tight breath. The weight of nearly losing Vlad, of maybe missing something that could kill even more people, pressed down on him.

This was a wake-up call. No more tunnel vision. No more convenient theories.

He couldn't leave now. Whatever was happening here, he was going to figure it out. He had to.

For Brent. For Vlad.

For all of them.

12

That night, the bonfire crackled high into the cool high desert air, casting golden light over the gathered faces. Someone strummed a guitar, and laughter rippled through the circle. The mood was celebratory, relieved, joyous.

Cyrus edged closer to the fire, the warmth on his skin a match for the glow in his chest. People clapped him on the back, thanked him, toasted him. For once, he didn't deflect it. He let himself smile. Let himself feel proud.

Maybe I do belong here, he thought, watching Dana laugh with someone across the circle, her eyes occasionally drifting back to him with quiet admiration.

I had forgotten what it feels like to be part of something.

James, the man Cyrus had helped with the composting, took a seat beside him.

"Gus just got back from the hospital," James said, grinning. "He said Vlad's doing great. Doc Bronson convinced him to stay overnight for observation, just to be safe."

Cyrus nodded, relief washing through him.

But then James's smile faltered. His face went still, then slowly shifted, his eyes widening.

He was looking over Cyrus's shoulder.

Cyrus turned around, alarmed by James's look.

Grady stood stiffly with his arms at his sides, staring at Cyrus. Cyrus rose in disbelief, his mind bracing for the fight they had nearly started that morning.

But instead, Grady took a deep breath, stepped forward, and extended his hand.

"Doc," he said, his voice surprisingly steady. "I'm sorry for giving you such a hard time since you got here. I was wrong about you. We've had so many outsiders try to take advantage of us that I guess I let my imagination run away with me. Thank you, for what you did, both for Brent and for Vlad."

For a moment, Cyrus stared at him, caught off guard by the unexpected truce.

"Thank you, Grady," Cyrus said, adjusting uncomfortably in his place. "I really appreciate that. You want to sit with me?"

Grady nodded slowly, clearly still shaken, and sank down beside him.

No words passed between them, the fire popping gently, the celebration continuing.

Then came a voice from behind them, deep and steady, but now tinged with something urgent.

"*Doc?*"

Cyrus turned. Grady did too.

Calvin stood just behind them, his usually calm face drawn tight with worry. Beside him, his wife Cindy leaned heavily against his arm, her breathing short and rapid.

Seeing someone as solid as Calvin looking so afraid sent a jolt through Cyrus. He pushed himself to his feet and stepped toward them.

Cindy was coughing, her shoulders rising and falling in quick, shallow bursts. Her skin had a pale, waxy sheen in the firelight, and her neck veins were distended, clear and high.

Cyrus's mind clicked into gear.

CHF, he thought. *She told me two days ago, cutting back on fluids, but drinking more anyway because of the nausea. It's catching up with her.*

He steadied her with a hand clasp on her shoulder and looked at Calvin. "Let's get her somewhere quiet," he said. "I need a better place to evaluate her."

Cyrus turned to Grady and gave a quick nod. "Thanks," he said, his voice low but sincere. "I'll catch you later."

Grady gave a small, solemn nod in return as Cyrus kept pace with Calvin, supporting Cindy between them as they moved quickly toward the farmhouse.

Inside, the warmth and noise of the celebration was replaced by the dim hush of the empty house. Together, they helped Cindy into a worn recliner in the living room. She sank back with a grateful exhale; one hand pressed to her chest as she tried to slow her breathing.

Cyrus knelt beside her and gently rolled up the cuffs of her jeans to mid-shin. He pressed a finger into the soft tissue above her ankles, first one leg, then the other. Each time, a deep indentation remained, slowly filling back in.

"Pitting edema," he said to himself, but loud enough for Calvin to hear. He looked up. "Cindy told me the other day she has congestive heart failure."

He turned his gaze back to her. "Cindy, are you still drinking a lot of water? Eating anything high in salt?"

Before she could answer, Calvin spoke. "She's been drinking a lot, three, maybe four liters a day from the spring. And she's been eating a lot of the soup the kitchen crew has been making lately. I'm guessing there's salt in it."

As he said it, Cindy was seized by another coughing fit, her shoulders curling inward with the effort.

"Let's get you up, Cindy," he said calmly. "It'll help you breathe."

As the coughing subsided, Cyrus helped Cindy sit more upright, adjusting a pillow behind her back. Then, without a word, he leaned in and pressed his ear gently to one side of her back, listening intently, then moved to the other side.

Her breathing crackled faintly beneath the surface, wet, labored, unmistakable.

He straightened, looking from Cindy to Calvin. "She's got all the signs of fluid overload," he said. "We have to get the fluid off her."

Calvin and Cindy looked at him, confused, worry in their eyes.

Cyrus kept his voice steady. "When someone has congestive heart failure, it means the heart isn't pumping blood around the body the way it should. Either the muscle is too weak, or the valves aren't working right. When that happens, fluid can start to build up, sometimes in places you can see, like the legs, but other times in the lungs, filling the air spaces with fluid instead of air."

He glanced at Cindy, then back at Calvin. "That's what I think is happening. Based on what I'm seeing, she doesn't have the luxury of waiting to see Dr. Bronson tomorrow."

He paused, letting the weight of it settle. "She needs to go to the hospital. Tonight."

~

Night had settled over Lakeview Hospital, the air cool and still under the parking lot lights as Brent's old white pickup truck pulled in.

Cyrus ran to the entrance, fetched a nearby wheelchair, and then helped Calvin ease Cindy into it. Her breathing still sounded shallow and labored. Inside, the waiting room was nearly empty. Cyrus pushed the chair to the front desk.

Behind the registration desk sat Betty, the same woman that had previously greeted Cyrus.

She looked exactly the same as she had when Brent and Cyrus

were there, as if someone had pressed pause when he left. Her graying hair was parted neatly down the middle, styled in the same casual way. Her eyes flickered with recognition, though her expression stayed carefully composed.

"She's in heart failure," he said calmly. "She needs help now."

Betty barely reacted. With the same calm efficiency, she typed away at her computer, her face showing the kind of unflinching expression from having seen this all too often. Without missing a beat, she pointed toward a corner of the waiting room. "You can wait over there," she said, her tone flat and unfazed, as if this was the millionth time she'd handled this issue.

As Calvin turned to push Cindy toward the seating area, Betty called to them, "Oh, Dr. Bronson may be a little annoyed. He just finished seeing someone here and went home. He's not happy when he's on call for the ED and has to come back in right after he left."

Cyrus nodded, sitting in a chair next to Calvin and Cindy, settling in for what could be a long wait. He knew many small-town hospitals weren't busy enough to hire full-time emergency physicians; instead, the local doctors rotated call to cover the ED. Back when he worked in Corlen, Virginia, he'd done the same, dragging himself in from home in the middle of the night more times than he cared to remember.

They sat there for what felt like hours, the minutes dragging on in the sterile, brightly lit room. Finally, Cyrus's attention was alerted by the clip-clop of clogs. Moments later, Dr. Bronson rounded the corner from behind the registration desk.

He looked the same as last time, annoyed, with his silvery, unkempt hair sticking out in every direction. He again wore green scrubs and a long white lab coat.

Instead of addressing Cindy or Calvin, Dr. Bronson barked at Cyrus, "What the heck is going on this time?"

Cyrus didn't have the energy to deflect. "I think Cindy's having a CHF exacerbation, Dr. Bronson. She's been dyspneic, she's got elevated JVD, pitting edema, and crackles on lung exam."

The look on Cyrus's face was pure exhaustion.

At first, Dr. Bronson furrowed his brow, looking from Cyrus to Cindy. But as he took in the scene, the exhaustion on Cyrus's face and the frightened, sickly look in Cindy's eyes, a flicker of empathy softened his features. His frustration gave way to understanding.

Then he turned to Cindy, taking hold of the wheelchair. With a quick glance to Calvin, he gave a subtle nod, signaling him to follow. Calvin didn't hesitate; he fell in beside Dr. Bronson as they pushed Cindy through the automatic doors and into the emergency department, the urgency in their steps matched by a shared, unspoken determination.

Cyrus sat in the waiting area for about an hour, tapping his foot nervously on the floor, before the automatic doors swung open. A nurse in faded purple scrubs came through. Her blonde hair was pulled back in a ponytail, and her friendly smile put Cyrus at ease despite his anxiety. Her nametag read "Alicia Pence, RN," and she looked young enough to be fresh out of nursing school.

She approached him with purpose, then gestured for him to follow. "We admitted Cindy to our med/surg unit. Let me show you where she is," she said. Instead of leading him back into the ED, she guided him through a series of hallways to the medical wards.

As they entered the room, Cyrus saw Cindy lying in the bed. They'd connected multiple IVs to her arms, and electrodes dotted her chest monitoring her vital signs and the electrical activity of her heart. The soft, steady tones of the telemetry monitor filled the room, a quiet but constant reminder of the fight her body was engaged in.

Beside the bed, Calvin sat in a chair, his large hand gently wrapped around hers. His posture was rigid, eyes fixed on Cindy's face, the stress and strain etched deep across his features.

"Thank you for your help, Alicia."

The nurse gave him a warm smile before returning to the hall.

Cyrus moved to the other side of the bed and reached for Cindy's shoulder, giving it a light squeeze. Her skin felt cool and fragile, but she opened her eyes just enough to see him there. He offered a reassuring smile, then leaned in, speaking softly. "You're in good hands now," he said. "Just rest."

Across from him, Calvin gave a slow nod and Cyrus continued. "They treat this kind of thing all the time," he explained, "people come in with heart failure, get diuretics like Lasix, they pee out all that extra fluid, stabilize, go home again. It's common."

The room fell quiet then, the only sounds the rhythmic beeping of the telemetry monitor.

Cyrus's eyes wandered to the telemetry screen that showed the electrical activity of Cindy's heart's.

He leaned in, eyes narrowing on the rhythm strip.

Was that . . . a prolonged QTc?

Something was off about the tracing; an abnormality like Long QTc could describe abnormal cardiac electrical activity. The kind that could lead to arrhythmias. The kind that killed people.

For a split second, his thoughts shot back to Brent, the panic, the crash, the helplessness.

He closed his eyes and breathed slowly. QTc was hard to measure on a telemetry monitor. Too much noise, too many variables. He must be mistaken.

Still, the unease lingered.

From down the hallway came the sharp, even rhythm of clogs on linoleum. A few seconds later, Dr. Bronson stepped into the room, looking tired. Still, he offered a quick nod and a reassuring smile.

"How's our girl doing?" he asked, already glancing toward the monitor.

Cindy stirred in the bed, her voice faint but with a trace of humor. "I think that Lasix is already kicking in," she said. "I feel like I've already peed a gallon!"

Dr. Bronson gave a small chuckle and nodded. "That's a good sign. Means your kidneys are still listening."

Cyrus, still holding her hand, glanced up at the monitor again. "I thought I saw Long QTc on her telemetry monitor," he said, keeping his voice low but edged with concern. "Have you had a chance to check her electrolytes or confirm with an EKG yet?"

Dr. Bronson's face tightened, and he snapped, "What do you think I am, an idiot? I don't know what you used to do, but correcting electrolyte imbalances and getting an EKG are the first things any real doctor does in a situation like this."

His defensive tone stung, but the tension between them was cut by the weight of the situation at hand.

Cyrus didn't want to cause Cindy any more stress. "I'm sorry, I didn't mean it like that."

Dr. Bronson's face was unchanged. "Well, I've got her on IV Lasix, and we're checking and replacing electrolytes like clockwork. Let me know if you have any other consultation suggestions." He turned and went out of room.

Cyrus wanted to ask about Vlad but thought better of it. Alicia came in and started fiddling with Cindy's IV, possibly trying to find some work to do to not draw attention from Dr. Bronson.

She saw Cyrus watching her and shrugged lightly. "Dr. Bronson had just gotten home when he got called in about Cindy. He's been Cindy's doctor since she moved here, he really likes her, and I think his irritability is because he cares so much and is frustrated that she's sick." It sounded more like the sage advice of a seasoned nurse than that of someone as young and inexperienced as she appeared.

"I get it," Cyrus said, impressed with her insight.

Cyrus sat with them for a while longer, the steady rhythm of the monitor and the hushed sounds of the hospital filling the room. Every so often, his eyes flicked to the telemetry screen, uneasy about what he thought might be a prolonged QTc interval. Still, the hours wore on, and the medicine for Cindy's fluid overload kept her up, needing help to and from the restroom. The more it happened, the more Cyrus felt like he was in the way, an outsider in a private moment. At last, the sense of being an intruder outweighed even his concern about the monitor, and he decided it was time to go.

By the time the first light of morning touched the edges of the window, he stood up from his chair.

"I should head back to Reckoning Grove," he said. "Try to catch a little sleep."

Cindy gave him a tired but genuine smile. "You should. And if you can, stop by and see Vlad. He should be going home this morning."

Cyrus nodded. "I will. You rest, okay?"

He turned to Calvin and gave him a quiet nod of farewell, then slipped out of the room, the door clicking softly shut behind him.

13

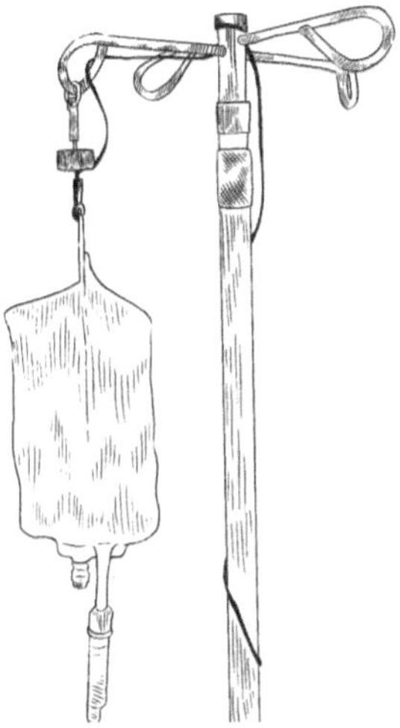

The air outside Cindy's room felt cooler somehow, the fluorescent lights humming softly above him as he made his way down the corridor. As he did, he walked past the small hospital's ICU and looked inside. Monitors beeped steadily, and the soft whoosh of a ventilator rose and fell in rhythmic breaths. The sterile light cast everything in pale blue and white. Tubes, machines, silent figures in beds.

The sounds pulled something from deep inside him.

His mind wandered back to a similar small-town hospital room, when he'd sat, fatigued, tears in his eyes, next to a patient who had died only moments before. Betty Painter had been only sixty, but her years of smoking made her look much older. He'd stayed up the previous night with her. He had known her ever since he moved to Corlen to practice medicine, caring for her many times over the years. But this time had been different.

Betty had been admitted for a respiratory illness he believed he could treat. She came in short of breath, presenting a typical COPD exacerbation, a flare-up of a chronic lung condition causing inflammation in the lungs. Normally, Cyrus had managed such episodes countless times. Yet from the start, something about this one felt wrong. The flare was sharper, more aggressive, as if it carried a violence he couldn't quite define. When he leaned close, he caught a chemical tang on her breath, strange, acrid, not like the usual heaviness of a COPD flare. He couldn't place it, but the scent unsettled him, gnawing at the back of his mind even as he escalated her treatment.

"Betty, your breathing is getting worse, so I need to put you on BiPaP. It's a device that pushes air into your lungs because you can't draw in enough right now."

She was barely able to talk with so much shortness of breath. "Whatever you say, Dr. Darian," she said, breathing heavily through the plastic oxygen mask. "I can't breathe."

Cyrus had his respiratory therapist put Betty on the breathing device. A bulky mask cinched tight over her small face, a hose running to a loud box by the bed that shoved air into her lungs with every breath. However, within hours her condition grew worse. Despite being on the highest BiPaP setting and receiving additional medication, she was still barely getting enough oxygen. Her condition was worsening by the minute.

Warily, Cyrus sat on the edge of Betty's bed holding her hand. A plastic pulse oximeter sensor was taped to her finger, and the cold plastic pressed into his palm. "Betty, I'm so sorry, but things are rapidly getting worse, and I need to put you on a ventilator. We've talked about this in the past. A breathing tube goes down your throat, and a machine will breathe for you. I'll have to put you in a medically induced coma until you get better and can breathe on your own again."

Betty didn't speak. All Cyrus could see was her chest rising and falling at an alarming rate, like the frantic fluttering of a trapped bird's wings. Each breath carried the faint whistle of wind squeezing through a cracked window. He adjusted her oxygen, recalculated the medications, forcing the treatments to climb higher and higher, but the unease gnawed at him. Something about this wasn't right, worse than any flare he'd managed before. What was it? Why did this exacerbation feel so different from all the others?

Finally, she spoke, her soft voice muffled by the oxygen mask. "I've been alive a long time, Dr. Darian." After catching her breath, she continued, "When you're young like you are now you have a family and career and energy. I've done all that. My kid is happy and set on his way."

As she paused, the hiss of oxygen filled the room. Cyrus leaned closer, listening, and the strange tang in her breath hit him again. This time, recognition stirred, sharp, acrid, almost like chlorine. The thought unsettled him. Chlorine didn't belong here, not in a hospital room, not on the breath of a patient with COPD.

She went on, her voice thinner now. "I'm sick of this circle, every other month being in the hospital. It's not how I want the last moments of my life . . . ." Her words trailed off, smoke from a dying fire.

Cyrus was conflicted. On one hand, he knew what she was saying was the right thing, her goals, her dignity, her decision to stop the endless cycle of admissions should be respected. But his gut screamed that this wasn't just another flare, not the same old COPD.

Part of him wanted to push harder, to treat aggressively, to keep her alive until he understood what made this different. It was the reason he had become a doctor in the first place, to fight for his patients, to fix what was broken. Yet now, faced with her frailty and her quiet resolve, he felt paralyzed between honoring her words and chasing the instinct that something more sinister was at play.

Betty shifted slightly, her voice imploring him despite her shortness of breath. "I don't want a tube down my throat or to be hooked up to a ventilator. I know what that means. Without all that, I'll die. But I'm ready for it. I want to be comfortable when the time comes."

Cyrus tightened his hand around her cold fingers. "Okay, Betty, I understand," he said with a tear in his eye.

Although a part of him felt he was giving up on her, he knew that whatever was different about this illness, resolving it would ultimately require intubation and mechanical ventilation. That was something Betty had made clear she never wanted. So, even as every instinct urged him to fight, he forced himself to do what was right, not as a physician desperate to fix, but as a caregiver honoring her goals of care. He transitioned her treatment toward comfort, swallowing the bitter truth that respecting her wishes meant stepping back. Shifting from trying to cure to trying to comfort, giving medicines to ease the air hunger, calm the panic, and take away pain, so she could die without suffering.

With Cyrus sitting at her bedside, she passed peacefully in the early morning. No family bothered to show up, despite repeated calls, and for moments after she passed, he stared at her still form. Her face, though pale and unmoving, appeared peaceful, as if she had simply drifted off to sleep. He found comfort in the way her features rested, a faint hint of a smile touching her lips. As though in her final moments she found contentment or release, which brought a quiet reverence to the air around her.

Moments later, the door creaked open, and a rugged man stepped into the room. He was lean and muscular and wore a dirty flannel shirt. His worn jeans were smudged with grime, and his unshaven face gave him a rough, disheveled look. The stench of cigarettes preceded him as he walked closer. Cyrus recognized him immediately as the woman's son, Mike Painter, the one who always seemed indifferent to his mother's condition despite Cyrus's many conversations with him.

Mike barely glanced at his mother as he stepped closer to Cyrus, casually handing over a pair of glasses. "My aunt told me to bring these over on my way to work," he muttered, his voice flat, indifferent.

Cyrus stood slowly, clutching the glasses, a mix of frustration and sadness rising in him. "Mr. Painter, I tried calling you all night," Cyrus said, his voice steady but strained. "Your mom passed away just a little while ago."

Mike looked over at his mother for the first time, and his demeanor changed in an instant. His face darkened, fists clenching as his anger surged.

"What do you mean she's dead?" he snapped, his voice rising, full of rage and defensiveness. "Why the hell didn't you tell me sooner?" His frustration boiled over, as if the truth was too much for him to accept or face.

"Like I said," Cyrus continued firmly, "I've been trying to call you all night. Your mom requested that we not pursue any further aggressive treatment. I had to switch her to what we call comfort measures. I focused on making sure she didn't have any pain or discomfort as she passed."

He hesitated, because the rest of it wouldn't sit right in his mouth unless he said it. "But, and I hate to put it this way, her death felt . . . peculiar. During her earlier admissions, the things I'd been able to fix before, none of them responded the way I would have expected. I don't know why. I don't know what happened."

What he didn't add was the part that still gnawed at him, the peculiar smell on her breath, sharp and acrid, almost like chlorine from a swimming pool. And hadn't Mike been the one looking after his mother's trailer park, the same place with that aging pool out back? The thought flickered, unsettling, but Cyrus kept it to himself.

Mike's face went hard, defensive in a way that made Cyrus flinch. "Sounds like you're blaming me," he snapped. Then, as if that accusation gave him cover, he flipped it. "You know what? You're the fake doctor around here, screwing up our town. Who do you think you are, telling me my business?"

Cyrus held up his hands. "No, I'm sorry. I didn't mean it like that. I wouldn't blame you. I'm not blaming you. I just mean her symptoms were off, and I'm trying to understand."

Mike's jaw tightened. "Well, here's what you're going to do: You screwed up *my* family, now, get the hell out of town, before something happens to you and *your* family."

Cyrus felt the breath leave him in a slow, measured way, as he tried to herd his thoughts into order. Meanwhile, Mike stood inches away, chest heaving, breathing loud enough that Cyrus could count the ragged pulls. Why so defensive? Was all this show because he was feeling guilty about not being there for his mom when Cyrus had called? Or was there something else? Was he trying to hide something? Didn't he take care of his mother's medications?

In Corlen, he and Juliette had taken care of most of the town between them, shared patients, shared stories, shared the quiet shorthand that came from years of practice. Mike Painter had been Juliette's patient. She'd always described him as a hothead, all noise and bluster, someone who talked big but burned out fast. What Cyrus was seeing now didn't fit that picture.

A worse possibility slid through Cyrus like a chill he couldn't shake. Footsteps sounded in the corridor; the security guard was coming. Cyrus let his eyes flick to the doorway and back to Mike's face, where the anger sat like a stone, waiting.

Just then, a nurse hurried into the room, followed closely by a security guard. The guard, who had clearly just started his shift, still had a cup of coffee in his hand. Setting it down calmly, he took a step toward the irate man, his tone firm yet familiar.

"Mike, come on now," the guard said, holding up a hand in a

calming but authoritative gesture. "We've known each other since high school. I'm gonna have to ask you to leave now."

Mike's face twisted with anger, his eyes darting back to Cyrus. "You little quack," he spat, his voice seething. "You're the reason my mom died."

Cyrus froze, shocked by the venom in the man's words, but the security guard moved quickly. Without further escalation, he guided Mike toward the door, his tone remaining steady. "Let's go, Mike," he said as he escorted him out of the room, the tension in his wake punching Cyrus in the gut. "Let's go outside where you can cool off."

Footsteps echoed softly down the hallway beyond Cindy's room, breaking into his thoughts. Cyrus turned slightly, the moment slipping away like a thread lost in the wind.

Still, the memory lingered, heavy, unsettled.

It was a time when the stress had piled high, when everywhere he looked there was mounting strain. The same kind of pressure he felt starting to build now, at the commune, around these people he barely knew but somehow felt responsible for.

Being here, back in the sterile air, the rhythm of beeping machines, it stirred something he thought he'd left behind.

I'm not sure how I'll handle this, he admitted to himself. *Not again.*

14

Cyrus continued to walk along the hospital hallway until he found the nurses' station. Alicia was there, typing into the computer, eyes flicking across the screen. She looked up when she saw Cyrus approaching.

"Hey there, Doc," she said with a brief smile.

"Hey," Cyrus replied. "I was wondering, do you know where my friend Vlad ended up?"

Alicia raised an eyebrow and smirked. "At this rate all your friends are gonna end up here." She nodded toward the opposite end of the hall from Cindy's room. "He's in 118. Just around the corner. I should be in there soon to give him his discharge paperwork."

"Thanks." Cyrus gave her a small wave as he headed that direction.

Room 118 was quiet, the air faintly cool. Cyrus knocked once and pushed the door open.

Vlad was already sitting upright on the edge of the hospital bed, feet planted firmly on the floor, elbows resting loosely on his knees. He wore his street clothes, jeans and a faded flannel shirt, with a fresh white bandage taped to the side of his neck above the collarbone. He shifted toward the door and the bed beneath him creaked in quiet protest. He looked comically oversized, a circus bear crouched on a child's tricycle, all bulk and gravity in a space that clearly hadn't been designed with him in mind.

As soon as he saw Cyrus, his face lit up. "There he is," he said, his voice warm. "I've been thinking about you. What are you doing here?"

Cyrus gave a crooked smile and stepped into the room, letting the door shut behind him. "Cindy is feeling a little sick. She needs some medical treatment but should be just fine."

Cyrus pointed at the bed. "I didn't know they made hospital furniture in 'fun-size.'"

Vlad chuckled and patted the edge of the bed. "Yeah, I told the nurse I'd split the frame if I sneezed too hard. She didn't laugh." He tilted his head faintly, wincing at the stretch that occurred near the bandage. "I'm really sorry about Cindy."

Cyrus's eyes flicked to the bandage. "How's that feeling?"

"Like someone jabbed me with a hot screwdriver." He shrugged. "But better than not breathing."

Cyrus pulled the visitor chair up beside the bed and sat, the vinyl cushion squeaking beneath him.

"Just waiting on the nurse to bring in my discharge papers." He shifted on the mattress with a grunt. "Then I'm out of here."

Cyrus nodded, glancing again at the bandage on Vlad's neck.

Vlad noted his gaze. "I don't remember any of it, by the way. Not the collapsing, not getting to the hospital, nothing. Gus filled me in." He turned to face Cyrus more fully. "He said you're the reason I'm still breathing." He extended his hand. "Thank you, man. Seriously."

Cyrus hesitated for half a second then reached out and shook it. The moment their hands met, he winced, Vlad's grip was like a hydraulic clamp.

"Jesus," Cyrus muttered, trying to keep it light.

Vlad pulled back instantly, wincing. "Sorry. I forget sometimes."

Cyrus flexed his fingers once then gave a half-smile. "No worries."

The door opened and Alicia came in, a clipboard in one hand and a small orange pill bottle in the other.

"Well, Mr. Markovic," she said with quiet reassurance, "you're lucky to be alive."

Her eyes flicked briefly to Cyrus, and for a beat, so did Vlad's. The moment passed quickly, but the effect lingered.

Alicia set the clipboard on the side table and handed Vlad the bottle. "These are antibiotics. Take one now, and then twice a day with food. You'll feel pretty wiped for a few days, but if anything seems off, come back in right away."

Vlad nodded, glancing at the bottle in his hand. "Got it."

Cyrus sat back in the chair, watching quietly, the weight of their shared glance still hanging in the room like dust that hadn't settled.

Alicia gave Vlad a final nod before slipping out of the room.

Cyrus rose from his chair, stretching his back with a quiet sigh. "So . . . how are you getting home?"

Vlad blinked. "Honestly? I haven't gotten that far yet."

Cyrus smirked and pulled his keys from his pocket. "Well, you're in luck. I've got Mystique parked out front."

Vlad chuckled. "The legend herself."

THE OLD TOYOTA pickup jolted as Cyrus pulled onto the road, the tires humming against the asphalt. Vlad sat in the passenger seat, his broad shoulders pressed awkwardly against the door, one knee up higher than the other as he tried to angle his legs away from the dashboard.

The silence between them was easy at first, both men tired and content to let the road speak. But after a few minutes, Cyrus said, "You seem like you're no worse off for the experience you just went through. Do you remember when the rash first started? Did you have any other symptoms around then, nausea, fatigue, maybe even some numbness?"

Vlad glanced sideways at him, frowning faintly. "I don't remember much. Just that it started small, like a patch on my skin. Then it spread to my neck and got worse. It started itching along my neck. Like a kid with a scab, I couldn't stop scratching at it, and Dr. Bronson said it developed an abscess that blocked off my windpipe."

Cyrus kept his eyes on the road. "And no nausea, fatigue, or numbness?"

Vlad hesitated. "No . . . why do you ask?"

"Because some of the others at the commune are showing those symptoms," Cyrus said quietly. "Cindy, her husband Calvin . . . even Brent before he died. It worries me."

Vlad said nothing for a moment, then nodded. "I appreciate you being here for us, Cyrus. If I can help with anything, anything at all, just say the word."

Vlad paused, his gaze drifting to the pine trees slipping past along Highway 140 as they headed back toward Reckoning Grove. "I'm used to being this big strong guy. Someone who can overcome everything with my own strength. This was kind of a wakeup call for me."

Cyrus let the weight of Vlad's words settle for a while as he drove, his eyes tracing the faded centerline that stretched endlessly ahead . . . along a path he wasn't sure he chose.

Then he said softly, "I guess we all need help sometimes. I'm even trying to come to terms with that."

The moment lingered between them, but it wasn't awkward. It was an understanding, the kind that forms when two people recognize a wound they share but rarely name. They let it sit there a moment longer, unspoken but mutual.

Just then, Cyrus remembered the canned green beans he'd dropped off at the health department a couple days earlier. Since then, he'd already crossed botulism off his list of likely causes, but the thought nagged at him. As a physician, he knew better than to rely on assumptions, every diagnosis deserved proof. He promised himself that once he got Vlad home, he'd call the health department to make sure the samples had been tested, to confirm his hunch instead of treating it like a settled fact.

He gave a slow nod to himself.

"I'll check it out," he murmured.

Vlad didn't respond. He just leaned his head against the window and closed his eyes, as if the thought had already drifted away.

Shifting gears, Cyrus glanced over and asked, "So how'd you end up at Reckoning

Grove, anyway?"

Vlad exhaled through his nose, his fingers absently grazing the edge of the bandage on his neck. "I was living in Virginia for a while. Outside of Roanoke. Worked at a long-term care home, mostly older vets, a few dementia cases. It was a rough job, but it felt like it mattered, you know?"

Cyrus nodded, letting him talk.

"There was this little place up in the hills, not far from the shoreline. Kinda tucked away. Quiet. Fog rolled in some mornings like you were the only one left in the world." Vlad smiled at the memory. "I liked it there."

Cyrus blinked, the story not quite adding up. *Shoreline?* Roanoke was a few hours from any coast. But maybe Vlad meant a lake or river, or maybe he was mixing up places. He'd just come out of the hospital, after all.

Cyrus didn't press it.

Vlad shifted in the seat. "Then the home shut down without notice, and the owners bailed. I bounced around for a while. Did some contract work, picked up what I could. I heard about Reckoning Grove from a guy I met in Idaho, said it was a place where people looked out for each other. No clocks. No noise. Just life at its own pace."

He looked out the window, voice softer. "It sounded like the kind of place you go to put your pieces back together."

Cyrus gave a slow nod. "Yeah. That's what it is."

The truck rumbled on, dust rising in their wake. There was something easy about being around Vlad, something grounded and accessible. Cyrus found himself liking the man more than he expected, drawn to his openness, the way he carried his past without making it heavy.

The tires of the truck crunched against the gravel driveway as Cyrus pulled back into Reckoning Grove. He shifted the gear into park and turned off the engine. For a beat, neither of them moved.

Vlad exhaled then looked over. "Seriously, thank you. For everything."

Cyrus gave a small nod. "Yeah. Of course."

Vlad climbed out, stretching his long frame as he closed the door with a quiet *thunk*. He gave Cyrus a final salute then made his way toward the white farmhouse, his boots kicking up small clouds of dust before he disappeared inside.

Cyrus remained in the truck, hand still resting on the steering wheel. In the stillness, the weight of unspoken thoughts pressed in around him. The adrenaline that had carried him through the hospital and the drive drained from his body in one slow wave. His limbs felt heavy, every muscle reminding him of how long the day had been. The angle of the sun said it was around late afternoon, his stomach churned like a rock polisher, but the thought of food barely registered. He was exhausted, bone-deep tired, but his mind refused to let go of thinking about Cindy.

Even as he'd left the hospital, the image of Cindy's telemetry screen stuck with him. The rhythm hadn't looked right, irregular, erratic. *Long QTc arrhythmia,* he thought. *Could be from electrolyte abnormalities. But what caused all this in the first place?*

He shifted his gaze to the glowing digits on the dashboard clock. 4:30. Less than half an hour before the Health Department office closed. The knowledge pressed against his fatigue, urging him to act even as his body begged to shut down.

15

Cyrus sat on the old swinging chair in front of the farmhouse, the wood creaking beneath him as he cradled a cell phone borrowed from Gus. He had just spent five minutes clicking through an endless phone tree, only to land on hold with tinny music hissing in his ear. Finally, the screen lit up: 4:55.

A click, then a rushed voice. "Health Department, this is Justin." Papers shuffled in the background, drawers sliding shut, the hurried sounds of someone eager to leave for the day.

"This is Dr. Darian," Cyrus said quickly, leaning forward as if that might push the words through faster. "We spoke a couple of days ago. I dropped off a canned green bean sample for botulinum testing."

A pause. Then Justin's voice came back, flat, distracted. "Can't say I remember that."

"I was just there," Cyrus pressed. "It was from Reckoning Grove."

"Oh. Right." The way Justin said it carried no real recognition, just a sour note, like the name itself left a bad taste in his mouth.

"Look," Justin continued, "I've got a hundred things stacked up on my desk. Honestly, that sample probably got lost in the fray. If it's really that important, you'll need to drop off another one."

Anger flared in Cyrus's chest. "One person has already died, and another is sick in the hospital. This isn't something you can just brush off."

"Then if it's that serious," Justin snapped back, "notify the treating doctors and have them contact me tomorrow. That's the protocol."

The line went dead.

Cyrus lowered the phone, his knuckles white around it. On the screen, the time glowed back at him: 4:59.

Cyrus stared at the phone a moment longer, his jaw tight. The fact that they hadn't confirmed whether or not this was botulism didn't bother him as much as the attitude behind it. The conversation with Justin only confirmed what he already suspected—he was on his own. He had tried Dr. Bronson, tried the health department, and every time the response was the same: dismissive, as if the concerns from Reckoning Grove didn't warrant real attention. The fight drained out of him almost as quickly as it had risen. He didn't have the energy to chase down another sample tonight. Even if he did, it wouldn't change anything. He was sure this had nothing to do with canned foods anyway. What he could do, what he had to do, was get back to the hospital and check on Cindy.

A heavy wave of exhaustion hit him. He needed a nap, just a couple hours, then he would go see Cindy.

Back at the RV, he paused at the broken stairs. Morning. The note. *Time is up. Leave first thing tomorrow morning.* He was still here, and nothing had happened. Maybe it had been a bluff.

He climbed in carefully, stretched out on the narrow bed, and let his eyes close. He was asleep in seconds.

Cyrus jolted awake, disoriented in the darkness that enveloped him. For a moment, he was confused, unsure of where he was or how much time had passed. But as his eyes adjusted, the familiar surroundings of the RV came into focus, and the events of the last few days rushed back to him. Through the haze of waking, he realized it was dark outside, and he had slept through the afternoon and into the night, breaking his promise to Cindy to return. A pang of hunger gnawed at his stomach, bringing another realization: he hadn't eaten in a while.

Remembering that he'd seen Brent's stash of granola bars and chocolate bars next to his bed, he swung his legs over the side and stumbled toward the small space. The dim light from the moon through the windows barely illuminated his path, but he found the stash and grabbed a granola bar, tearing it open with eager hands.

Sitting in the dark, he took a bite, the chewy texture offering a small comfort. As he chewed, the faint red glow of the LED bedside clock caught his eye, 3 a.m. The hour felt surreal, a reminder of how much time had slipped away.

From his bed, the distant sound of a car carried through the night, growing louder until the crunch of tires on gravel told him it had turned into the driveway.

Cyrus froze for a moment. It was late, too late for anyone to be moving around without a reason. A flicker of suspicion pushed him to act. He eased open the RV door and paused, eyeing the damaged steps. They were still useless. He swung himself down instead, landing lightly on the ground and steadying his balance before moving off. The air was cool, and moonlight washed over the grounds of Reckoning Grove, leaving most of it in shadow.

He moved slowly, his steps cautious as he followed the faint sound of voices. As he neared the driveway, a deep black SUV came into view, its glossy surface reflecting the pale moonlight. It looked out of place, unfamiliar, and instantly heightened his wariness. Squinting, Cyrus made out figures standing near the vehicle, their pale shapes silhouetted against its dark sides.

Curiosity pulled Cyrus forward, but he moved slower now, placing each step with care as he edged closer to the driveway. He was almost near enough to make out faces when his boot brushed a dry twig. It snapped sharply in the still night.

Cyrus froze.

The figures by the SUV went quiet and turned slightly in his direction. In that instant, moonlight flashed off a pair of round lenses. James. The recognition hit hard and sudden.

Cyrus slipped back behind the nearest tree and held still, heart hammering, breath locked in his chest. A second passed. Then another. The two men looked at each other, then turned back to the vehicle as if nothing were there.

Relief crept in, thin and uneasy.

Their voices dropped again, low and indistinct. Cyrus stayed where he was, watching. The other man leaned into the back of the SUV and pulled out a small container, its shape hard to make out in the moonlight. He handed it to James, who took it without hesitation.

The man said something lightly and both of them chuckled. The sound only sharpened Cyrus's unease.

The laughter faded. The man closed the rear hatch and climbed into the driver's seat. The engine started, and moments later the SUV rolled away, leaving James alone in the dark, the container still in his hand.

Cyrus remained hidden, his mind filled with questions as James lingered in the stillness, shrouded in the settling dust, as if the night had revealed a secret it wasn't meant to share.

James glanced around cautiously before he began moving again. He walked carefully, his footsteps muted as he passed by the house and the garden, apparently heading toward the spring situated at the edge of Reckoning Grove. Cyrus followed at a safe distance, his own steps deliberate, heart pounding as he made sure to stay hidden in the shadows. Every rustle of leaves or snap of a twig seemed louder than usual, but James didn't act like he noticed. Perhaps he was too focused.

When James reached the spring, he paused, scanning his surroundings once more. He seemed wary. Cyrus ducked behind a tree, holding his breath as James's gaze swept over the area where he hid. Satisfied he was alone, James knelt at the edge of the spring, the moonlight casting a soft glow over the clear water.

Cyrus watched as James carefully unscrewed the cap of the small container and with a slow, deliberate motion, poured its contents into the spring. The liquid mixed in and vanished into the water instantly. James hesitated for a moment, watching the ripples spread, then screwed the cap back on, taking a deep breath as if releasing unspoken tension.

Standing, James brushed his hands off and, with a casual air, walked back toward the house, his posture relaxed as though nothing unusual had occurred. Cyrus remained frozen in the shadows, unsure what he'd witnessed, the tranquil surface of the spring hiding whatever James had poured into it.

When Cyrus got back to the RV, he collapsed onto his bed, but sleep was impossible. His mind swirled with theories. James, the container, the spring, it all replayed in his head over and over, each detail adding to his growing unease.

He tossed and turned, staring at the ceiling and the walls, trying to make sense of it. What had James poured into the spring? Why did it feel so secretive? The questions looped endlessly in his mind and refused to let him rest.

At first, Cyrus had thought the mystery illness at the commune was tied to some kind of infection, something unintentional, even innocuous. Later he was focused on their canning process. But tonight changed everything.

He had seen James. No doubt about it, James, crouched low in the moonlight, pouring something from a bottle into the commune's drinking water. The memory replayed in flashes: the gleam of liquid, the furtive way James moved, the way he glanced over his shoulder.

Poison.

The word settled on his chest like a weight.

Still, something didn't fit. Why would James do this? Cyrus turned the question over in his mind, searching for a thread to pull. His thoughts drifted back to the night of his arrival, the first bonfire under the dark sky. He remembered sitting next to Gus, Vlad's roommate, the ex-lawyer with the sharp laugh, listening as he talked about how people had tried again and again to drive the commune members out. And then Gus had mentioned a church. Some preacher who'd declared Reckoning Grove "holy land," claiming the commune was desecrating it. The name came back to Cyrus now, stark and unwelcome: *Church of the Sovereign Covenant.*

A cold weight settled in his stomach. Gus had added, almost offhandedly, that James used to belong to that church.

Cyrus's mind kept spinning. If James really was poisoning the water, then why weren't more people sick? Why hadn't the whole commune fallen gravely ill, or worse, died?

He turned onto his side and stared at the curved wall of the RV. Maybe it wasn't meant to kill. Maybe it was something microbial, some engineered sludge, a bio-toxin with subtle effects. But that didn't explain Cindy's hair loss, or nausea or fatigue or the pattern of other symptoms that seemed too clean, too deliberate.

Heavy metals, he thought. Arsenic, lead, mercury, thallium, they could do it. Rash, nausea, tremors.

His pulse picked up.

Was tonight just another dose in a slow, sickening plan?

Or had James finally poured in enough to tip the balance?

"Fuck!" Cyrus hissed under his breath. "I should have taken a sample of the water to the health department too." The thought of Justin flickered back, his rushed, dismissive voice, the way he'd brushed off the canned beans. Even if Cyrus had brought the water now, Justin wouldn't take it seriously.

The first light of dawn seeping through the RV windows cast a soft, glow over the small, cluttered space. The faint warmth of the early morning light played across the room, Cyrus stirred, his body enervated from his stress as he dragged himself out of bed. His movements were slow, weighed down by the restless night behind him. With groggy determination he stretched and rubbed his face, steeling himself for the day ahead. He needed to get to the hospital to check on Cindy, but first, his empty stomach reminded him, he needed to find something to eat.

He reached for an unopened water bottle from Brent's stash. Seeing James pour something into the drinking water made him paranoid. Then at the house, he used the bottled water to make a quick cup of coffee before filling a plate with scrambled eggs. Even though he was starving, he just wanted a quick bite before rushing off to check on Cindy.

As Cyrus entered the dining room, food and coffee in hand, he saw James sitting alone at a nearby table. His stomach tensed as James looked up at him, but then the other man's face broke into a welcoming smile, and he gestured Cyrus over. Veiling his suspicions, Cyrus walked over and sat down with his coffee and breakfast. He took a bite of the scrambled eggs, barely tasting them as his thoughts churned. He couldn't shake the worry that James might have seen Cyrus in the dark, watching as he poured the solution into the spring.

James spoke up, asking casually, "So how'd you sleep last night?"

Cyrus froze mid-bite, his heart racing, nervous James might have caught him spying after all. "Huh?" he blurted out.

James didn't seem to notice the hesitation. He leaned back and took a sip of his Diet Coke. "I slept amazing. Out cold the whole night after the bonfire, didn't even wake up once."

Cyrus let out a hopefully imperceptible sigh of relief. James didn't know. In fact, he was covering for what he had done, though Cyrus kept his face neutral.

"Yeah, well, you probably heard I had to take Cindy to the hospital yesterday," Cyrus said. "I crashed when I got back. I'm planning to check on her right after I finish breakfast."

James raised an eyebrow, leaning forward slightly. "Tell her I said get better soon." He added with a grin, "At this rate, you're going to end up saving everyone at Reckoning Grove. Might as well slap a superhero emblem on that backpack of yours."

A faint smile tugged at Cyrus's lips. "Superhero?" He shook his head lightly. "More like the guy who just patches things up until they break again. Pretty sure I'm no one's first call for saving the day."

James laughed, leaning back in his chair. "Don't sell yourself short, Doc. Even superheroes have their off days."

Cyrus chuckled faintly, though the tightness in his chest didn't entirely ease. "Yeah, well, we'll see." He finished the last of his coffee and stood, picking up his plate. "I should get going."

"Take it easy," James said, lifting his Diet Coke in a mock toast.

Cyrus headed outside to Mystique. Climbing into the driver's seat, he sat for a moment, gripping the steering wheel, his thoughts flickering back to James's easy smile.

He doesn't know anything, Cyrus reassured himself, though the lingering tension in his chest wouldn't let him relax completely.

CYRUS PULLED the truck into the hospital parking lot, subconsciously choosing the same spot he'd parked in the last two times. Guilt gnawed at him as he hurried inside, remembering his promise to visit Cindy the day before, the day that he'd slept through. He made his way quickly to Cindy's room, his pulse quickening as he approached the door.

But when he stepped inside, he froze. The room was empty. Cindy's bed was neatly made, its white sheets perfectly tucked in, corners squared with precise folds as if no one had ever disturbed them. The pillow was fluffed and centered, lying untouched under the stark fluorescent light. Even the thin hospital blanket, folded at the foot of the bed, showed no sign of creases or wrinkles, just clean, sterile lines against the pale sheets. The monitors were powered down, screens dark, cords coiled neatly at the bedside, lending an unsettling stillness to the room.

The room itself was unnervingly quiet, though faint hospital sounds drifted in from the hallway, the distant murmur of voices, a soft beeping, the shuffle of footsteps. Cyrus stood staring at the empty bed, an uncomfortable chill creeping up his spine. Hundreds of scenarios filled his mind, maybe Cindy got so sick they had to transfer her to a bigger hospital? Maybe she had left for home already? But if that were the case, he would have seen her at Reckoning Grove, and Cindy didn't have a vehicle to get back anyway. And where was Calvin?

Anxiously, Cyrus turned and made his way back to the nurses' station, a gnawing worry growing in his chest. As he approached, he spotted the young nurse he'd spoken to the day before, Alicia. She looked up at him with a flash of surprise, her eyes widening slightly as their gazes met.

"Oh, hi," she said, standing up from her desk. "I didn't expect to see you here."

Cyrus wasn't sure why she would say that, and dread filled his voice as he asked, "My friend Cindy isn't in that room anymore. Did she get moved or something?"

A shadow of sadness fell across the nurse's face, and she looked down for a moment before meeting Cyrus's gaze again. Her voice softened. "I'm so sorry, but . . . your friend passed late last night." She hesitated, watching him, then continued, "I wasn't here, 'cause my shift had ended, but when I took over for the night nurse this morning, she told me Mrs. Ellingson developed some kind of arrhythmia.

They had to code her . . . they worked on her for almost an hour." She paused, swallowing. "I heard that Dr. Bronson didn't want to give up. He pushed them to keep going, but . . . in the end, he had to call it."

Cyrus stared at her in horror, not knowing what to believe. Cindy had been relatively healthy; there was no way she would succumb like that. He'd taken care of hundreds of people with CHF exacerbations. It was a dangerous diagnosis, but he just didn't believe Cindy could have died from something like that.

Cyrus excused himself from the nurses' station, his mind numb as he drifted down the hall. He found a bench and sank onto it, sitting stunned as he tried to process what he'd just heard. The thought circled back, relentless. This was exactly what had happened with Brent. Treated for one problem, stabilized, even showing signs of recovery, and then snatched away by an arrhythmia, sudden and merciless. The same cruel pattern repeating itself. And now, sitting alone in the dim corridor, Cyrus felt the weight of it land squarely on him: he was the one who had to find out why. The duty he thought he'd left behind had returned. People needed help, and he couldn't look away.

16

With his face in his hands, he listened to someone typing on a computer at the nurses' station, and his mind drifted to an earlier time at his small hospital in Virginia.

The soft hum of the computer screen filled the quiet nurses' station as Cyrus typed, his fingers moving quickly over the keys. It was just another day in the rural hospital, a place where Cyrus knew almost everyone, not just as patients, but as neighbors, friends, and, sometimes, people who had helped him with his own errands.

He paused for a moment, leaning back in his chair, scanning the notes on the screen. Forty minutes ago, he'd rounded on Mrs. Tester, a broad-shouldered 66-year-old woman with a warm, easy laugh, who still babysat for Cyrus's kids from time to time. She worked at the local tire store now, and when he'd stopped in for new tires last month, they'd joked about how she probably knew every car in town better than the people driving them. She had recently been admitted for pneumonia, but her clinical course had been worrying Cyrus.

She was on all the appropriate treatments, but her respiratory status had been tenuous during the last twenty-four hours. Cyrus had placed her on broad spectrum antibiotics; she was on the maximum medical therapy possible, and Cyrus was wondering which way her course would go, she would improve or . . . well, Cyrus didn't want to think about the other direction.

That thought was interrupted by hurried footsteps.

"Dr. Darian!"

Cyrus turned, startled, as a young nurse, Tracey, rounded the corner. Her light blue scrubs were spotless and new, a subtle testament to her recent graduation from nursing school. Her face was pale, her hands trembling as she clutched the edge of the counter.

"It's Mrs. Tester," she said. "She, she's looking a lot more tachypneic!"

Adrenaline hit Cyrus like a jolt of electricity. He pushed himself away from the computer and was moving before the chair fully spun back.

The scene in Mrs. Tester's room hit him hard. She sat hunched forward in her bed, her chest heaving as she fought for every shallow breath. Her round face was drenched in sweat, and her eyes darted toward Cyrus with raw panic.

Cyrus's mind worked in overdrive. This was respiratory distress, severe. Although this was not unexpected, and Cyrus had done everything he could to prevent it. Unfortunately, the pneumonia was worsening by the second. Mrs. Tester's lungs were failing her, and it wouldn't be long before her body gave up entirely. Cyrus didn't have the luxury of time. The only option Mrs. Tester had now was to be placed on a ventilator. Mechanical breathing would give her the time needed for the antibiotics to banish the pneumonia.

"Tracey, call a code blue!" Cyrus barked, not looking away from Mrs. Tester.

As another nurse ran in, Cyrus ordered, "Grab the bag valve mask. Start bagging her now."

The nurse moved quickly, pulling the equipment from the wall, easing Mrs. Tester down onto the bed and fitting the oxygen mask over her face. Cyrus stepped closer, assessing the situation. Every breath Mrs. Tester took was labored, her chest barely moving despite the oxygen being pushed into her lungs.

Footsteps pounded against the hallway floor, and another figure rushed into the room, Maddie, the nursing aide. Maddie was older, with a no-nonsense demeanor honed over decades of experience in this very hospital. She didn't need instructions to understand the gravity of the situation.

"Maddie," Cyrus said, his voice steady despite the chaos. "Tell Dr. Fisher to get in here now. I need him to help me intubate Mrs. Tester."

Dr. Fisher was the only other physician in the building that day, a battle-tested ED doc with decades of experience and nerves that didn't rattle easily.

Maddie nodded once and was gone in an instant.

Cyrus turned back to the nurse pushing air into Mrs. Tester. "Keep bagging her. You're doing great," he said.

The nurse nodded, her eyes wide but determined.

Cyrus turned as another nurse rushed in with the code cart. Cyrus planned in his head what he would do. He'd done this hundreds of times; last weekend alone, he'd intubated an obese elderly woman and arranged for her to be airlifted to a larger hospital. This time, though, it felt different.

This was Mrs. Tester. The woman who looked after his kids, who slipped them extra dessert and left notes about how well they'd behaved. Who worked the tire shop and waved whenever he drove by.

The room buzzed with tension, but Cyrus's mind stayed calm, sharp. He would get Mrs. Tester through this; there was no other option.

The nurse set the code cart alongside the bed. Its drawers were packed with everything they would need to manage the crisis: medications, intubation tools, and even the defibrillator, should it come to that. Another figure quickly entered the room, a respiratory therapist, an older man with salt-and-pepper hair and a face weathered by years of experience. He nodded briefly at Cyrus, his raspy voice carrying a tone of grim determination.

"I've got this," he said, stepping in to take over the bag-valve mask from the nurse.

Cyrus caught a faint whiff of tobacco as he handed off the mask. He had always found it ironic that a respiratory therapist, a man responsible for preserving lung function, struggled with a smoking habit. But there was no time to dwell on that now.

The nurse who had brought in the code cart stood beside him, her eyes flickering between Cyrus and the patient.

"Which meds, Dr. Darian?" she asked, hovering over the medication drawer.

Cyrus didn't hesitate. "This'll be rapid sequence intubation, so give her 140 mgs of succinylcholine and a hundred of propofol."

She immediately started drawing up the doses.

"Dr. Darian," the respiratory therapist said. "I'm sorry, but she's got very little chest rise, and I can't get a good seal. Bagging isn't working."

Cyrus glanced at Mrs. Tester. Through the plastic face mask her lips were tinged blue, and her chest heaved weakly as if every breath were a losing battle. Cyrus's heart sank. Because the respiratory therapist couldn't get the bag mask to work, there was no other option but to intubate Mrs. Tester, as quickly as possible.

"All right," Cyrus said, his voice calm but commanding. "We intubate now."

He reached for the intubation kit on the code cart, his hands moving with the precision of experience. From the tray he selected a #3 Miller blade, a tool he knew well and trusted.

"Get the meds in now," he told the nurse, who was already injecting them into the IV line. "And where the fuck is Dr. Fisher?"

Cyrus moved to the head of the bed, positioning himself above Mrs. Tester. He tilted her head back gently but firmly, aligning the airway. The room tightened around him, the air thick with tension.

Cyrus was confident in his skills but always liked having backup available. He'd hoped to have Dr. Fisher backing him up in case things got complicated. But there wasn't any more time to wait.

The therapist hovered next to him, bagging as best he could until Cyrus gave the signal.

"All right let's do this," Cyrus said, gripping the Miller blade and positioning it inside Mrs. Tester's mouth.

Cyrus leaned over the patient, carefully maneuvering the Miller blade past the teeth. He was meticulous, steadying the blade to avoid causing any damage. But as he advanced, a knot formed in his stomach. Something wasn't right.

The airway was unrecognizable. Significant swelling obscured his view, and no matter how he adjusted the blade, the landmarks he relied on, the vocal cords, remained hidden. Sweat beaded on his forehead.

Behind him, the raspy voice of the respiratory therapist cut through the tension. "Sat's down to ninety percent."

Cyrus gritted his teeth. Only a few seconds earlier, the respiratory therapist had reported her sats were at one hundred percent. Cyrus adjusted the blade again, trying desperately to find any familiar structure. But nothing came into view.

"Eighty-two percent, Dr. Darian," the therapist said, his tone laced with urgency. Her oxygen saturations were dropping fast. The frantic beeping of the monitor in the background emphasized the point.

Then he saw it.

A flash.

The vocal cords appeared for a fleeting second before swelling obscured them again. Cyrus's gut clenched, but he had no choice. He had to act.

"There!" he shouted, guiding the endotracheal tube into the space where he'd seen the cords. Without looking away, he grabbed the endotracheal tube sitting next to him with his free hand and with one smooth push, he advanced it, praying he was in the right place.

He stepped back as the respiratory therapist immediately

attached the bag-valve mask to the tube and squeezed. "CO2 detector's yellow, Dr. Darian."

Cyrus held his breath until Mrs. Tester's chest finally rose. Relief surged through him, momentarily loosening the crushing weight on his chest. He grabbed his stethoscope, pressing it to her chest and listening intently for breath sounds.

Air moved clearly on both sides. For the first time in what felt like hours, Cyrus let himself exhale. "We've got it," he said, his voice shaking with a mix of exhaustion and relief.

But then the relief shattered.

The shrill, continuous beep of the heart monitor sliced through the room.

Cyrus froze. His eyes darted to the monitor, where the once-erratic rhythm had changed into a jagged saw.

"V-fib!" a nurse shouted.

"Damn it!" Cyrus growled, throwing off his stethoscope and stepping back to the bedside. He immediately felt Mrs. Tester's carotid artery for a pulse . . . nothing. He turned to Maddie, his voice commanding. "Start CPR! That's a shockable rhythm. Get the defibrillator pads on! Now!"

In a chaotic dance, nurses and aides ran around the bed. Cyrus ordered each person to do their specific jobs, CPR, airway, meds, taking notes. Immediately, a nurse hopped onto a stepping stool next to Mrs. Tester's chest to do chest compressions. With each push, the chest pumped up and down like a bellows desperately pumping air into a dying flame.

In moments, the equipment was ready for a shock. Cyrus followed the ACLS protocol for codes as he had been doing since medical school. He ordered a shock of electricity. "Clear!"

The nurse pressed the button on the defibrillator. The machine emitted a loud whine then delivered a jolt of electricity that made Mrs. Tester's large body jerk slightly on the bed. Everyone in the room held their breath, eyes flicking to the heart monitor for a sign of life.

Nothing.

Instead, a new waveform appeared on the monitor, a series of disorganized lines. Cyrus's chest tightened, and he snapped back into action.

"Restart CPR," he ordered, as he felt no pulse with his fingers.

The respiratory therapist leaned back, giving room for the nurse to resume compressions. The chest rose and fell under the relentless pressure of her hands, like an old door groaning open and shut, fighting against the weight of inevitability.

When it was time to check again, Cyrus stepped closer, his fingers finding the spot to the right of Mrs. Tester's groin, pressing down to search for a femoral pulse. He ordered CPR to stop and felt nothing, no resistance, no reassuring thrum of blood pumping.

"This is PEA, guys," Cyrus announced grimly, naming the electrical activity on the monitor. His heart sank further. PEA wasn't just bad, it was dire.

"Give a milligram of epi," he ordered.

Time stood still, stretching endlessly as though the room existed outside its bounds. Each second took an eternity, marked only by the rhythmic compressions of CPR and the unchanging, ominous beeping of the heart monitor.

The code dragged on, medicine after medicine pushed into Mrs. Tester's failing body. Nurses swapped places to perform chest compressions, their faces flushed and dripping with sweat, their movements driven by duty and desperation.

Cyrus stood at the head of the bed watching the scene unfold with a sinking heart. Rationally, he knew it was hopeless, thirty minutes had passed, and nothing had changed. But emotionally, he couldn't bring himself to say the words.

"Another round of epi," he muttered, his voice barely audible.

The staff hesitated. They exchanged uneasy glances, their fatigue showing in every line of their faces. But no one spoke. No one challenged him.

Then Cyrus felt it, a soft hand on his shoulder, grounding him, pulling him back from the edge.

He turned slightly, and there was Dr. Fisher, his face full of quiet resolve. His voice was calm, steady, almost fatherly as he said, "Cyrus, you have to call it."

The words hit like a blow to the chest, and for a moment, Cyrus couldn't breathe.

"Okay," he whispered. His voice broke, but the room was quiet enough that everyone heard.

The compressions stopped. The machines were powered down. One by one, the nurses and the respiratory therapist stepped back, their faces a mix of sorrow and exhaustion. The relentless fight was over.

Cyrus looked down at Mrs. Tester, his hands trembling at his sides. She lay still. Although she was dead, her face remained contorted as if she were still in pain, the stress of her final struggle etched into her features. A plastic endotracheal tube protruded from her mouth with dried blood crusted at the corners of the lips, a stark reminder of the desperate battle to save her.

The sight was devastating, but what made it worse was the quiet that followed. The room, once alive with frantic energy, now felt oppressively still, as though even the air refused to move.

Cyrus couldn't help but feel responsible. This woman's death was his fault. He was responsible for curing her, for fixing her, but he had failed. This woman had died because of him, and he could not forgive himself. Ever.

"I'm sorry," Cyrus said softly, his voice barely above a whisper. The words caught in his throat, heavy with guilt and grief.

A tear rolled down his cheek, and he let it fall, unashamed. He stood there for a moment longer, his chest tight and his heart aching, before finally stepping back, leaving the woman who had been both a patient and a friend in the stillness of the room.

As Cyrus opened the door to leave, he saw Mr. Tester. He was also in his sixties, a bit overweight, with clothes hastily thrown on as if someone had called him to come in on short notice. His frantic expression made it clear, he knew. He knew his wife was gone.

Their eyes met, and in that moment, the sorrow turned to rage. His face twisted, and without a second of hesitation, he shoved his pointer finger into Cyrus's chest.

"This is your fault!" he screamed, his voice cracking with fury. "You let my wife die!"

The weight of his anger pressed down on Cyrus. He didn't move. He couldn't. His face betrayed nothing but defeat, the exhaustion of a hundred failed attempts to save Mrs. Tester still hanging heavy in the air.

From the corner of his eye, he saw the nurses and staff watching the scene unfold like an accident they couldn't look away from. The room was deafeningly quiet, each of them a bystander to the moment that would stain his career, his life.

"I know my rights, this is your fault! I'm going to notify the medical board and the newspaper. Everyone in town will know what a quack you are!" Mr. Tester's voice was high-pitched now, as his finger jabbed into Cyrus's chest with each accusation.

A sharp, rhythmic beeping from a monitor down the hall tugged him back to the present moment. Cyrus sat on a bench in the dim corridor of Lakeview Hospital. The overhead lights buzzed faintly, casting long shadows across the scuffed linoleum floor.

He had replayed that night with Mrs. Tester countless times since then. Eventually he came to accept that her death hadn't been his fault, but like so many physicians, his first instinct whenever a patient died, or even suffered a bad outcome, was to shoulder the blame. That reflex was why he hadn't defended himself when Mr. Tester's grief turned to accusation. He remembered the feeling vividly when she had died, like being swept out by a riptide while still attempting to swim. He'd sat in the call room with his head in his hands, convinced he wasn't cut out for medicine. That he was doing more harm than good.

But here, in this hospital, everything felt different—his friends were dead, and the circumstances around their deaths were all wrong. He thought he might actually be able to do something, to help the commune.

Down the corridor, the monitor continued to beep faintly, steady, indifferent.

He leaned forward, elbows on knees, and exhaled slowly. His recent experiences had stirred the urge to help again, though the doubts born of earlier failures still lingered.

17

Cindy's death wasn't a case of doing everything right and still losing the patient. Cindy hadn't died from bad luck or the limits of medicine. Cyrus was almost certain now that it had been some kind of toxin. A deliberate act. And that gnawing uncertainty, the not knowing when, or how, or why, was worse than any clear-cut failure. It meant the danger wasn't over.

Cyrus was lost in a whirlwind of thoughts when he heard the distinct sound of clogs echoing down the hallway. When he looked up, Dr. Bronson was standing before him. The man appeared utterly exhausted. The deep lines etched into his face and the dark circles under his eyes spoke of long hours and hard decisions. Yet, despite his fatigue, a flicker of pity entered his gaze as he took in Cyrus's distressed expression.

Cyrus stood, and Dr. Bronson extended his hand. They shook, the older doctor's grip cold and firm. "I'm sorry this happened," Dr. Bronson said, his voice laced with a weariness that resonated in the air between them.

"Before I left the other day, I thought I saw some abnormalities on Cindy's telemetry monitor," Cyrus said, his voice shaky but resolute.

At that, Dr. Bronson's expression shifted, his tired eyes sharpening with something closer to alarm. He exhaled sharply and murmured, "Son . . . follow me."

Without another word, he turned and strode down the hallway, his footsteps fast and precise.

Cyrus blinked and hurried to keep up, surprised by the man's sudden haste. For someone who looked like he hadn't slept in days, Dr. Bronson moved with purpose, his clogs clicking against the tile with surprising energy.

They rounded a corner and stopped at a door marked Doctors' Lounge. Dr. Bronson pushed it open and stepped inside.

It was a smallish, functional room, the kind that had seen better decades. A sagging, brown fabric couch hugged the wall opposite the door, its arms worn to threadbare patches. Opposite it sat a scratched wooden desk with a hospital computer terminal. A narrow, neatly made bed had been pushed into one corner. A harsh fluorescent light buzzed overhead, casting everything in a tired bluish-white glow.

Bronson motioned toward the couch. "Sit," he said.

Cyrus didn't argue. He sank onto the flattened cushions, his body finally acknowledging the weight of everything, fatigue, confusion, grief. He leaned forward, elbows on his knees, watching as Bronson settled into the desk chair with a grunt.

Dr. Bronson leaned back in the chair, his gaze drifting to a spot on the far wall, as if he were seeing something far older than the beige paint.

"A long time ago," he began, "my best friend was also my partner in practice. We opened a small clinic together out in Bly, two young idiots with more ambition than sleep. We covered for each other, handed off patients, built something we were proud of."

He paused, rubbing a hand over his face.

"One day, he mentioned he'd been feeling off. Just tired, a little winded, maybe some pressure in his chest. Nothing dramatic. I did what I could, labs, EKG, even brought him in for a treadmill stress test. All normal. A week later, he collapsed at home. Massive heart attack. Dead before the paramedics even got there."

Cyrus said nothing. The only sound in the room was the soft hum from the old ceiling vent.

"I spent the next year tearing myself apart over it. I was sure I'd missed something; some little sign, some detail I hadn't thought to look for. It haunted me. But eventually, I sat down with another doc, cardiologist in Eugene, and we went through everything together. Objectively. I hadn't missed anything. It was just one of those things."

He turned to Cyrus, meeting his eyes for the first time since they sat down.

"What I'm telling you is this: sometimes people die, even when you do everything right. This job will crush you if you carry every loss like it's your fault. All you can do is your best, and then leave it all on the field."

Cyrus nodded, slowly. He knew what Bronson was saying. It was the first lesson every doctor learned, the one drilled into you early and repeated often. You do what you can, you accept the outcome, and you move on. Otherwise, the losses pile up and break you. He'd told the same thing to interns and residents more times than he could count. Bronson meant it kindly, offering reassurance, mentorship, a way to survive the job without being hollowed out by it.

But Dr. Bronson didn't understand.

Cyrus could feel it, this wasn't about guilt. Cindy's death was not natural.

Dr. Bronson was trying to be a father figure, passing down hard-earned wisdom from one doctor to another. But he hadn't heard what Cyrus was really asking.

And what Cyrus feared wasn't past mistakes, it was what was happening right now.

Cyrus looked down at his hands for a moment, then back up at Dr. Bronson. "Thank you," he said quietly. "I mean it. I've seen how the nurses talk about you, how Brent and Cindy thought about you. You're the kind of doctor I always hoped I'd become."

Bronson's expression softened slightly, the edge of his jaw unclenching.

"But I think you may have misunderstood me," Cyrus continued, his voice cautious but firm. "This isn't just me blaming myself. I've been staying at Cindy's commune these past few days. I've seen people with strange, seemingly unrelated symptoms, GI issues, fatigue, rashes, neuropathy, even hair loss."

Dr. Bronson blinked, his brows beginning to knit.

"At first, I thought it was just malnutrition or some kind of community infection, but now . . . " Cyrus hesitated. "Now I think they're being poisoned. I saw someone, someone I know, adding something to the drinking water at night. And Cindy was relatively healthy. Yes, a CHF exacerbation can cause arrhythmias, but I saw QTc prolongation on the telemetry monitor . . . that shouldn't happen. Something else had to be going on."

He looked up, eyes searching Dr. Bronson's face. "I was hoping you might help me figure it out. Maybe help me test the water or take a look at the labs. I don't know."

The older doctor stared at him for a beat too long, then leaned back, his mouth tight. "Jesus, son," he muttered. "You have to let this go."

Cyrus opened his mouth to respond, but Bronson stood abruptly, the legs of the chair scraping loudly against the floor.

"I mean it," he said, louder now, frustration breaking through his fatigue. "I've seen this before, young doctors who can't live with not having control over every outcome. Who think every death is a conspiracy they're supposed to unravel."

He turned to the door and held it open. "I think we're done here. Good luck with your life."

Cyrus stood slowly, stunned. "Dr. Bronson."

But the older man didn't respond. He walked briskly down the hall without another word, leaving Cyrus standing just outside the lounge, alone.

From his previous interactions, Cyrus knew that Dr. Bronson tended to bristle whenever he thought someone was questioning his medical judgment or clinical skills. That must have been what just happened. Dr. Bronson had taken his words as a challenge rather than a request. Cyrus had known plenty of doctors like that over the years, people who grew defensive the moment doubt crept in, who protected their authority by shutting down instead of admitting uncertainty. Bronson wasn't being cruel, just rigid.

Cyrus wished he'd framed the question differently, made it clearer he was asking for help, not casting doubt. But the moment had already closed off, and it was too late to take it back. Which meant he was back to figuring it out himself. Cyrus paused, the echo of Dr. Bronson's anger still hanging in the air. For a long moment, he didn't move. The fluorescent lights buzzed overhead, too bright, too sterile.

Then he turned and headed for the hospital's front entrance.

Outside, the late morning light was flat and gray. On a bench near the parking lot, Calvin sat hunched forward, elbows on his knees, hands clasped tightly. His broad frame was motionless except for the slight rise and fall of his shoulders. The wisps of white in his close-cropped hair caught the light, and his eyes, when he glanced up, were dark and red-rimmed.

Cyrus walked toward him, slowing as he approached.

"I just heard," he said quietly. "Calvin . . . I'm so sorry. I can't imagine what you're going through."

Calvin didn't speak right away. His gaze drifted to the pavement. When he finally answered, his voice was rough but measured.

"She was fine two days ago. Laughing. Picking greens for dinner." He clenched his jaw. "Then this. Just like that."

He looked at Cyrus now, eyes hard. "Doesn't sit right. None of it."

Cyrus nodded slowly. "I've been thinking the same."

They shared a wordless pause for a few moments, the sounds of the parking lot distant and irrelevant.

"Do you want a ride back to Reckoning Grove?" Cyrus finally asked.

Calvin shook his head and stood. "I'll walk."

Cyrus blinked. "It's ten miles."

Calvin adjusted the collar of his coat. "I need the time. I'll let Reckoning Grove know about Cindy when I get there."

Then he turned and started down the sidewalk, shoulders squared, stride steady. Cyrus watched him go until he was just a silhouette against the overcast sky.

18

With sadness in his heart but determination hardening his resolve, Cyrus went to the only place he could think of for answers: the community library. It was a routine he'd grown accustomed to on his journey, whenever he found himself in a new town or settlement, he would locate the library, sign in, and settle at a computer. Most times, he was on Craigslist, searching for day jobs that paid cash, letting him slip by unnoticed and stay off the grid. But today was different.

The two-story library in Lakeview was on the small side but had a quiet dignity to it, its sandstone facade standing solidly amid the town's mainly wood frame buildings. Large Corinthian columns framed the entrance, and tall windows lined the walls, letting in streams of natural light that gave the interior space a warm, inviting glow.

Cyrus headed to the front desk, where an older man in dress pants and a button-down shirt awaited him. His white hair was parted neatly to the side, yet his expression was anything but welcoming as he looked at Cyrus with a disapproving squint.

"I'd like to sign up for a computer," Cyrus said, hoping for as little friction as possible.

The librarian adjusted his glasses before giving a brisk nod. "Do you have ID?" His tone wasn't unkind but carried the practiced firmness of someone used to following procedure to the letter.

Cyrus kept his voice even. "Do you ask everyone that question?"

"Library policy," the man replied, already reaching for a form on the counter. His expression stayed neutral, matter of fact.

Cyrus exhaled through his nose, weary. Exhaustion gnawed at him, thinning his patience. He pulled out his wallet, slid his driver's license onto the counter, and let it rest there with a quiet finality.

The man inspected it and then handed it back to Cyrus. "Sign in on the sheet here," he said, tapping a clipboard with a short, chewed-up pen clipped to it. "You can take any computer not in use."

As Cyrus scanned the sign-in sheet for the next blank line, a name near the top caught his eye.

Charlie Collings dated two days ago.

He froze for a moment, the name instantly familiar. It had to be the same conspiracy-minded Charlie who lived at Reckoning Grove.

Finished checking in, Cyrus found a computer where he'd be left alone. He signed in and called up several medical references he was accustomed to using and began searching.

He began by entering terms for poisons that could cause the range of symptoms he'd observed. The screen refreshed, and results appeared. His eyes flicked over search results, tabs multiplying as he chased one toxic lead after another.

At first, the list was chaotic, with dozens of poisons, some obscure, some terrifying. Synthetic chemicals, environmental contaminants, even biotoxins. But gradually, as he cross-referenced symptoms like nausea, fatigue, tremors, hair loss, neuropathy, arrhythmias, rash, one thing remained.

Heavy metals.

He zeroed in: mercury, thallium, lead . . . and arsenic.

An older article caught his eye, chronic low-dose arsenic exposure through contaminated water supplies, causing vague symptoms that often slipped past early detection. Rash, GI issues, neuropathy, arrhythmias. Over time, the toxin built up in the system.

Just like what he'd seen.

His pulse quickened. He sat back, staring at the screen. This wasn't just a theory anymore.

Whatever James had poured into the water supply, this might be the answer.

But he kept coming back to a question, linking all these symptoms to a poison still didn't mesh with the social harmony of Reckoning Grove. Why in the world would one of the residents poison the water supply and harm the others? Furthermore, none of these poisons helped explain anything; either they would kill you or make you sick, but if the poison used killed all the commune members, it would be easy to figure that out. The police investigators could probably trace something like that. So most likely the poison was being used to make people sick. But why? Why in the world would someone want people sick? Cyrus felt like figuring this out didn't get him closer to a real answer,

Why would James poison everyone just to make them sick? That didn't make sense.

He got frustrated and focused on James. James came off as such a nice guy, sitting at the dining room table with his usual Diet Coke.

Huh, Diet Coke; perhaps he never drinks water because he knows it isn't safe.

He paused only briefly at that thought before his fingers moved rapidly across the keys as he typed "James Rubin" into the search bar. Instantly, the screen flooded with hundreds of links, dozens of James Rubins, from doctors to accountants, actors to teachers. Each result felt like another dead end, and the list seemed endless. His frustration grew as he scrolled, trying to make sense of it all.

After a few minutes, he remembered his first conversation with James and narrowed the search to "James Rubin, chemical engineer, California." Finally, he found something, an old link to an article about a chemical engineering company in San Diego that quoted a James Rubin. The article was dated years ago, and the details were sparse, but it was something.

Cyrus leaned back in his chair, rubbing his eyes, and let out a frustrated sigh. He'd expected more, something clearer.

After a while, Cyrus felt the weight of exhaustion settle over him, a mixture of fatigue and frustration clouding his thoughts. Yet despite the swirling theories in his mind, the pieces wouldn't fit together. He was getting nowhere, and finally he pushed back from the desk, the screen still glowing with answers that weren't answers at all.

As Cyrus stepped out of the library, the sturdy columns caught his eye, and a wave of memories rushed back to him. He was transported again to rural Virginia, to a few days after Betty Painter had died and her son Mike threatened him in the hospital. A day after Mrs. Tester had died.

During his lunch break that day, Cyrus had decided to hit the gym. He parked his car in the lot of the strip mall, the harsh midday sun beating down on the asphalt. Halfway to the gym's entrance, he caught sight of a man approaching, Mike Painter himself.

Cyrus felt his heart skip a beat and a cold knot of dread tightening in his stomach. It had been a couple days since Mike's mother had died, and his unease had only grown. The circumstances gnawed at him, something about her decline didn't sit right, as if it had been engineered. Because of that, he had confided in his friend Dr. Jim Bales, a physician who had practiced in the county for three decades. Well known and deeply respected in the community, Bales carried the authority of both a trusted primary care and hospital doctor and the county's medical examiner. When Cyrus shared his concerns, Jim agreed to review her case. Still, the more suspicious Cyrus became, the more wary he grew of Mike Painter himself. And now, seeing Mike bearing down on him in the parking lot, Cyrus knew he had to get away before the confrontation turned ugly.

His eyes darted toward the neighboring department store, its broad columns rising like sentries along the entrance. If he could slip behind them, maybe he could loop back to his car. With quick, measured steps, he crossed the lot, pulse hammering in his ears.

He pressed his back against the cool stone, straining to hear, when the heavy footfalls closed in. A hand clamped onto his shoulder, iron-hard, yanking him around.

"You killed my mom," Mike hissed, his face twisted with rage, eyes burning. He leaned closer, his breath hot against Cyrus's cheek. "But I'll make you a deal. Leave town, walk away from this place, and I won't touch you or your family. Don't breathe a word of this to anyone, even your wife, otherwise," his lips curled into a cold smile. "All bets are off. Be a real shame if something happened to your pretty doctor wife. Or those two kids of yours."

Cyrus's heart hammered in his chest, every muscle locked in fear. The heat of the man's breath, the promise of violence in his words, paralyzed him. The world slowed, the air thick with tension.

But as everything was about to spiral into chaos, the door to the department store swung open. A figure emerged, a small elderly woman with a shopping bag gripped tightly in her hands. Her bright eyes caught sight of Cyrus, and with a smile, she called out, "Oh, Dr. Darian! I'm so glad I found you here!"

In small towns like Corlen, Virginia, it wasn't unusual for people to stop their doctors in grocery store aisles, at gas stations, or while picking up their mail to ask about strange aches, sniffles, or skin problems. Usually, it bugged him, made him feel like he never got to take the white coat off. But this time, Cyrus was grateful.

The suddenness of her appearance broke the spell. Painter's hand loosened on Cyrus's shoulder, his attention shifting.

"I have this rash that showed up yesterday, and I was wondering if you could take a quick look at it," the woman continued, oblivious of the danger she had unwittingly interrupted.

Painter's posture stiffened, and for a moment, his fury faltered. He took a step back, still glaring at Cyrus, but the threat in his eyes wavered. Slowly, he turned on his heel and walked away, disappearing around the corner of the strip mall.

Cyrus stood trembling, the adrenaline pumping through his veins, his heart thumping in his chest. The brief encounter left him shaken but unharmed. All Cyrus could think about was why Mike would do this.

Maybe he knows that I suspect something about him. Maybe he's trying to get me out of town so that I don't tell anyone. He must not know that I told Jim already.

Cyrus took slow deep breaths, the surreal feeling of the moment dissolved.

A car's brakes squeaked in front of the library where Cyrus now stood; he flinched, yanked from the memory abruptly, like surfacing too fast from deep water. The warm sunlight on his face felt foreign now, almost deceptive. That sick, coiled feeling in his gut hadn't gone away, it had only been waiting.

He knew this sensation. The way the air felt thinner, the way his instincts started whispering that something was shifting beneath the surface. It reminded him of before, when that man had threatened him and his family. When everything normal had turned suddenly, irreversibly unsafe.

And now, it was happening... again.

19

It was mid-afternoon when Cyrus arrived back at Reckoning Grove. As he parked the truck, he saw people working in the garden and smoke rising from the chimney of the farmhouse. He walked toward the house, his heart heavy. He had barely known Cindy, but felt a kinship with her. He felt responsible for her death; he should have caught the signs earlier and gotten help sooner.

The commune members would have to be notified about Cindy dying if Calvin hadn't made it back to the commune yet and done it himself. He decided, as he'd done with Brent, he could start with Dana.

"Here we go again," Cyrus thought.

He found Dana sitting on the front porch, gently rocking on a wooden swing. Her long, chestnut-brown hair cascaded over her shoulders, the soft waves catching the afternoon light and moving slightly with each sway. She wore a pair of faded denim shorts that ended mid-thigh, her tanned legs stretched out and crossed casually.

He made eye contact with her as she looked up. But instead of her usual warm, unguarded grin, she offered one that seemed restrained, her gaze slightly wary.

Cyrus hitched himself onto the porch swing and settled beside her. The bench shifted under his weight, then found a gentle rhythm as they swayed together without a word. Cyrus let the sounds of the creaking swing fill the strange vibe between them.

After a while, he spoke, careful with his words. If Calvin had returned before him, the commune would already know about Cindy's death. Wanting to gauge whether Dana knew, he asked, "Has Calvin come back from the hospital yet?"

Dana's initial tension vanished immediately as she turned to look at him, her dark brown eyes curious. "No, why?"

Cyrus took a deep breath. "I'm really sorry, but I found out in town that Cindy died last night. She had some sort of complication while they were treating her and died."

Her eyes widened. "What?"

He swallowed, his voice low. "Calvin wanted to walk back and then tell you all, but I guess I beat him here."

For a moment she stared at him, like the words hadn't quite landed. "What . . . what happened?"

"She had a complication from her congestive heart failure." Cyrus paused, rubbing a hand across the back of his neck. "She seemed to be responding, but then her heart went into an abnormal rhythm. She . . . she died last night."

Dana's face went still, the shock settling in her eyes. The swing creaked slowly beneath her. She didn't ask for details. Didn't cry out or demand to know more. Instead, she lowered her head into her hands for a moment, letting the news pass through her like a wave.

When she looked up, her eyes were wet, but her voice was calm. "I guess here we go again," she said quietly. "I'll need to tell everyone. We'll need to start planning."

Cyrus nodded, watching her. She didn't try to push the grief away, but she didn't let it paralyze her either. There was something deeply steady about the way she carried it. A kind of strength he respected, maybe even envied.

Cyrus didn't have the energy to join Dana and locate everyone, so he left her to find as many commune members as she could to tell. He learned later that they planned to gather at the bonfire that night to discuss holding a ceremony for Cindy, in addition to Brent.

Cyrus walked slowly toward Brent's RV, his thoughts heavy. As he neared the door, he heard footsteps and turned to see James approaching, cheerful and casual, a relaxed smile on his face. But as James noticed Cyrus's somber expression, his smile faded, giving way to a look of growing concern.

"What's wrong?" James asked, genuine confusion on his face.

Cyrus paused, studying James, wondering how he could seem so oblivious to Cindy's death, if he had any hand in poisoning her, wouldn't he know? After a moment, Cyrus decided to keep his suspicions to himself. "Cindy . . . she died last night . . . she had complications during her admission and died."

James's face went slack with shock. For a long moment he stared before he doubled over, hands braced on his knees, like he'd taken a blow to the gut. He looked back up, eyes brimming with tears. Without another word, he straightened, excused himself, and hurried back to the house.

Once inside the RV, Cyrus sat back on the bed, staring at the thin ceiling above him. His thoughts refused to stay in the present. They tugged him backward, toward a memory that had never left him, one that had seemed to mark the beginning of everything.

It had been two days since Mrs. Tester coded and died at the hospital, and a week since Betty Painter's death had unleashed her son's fury. Cyrus could still see Mike Painter outside the department store, spitting threats that clung to him like smoke. The weight of it all followed him home that evening, pressing down on him as he pushed open the front door.

Juliette was on the couch, her posture stiff, her hands clasped tightly in her lap. The worry in her eyes struck him even before she spoke.

"What's wrong?" he asked, his chest tightening.

"I don't know," she said carefully. "But when I went into our bedroom, I saw your suitcase sitting on the bed. Some of your clothes were laid out beside it. I thought. . . maybe you were planning something?"

Cyrus felt a chill cut through him. He hurried past her, his heart pounding as he entered the bedroom. There it was, his canvas suitcase, unzipped, a few shirts and pants folded neatly beside it. He hadn't done this.

A cold sensation spread through his body as his thoughts snapped to Mike Painter was sending him a message. He turned on his heel, rushing back to the front door. No broken lock, no splintered frame, no sign of forced entry at all.

It was clear this was Mike's doing, sending him a message to leave.

He looked back at Juliette, still sitting on the couch, her brow creased with concern. Mike's warning echoed in his head, *Don't breathe a word of this to anyone. Not even your wife.*

In the days since Betty Painter's death, Cyrus had begun to see what he had missed at first: details that didn't add up, signs of something darker. His friend and colleague Jim Bales, the county medical examiner, was now digging into it, and the more they compared notes, the more it looked like foul play in Betty's death. If that were true, then Mike wasn't just grieving, he was dangerous. The irony of it was that Cyrus had already told someone about it. But if Cyrus told Mike that Dr. Bales knew, then there might be even worse retribution.

When Cyrus stepped back into the living room, Juliette was still on the couch, arms folded loosely in her lap, her expression caught somewhere between curiosity and concern. The question she'd asked moments before, about the suitcase on their bed, still hung in the air, unanswered.

"Oh, another thing," she said, lifting her gaze to meet his. "Freddie said a nice man gave this to him after school," she said quietly. "He was waiting for the bus." She held the note out toward him, her hand trembling just enough for him to notice.

Standing next to her on the couch, he smoothed it open, his eyes running over the words: *Tell Dad I'm worried about you all. I only want to protect you. He knows what we talked about, that's the safest way.*

Cyrus lowered the note slowly, then sat beside Juliette.

"My patient, Mrs. Painter, died the other night," he said quietly.

"I remember," Juliette answered, her voice steady, though her brow furrowed.

At that, Cyrus told her everything, his suspicions of foul play, Mike's threats, the confrontation in the gym parking lot. Cyrus added that he was convinced that Mike Painter must have thought that if he got him out of the picture then maybe wouldn't be able to tell anyone about his suspicions. He explained that he had already gone to the police about Mike's assault, but with no witnesses and no proof, they had only opened a file.

Cyrus exhaled, pressing the note into her hand. "It's clear Mike came into our home and left the suitcase as a message. This note too. But there's no sign of forced entry, nothing stolen. I don't think the police will be able to do anything about this either." He met her eyes, voice tightening. "Mike's dangerous, Juliette, we all need to pack up and leave, now. We're not safe if we stay."

The unspoken tension thickened between them. Cyrus could see a tear glinting in Juliette's eye as she took a slow, steady breath.

"This isn't the best time or place to tell you," She began, her voice soft but deliberate, "but I've missed my period for the last couple of cycles. That's not unusual for me, but I checked." She paused, watching his face. "I'm pregnant."

Cyrus stared at her, stunned. The words landed like a blow he hadn't expected, hollowing out the air between them.

Juliette pressed on. "I love my job here, Cyrus. This, being a doctor in this small town, it's what I've always wanted. My dream job. And now, with me being pregnant, I think leaving would be the wrong thing. I just don't believe what you're saying about Mike."

"Juliette, I'm positive he killed his mother." Cyrus cut in, his voice sharp. "Mike thinks I'll figure it out if I stay, so he's trying to get me out of the picture."

She shook her head firmly. "Cyrus, you've explained why you think Mike killed his mom already. But Mike is my patient. I've known him for a long time. You gotta trust me, he's a lot of talk but he's harmless. We should stay and let the police handle this."

Her tone softened, almost pleading. "I know you've been under a lot of stress lately, with the kids, your work. And now another baby, even though we didn't plan it. And yesterday, you got that letter from the medical board . . . an investigation over that other patient's death. I get how oppressive that feels." She reached for his hand but held his gaze. "But I don't believe Mike is truly a threat. I'm not leaving."

Cyrus leaned forward, his voice ragged with urgency. "Juliette, please, you have to believe me. We're in danger. Mike isn't harmless, he's already warned me, and now he's breaking into our house. Listen, I've spoken to Jim Bales, he's working on it. Mike clearly doesn't know I've already told someone and the longer we stay . . . it's only a matter of time before something happens."

She squeezed his hand, her eyes earnest, though damp with tears. "Next week we're going on that ski vacation," she reminded him gently. "You'll get some rest, step away from all this for a little while. You'll come back with a new perspective, and you'll feel better. I'm sure of it."

Even in the memory, the world tilted beneath him. Life already felt precarious; now, with Juliette pregnant, all he could see was Mike's shadow over them, the threat of violence stretching toward his wife and their kids. The thought of protecting those three was overwhelming. And to top it off, the death of Mrs. Tester loomed. If her husband alerted the medical board like he threatened to do, they would investigate the death. If they decided the death was his fault, he could lose his license, and with it the very means to help provide for the family he was so desperate to keep safe.

A sudden rap at the RV door, three sharp knocks, snapped him back to the present. Cyrus blinked, the memory scattering like dust in the sunlight. His pulse surged.

20

Cyrus opened the door, and there stood Vlad, towering and solid, his face lit with a warm expression. The white bandage stood out on the right side of his neck. Cyrus stepped down from the RV, and without hesitation, Vlad scooped him up in a powerful bear hug, lifting him off the ground.

"Hey, Doc, I heard about Cindy, and I'm so sorry," Vlad said as he gave Cyrus one final squeeze then gently set him back on his feet. His eyes softened. "But I know you must have done everything you could. You saved my life, and I know you did your best for her."

Cyrus shifted uncomfortably, the weight of Vlad's gratitude settling uneasily on his shoulders. "I don't know, Vlad, it was so sudden, you know?" he mumbled, brushing off the thanks. He wasn't one for accolades, always feeling awkward when the focus was on him. "Anyway, how are you feeling since yesterday?" he asked, hoping to change the subject.

Vlad grinned, his deep voice relaxed. "I'm feeling great, actually. At first, I wasn't going to take the antibiotics Dr. Bronson gave me. You know me, I usually just tough things out, try to fix it myself. But after we talked in the truck on the way back here, I figured I should listen to the doctor for once." He shrugged, a hint of humor in his eyes.

Cyrus nodded, relieved to hear Vlad was doing better and going to follow medical protocol, but the lull that followed stretched between them. It wasn't uncomfortable, just an empty pause until Vlad's voice broke the stillness.

Vlad leaned toward Cyrus, a wistful smile tugging at his mouth. "You want to hear something funny about Cindy?"

Cyrus glanced over. "Always."

Vlad's grin softened as he leaned closer.

"Couple springs back, we'd just got a new batch of chicks. One morning the brooder tipped, and they scattered everywhere. Calvin and I are diving around the yard like fools, bumping into each other, swearing, can't catch a single one. They're faster than they look."

He chuckled.

"Then Cindy walks out, doesn't even try chasing. She just sits right down in the grass, sprinkles a little grain in her lap, and waits. Sure enough, one by one, the chicks wander back and pile right onto her skirt. Meanwhile, Calvin's still belly-crawling after the last straggler like it's combat, mud all over him. Cindy calls out, 'Sometimes you just gotta let them come to you, Chief.' He glared at her so hard I thought steam would shoot out his ears."

Vlad shook his head, smiling. "But she had every one of them nestled in her lap by the end, calm as could be. We were all amazed."

Cyrus smiled, the image vivid and oddly comforting. "Sounds about right."

They spoke for a while longer, the stories easing some of the weight, before Vlad left, allowing Cyrus a moment alone.

Cyrus returned to the bedroom of the RV and sank onto the edge of the bed, his body heavy with emotional exhaustion. He stared blankly at the wall, and one last memory crept in, uninvited, but impossible to hold back any longer. The memory of what happened on the disastrous trip to Colorado, moments that changed everything.

Cyrus sat alone on the ski lift, the soft hum of the cables the only sound around him. Snowflakes drifted lazily around him as he headed toward the summit, coating the trees and the vast expanse of mountains ahead. The crisp air bit at his cheeks, but he barely noticed. His mind was a whirlwind, the beauty of the Rocky Mountains distant and unreachable.

He had come to Colorado for a break, to unwind. But it hadn't worked out that way. The vacation had been a disaster. His wife and he argued constantly, the kids were unruly, and the tension in their rental condo was palpable, every moment the shadow of Mike Painter hanging over them. So, he came up here alone, riding up the mountain in the quiet cold, trying to find a moment of peace on the slopes.

But there was no peace to be found.

As the lift carried him higher, the stillness only gave his thoughts more room to press in. The medical board was investigating him over Mrs. Tester's death, and the guilt clung to him, convincing him he could have done more to fix her. If they decided against him, he feared he might lose his license, his ability to provide for his family.

Then there were Mike Painter's threats. Cyrus had gone to the police, handed over the note, explained what Mike had said and done. But the words were too vague, the threats too slippery, and with no witnesses, all the police could do was keep their "open file" open.

Now Mike had somehow gotten hold of his cell number. The texts came at random hours, short, ambiguous lines that looked harmless to anyone else but chilled Cyrus each time. He knew what they meant, even if the police didn't. Up there on the chairlift, the messages echoed in his mind, the weight of danger riding with him into the mountains.

If all that were not enough, his wife was pregnant with their third child, and all he could picture was Mike's rage finding its way to them, his two kids and his unborn baby caught in the crosshairs. He didn't understand why Juliette didn't see this threat for what it really was. Mike was a potential killer, and she seemed to be in denial about their safety.

The lift creaked as it ascended, nearing the top. Cyrus pulled his jacket tighter around him and took a deep breath, the mountain air cold and sharp in his lungs. His grip on the poles tightened as he made a decision.

When he reached the top, he would ski down as hard as he could, not for fun, but to release everything. The fear, the stress, the guilt. He would push himself to the limit, hoping the physical exertion would give him a moment of clarity, a chance to leave all of it behind, at least for a while.

As Cyrus got off the ski lift, he skied around to a trailhead called *Fright Trees.* Exactly what he needed: a fast, technical run that would demand all his focus. He had spent his life on skis, carving mountains since childhood, and the motions came to him as naturally as breathing. An expert, he didn't hesitate, pushing off with power, dropping into the run, edges biting clean into the fresh powder. Each turn was sharp and fluid, muscle memory guiding him past the towering pines until they blurred at the edges of his vision. For a moment, he was free.

In that instant, he left his worries behind him, falling away with each swift, clean turn. Exhilaration coursed through him, the tension in his body loosening with every movement.

But then, as quickly as it had come, the peace shattered. Cyrus misjudged the gap between two trees, his ski tips catching on a buried branch beneath the snow. The impact pitched him forward violently, his arms flailing in vain. He plunged head first into the hollow at the base of a towering pine, a tree well, where loose snow piled high around the trunk. The deeper he sank, the more it collapsed over him, sucking him down like quicksand. Skiers feared these more than cliffs; once trapped upside down, the suffocating snow could bury a person alive in seconds.

He was stuck upside down, headfirst in the well, arms pinned to his sides, his skis and boots the only parts of him visible above the snow. He was unable to move, buried in the icy, compacted snow around him as the blood rushed to his head. His breath came in shallow, panicked gasps, but the cold air tightened around him, drawing the breath away.

Panic surged through him as the reality of the situation set in. He couldn't move. He couldn't even scream. The snow weighed down his body, pressing around him, squeezing the life from him with every breath. The snow closed in around his head and face, cutting off the last of the fresh air. A suffocating hush crept in.

Time slowed to a crawl. He was going to die here, trapped in this frigid, snow-covered tomb. His life was slipping away, and with it, all his concerns. The threats, the pregnancy, his stressful life, they all seemed so small, so utterly insignificant now. In the face of this, his previous struggles became meaningless. He could do nothing. He was alone, and there was no escape.

Minutes dragged on, stretching into an eternity. Cyrus struggled against the weight of the snow, but every movement only made it worse. His arms were trapped, his body encased, unable to shift even a little. The snow around his torso pressed down with unrelenting force, and his panic only grew. There was no escape. His lungs ached as he gasped for air, but each breath felt thinner, colder. He was completely helpless, powerless against the suffocating grip of the snow.

When he thought he couldn't hold on any longer, he heard something, faint, distant at first, then growing louder. Digging. The sound of someone working furiously, breaking through the thick snow above him.

A voice, muffled but clear, came through. "You good?"

Cyrus couldn't answer. His throat was too tight, his body too rigid with cold. All he could do was inhale sharply, the air burning in his lungs, and then exhale, desperate, shaky breaths. The world closed in on him, but miraculously the snow around his face loosened. The thick, icy mass shifted, and for the first time in forever he could see.

Upside down, disoriented, he looked up to find a man above him, digging away the snow with frantic determination. The movement was so precise, so quick, Cyrus felt a rush of relief, the weight around his face was lifting, and there was hope, a glimmer of it, as the suffocating pressure on his chest eased.

Cyrus tried to respond, to speak, but his frozen mouth couldn't form words. Instead, he gasped, drawing in air like he had been starved of it for too long. The cold air tasted sweet, like the first breath after breaking the surface of water. All he could do was breathe, deep, shaky breaths in and out, his mind struggling to catch up to the sudden relief.

The man didn't wait for a reply. He kept digging, focused and relentless, as though there was no question Cyrus was getting out.

After what felt like an eternity, the man finally pulled Cyrus free, his strong hands lifting him from the snow and laying him gently on the ground. Cyrus's body, numb from the cold and the weight of the snow, felt like it belonged to someone else. He gazed up at the sky, the vast expanse of blue visible between the branches of the trees, the world suddenly bigger than it had been moments before.

The man's heavy breathing filled the quiet space as he caught his own wind, the only sound in the stillness. Cyrus barely noticed the cold now, his mind too full of shock to register much. He turned his head to study his rescuer.

The man was dressed in a forest green ski parka and black ski pants, the color contrasting with the snow-covered landscape. His black helmet was scratched and dented in a few places, evidence of past falls or collisions. Ski goggles were perched above his nose, reflecting the surrounding forest. He had a thick, brown beard, but it was frozen in patches of white ice, giving him the look of someone who spent hours fighting the elements.

Minutes passed, neither of them speaking. Cyrus breathing hard to catch his breath. His mind was still foggy from the panic, from the suffocating terror of being trapped.

Finally, the man spoke. "You doing okay? I was skiing and missed a turn on the trail and fell, I was getting up when I saw your skis sticking out. I don't think you would've made it if I hadn't seen you."

Cyrus, his chest still heaving, managed to take a deep breath, his voice barely above a whisper. "Thank you . . . ." He wanted to say more but couldn't find the words.

The man waved a hand dismissively, brushing off the gravity of the situation. "It's no big deal. Just doing what anyone would do."

He introduced himself as Thomas, and Cyrus, feeling the weight of the moment shift, said only his first name too. "Cyrus."

Thomas pulled a small backpack from his shoulders, rummaging through it before pulling out a chocolate bar and offering it to Cyrus. "Here. You should eat this, get some energy back."

Cyrus took the chocolate, his hands shaking as he unwrapped it. He took a small bite, the sweetness a welcome contrast to the cold settled deep in his bones. Thomas shifted back onto a patch of packed snow a safe distance from the trees, stretching his legs out in front of him and bracing himself with one arm behind.

Cyrus glanced at the man who had rescued him, a wiry figure with a scruffy beard and a calm demeanor that belied the intensity of the situation. "Do you ski here a lot?" Cyrus asked, his voice hoarse.

"Yeah, I'm here every day," he replied, kneeling to check Cyrus's gear for any signs of damage. He paused, brushing snow off his gloves, then added, "I used to be an investment banker." His voice was steady but carried the weight of something deeper. "Made millions. Had everything. But after a while, it didn't mean anything. So, I quit. Now I live as a ski bum. Honestly? I've never been happier."

Cyrus paused, the chocolate momentarily forgotten as he processed Thomas's words. The idea of walking away no longer seemed so far-fetched. Maybe Mike Painter had been right, maybe leaving was the only way to protect his family and himself. If he disappeared for a while, the threat might fade, the pressure might ease, and the storm that hung over them could finally settle. The thought carried a dark sort of logic: distance as protection, absence as relief.

He swallowed the last of the chocolate and stood, feeling stronger but more conflicted than before.

"Thanks, Thomas," he said quietly, his voice shaky but genuine.

Thomas smiled and clapped him on the back. "Take care of yourself, Cyrus. Life's short."

Cyrus watched, his thoughts now swirling, as Thomas clipped back into his skis, sidestepped onto the trail, and disappeared into the trees. When he made his way back to their condo, his wife barely looked up from the kids, who were arguing loudly across the room. "Can you get them to stop fighting?" she snapped, her tone dismissive. "You've been gone all day. This was supposed to be a family vacation."

Cyrus stood unmoving in the doorway. He wanted to tell her what had happened, to share the weight of the experience that had almost taken his life. But instead, he felt like an afterthought. His heart sank as she continued to ignore him, focused only on the chaos in front of her.

It was like he didn't even exist.

The next day, waiting at the departure gate in Denver International Airport, their tension boiled over in public. He sat across from his wife as they bickered in low, sharp bursts. The terminal buzzed around them, families herding children, the metallic voice of the PA announcing delayed flights. Juliette shifted Samira on one hip while wiping her nose, the diaper bag slipping from her shoulder. Freddie tugged at her sleeve, whining for a snack, nearly toppling the carry-on.

Cyrus watched, a knot tightening in his chest. It should have been an ordinary scene, just the messiness of traveling with two young kids, but he couldn't shake the dread. Every cough from Samira, every whine from Freddie, every exhausted sigh from Juliette only sharpened the thought that they were all vulnerable, exposed. If Mike Painter meant what he said, and Cyrus knew he did, then his wife and children weren't just weary travelers in a crowded airport. They were targets. And it was his fault.

When the announcement to board came, he fell into autopilot, bending to scoop up all the bags as usual: his kids' bags, his wife's, his own, all of them weighing down his shoulders and arms as he used a free hand to guide the stroller.

He felt the phone buzz against his thigh as he shouldered his way toward the narrow boarding tunnel. Juggling the stroller and a duffel, he fumbled it free, nearly dropping the bags, and held the screen up amid the tangle of straps. His phone buzzed again; the number was unfamiliar at first, then a cold little recognition clicked, Mike was using a burner phone so this couldn't be linked to him. The message read: "Leave. Go now and your family stays alive. Come home and you all die, even the one on the way."

The words seared into him, and in an instant everything else crashed down at once, Mike's voice in his ear, that low threat: *Don't breathe a word of this to anyone. Not even your wife.* Juliette's face when she'd asked about the break-in. Cyrus's friend and colleague Jim Bales's, the county medical examiner's cautious text during their Colorado trip: *"Cyrus, you were right. Something's off about Mrs. Painter's death. Be careful around her son."*

He had only been waiting for the right moment to share this information with Juliette. That moment had never come.

His breath caught now. His heart began to hammer, each beat violent, slamming against his ribs. The tunnel ahead looked suffocating, like being stuck in the tree well— too tight, too airless, the walls pressing in. The roar of the terminal behind him faded to a low, pulsing thrum, and all he could hear was his own ragged breathing. He tried to swallow, but his throat had locked, as if the air itself had turned solid. It was worse, if that were possible, than being stuck in the tree well.

The line of passengers pushed forward, their bodies brushing against him, jostling him closer to the mouth of the tunnel. Panic clawed through his chest, sharp and unrelenting. He glanced back at the terminal, at the wide-open space and the clean lines of light streaming through the glass, the promise of oxygen and escape.

Something inside him snapped. The bags slid from his shoulders, thudding onto the floor, handles spilling loose. Without a word, he turned and strode away from the gate, every step powered by one thought alone, he needed air, he needed space, he needed to breathe.

The memory faded and left him with only the stillness of the RV, so complete it felt almost accusatory. He felt hollow, his mind steeped in regrets and doubts.

How has my life unraveled to this point?

The quiet in the RV only magnified his sense of failure, the voice in his head whispering that he was a coward, unworthy of happiness or redemption. In that moment, he even considered leaving, disappearing from Reckoning Grove and giving up entirely.

Cyrus took a deep breath, a flicker of purpose cutting through the haze. Maybe it is too late to resolve things with my family, he thought, guilt pressing on his chest, but if I can help people here, figure out what happened to Brent and Cindy, maybe, just maybe, I can make something right.

The determination was small, fragile, but enough to keep him rooted, enough to stay.

Another knock startled Cyrus, pulling him from his troubled thoughts.

21

This time, when Cyrus opened the door, Charlie and Dana stood there, side by side, eyes narrowed and wary. They glanced at each other briefly before turning their gazes back to Cyrus, expressions openly laced with suspicion.

Dana was the first to speak. Gingerly, she said, "Hey, Cyrus, I broke the news about Cindy to everyone, and we'll discuss a ceremony tonight at the bonfire." She hesitated.

Charlie broke in, his tone firm. "The problem is, we need to talk, buddy." His gaze searched Cyrus's face, while Dana crossed her arms, her expression unreadable but intense.

The RV felt close and heavy as they both filed in. Cyrus gestured to his bed, and Charlie and Dana sat down on the crumpled sleeping bag, looking from each other back to him with measured concern. Cyrus leaned against the counter, crossing his arms, saying nothing and waiting for them to speak.

Dana took a deep breath. "Cyrus, a lot of strange things have happened since you got here." She glanced at Charlie, giving him the floor.

Charlie nodded, looking slightly embarrassed but resolute. "Well . . . I've got a subscription to Searchbug," he said, lowering his voice.

Cyrus raised an eyebrow. "What's Searchbug?"

Charlie shifted uncomfortably. "It's a website that private investigators use that pulls public, and sometimes private, information on people." His fingers worried at the edge of his mustache, and he cast a quick glance at Dana before continuing. "When Grady started saying things about you . . . being a sleeper cell terrorist and all, I thought maybe I should check into it." He shrugged apologetically.

Cyrus recalled seeing Charlie's name on the signup sheet at the library.

"So I looked you up. You were a pretty respected doctor in a small town back East, with two kids and a wife who's a doctor too." Charlie paused. "Then, a few months ago, there were some articles in a Colorado paper saying you had disappeared. They had a search party looking for you . . . you just dropped off the map." Charlie let his words hang there. "Now you show up here, and people die!"

Dana said, "Cyrus, we all come from different walks of life here. Because of that, we're welcoming of people who have different beliefs and different thoughts." She spoke deliberately, as though carefully choosing the right words. "But we try to be honest with each other, and I'm worried you're hiding something about your motives for being here."

Cyrus remained silent, brow knit, lost in a struggle that twisted his thoughts. Part of him wanted to turn his back, grab his things, and leave this place, too many memories and too much guilt for what he'd done to his family threatening to crush him. Yet a different part yearned to belong, to hold onto this fragile sense of family he'd found here.

As his mind churned, Dana rose, placing her hands gently on his shoulders, as his wife used to. Her touch startled him, a quiet anchor. She met his eyes and said softly, "We want to trust you, Cyrus. We want to think of you as family, like what I found here after my parents died."

Her words washed over him, and something in him softened. In that moment, he made his decision: he would tell them everything.

Cyrus took a deep breath. "Yes, I used to be a doctor in a rural town in Virginia. Kind of like Dr. Bronson," he added with a faint, tired smile. "In a place like that, you have to do everything, delivering babies, performing surgeries, making house calls. My wife and I were two of only four doctors in the entire county, and for the first few years, it felt like a dream. We were making a difference in a small, underserved community while raising our own family."

He continued, his voice quiet and weighed down. He told them how the work had grown darker, how a patient's death and the threats that followed left him carrying a fear he could barely voice. When he finally confided in Juliette, pleading with her to leave, she refused, he thought out of denial, unwilling to see the danger he saw so clearly. At the same time, a poor outcome with another patient shook his confidence to the core, leaving him unsure if he could protect anyone, not his patients, not his family, not even himself. And then came Juliette's news that they were expecting a third child, which only deepened his sense of being overwhelmed, stretched too thin to keep any of them safe.

Then, he said, it all came crashing down at once. The ski trip where he nearly died on the mountain, and then in the airport, the message from that man, sharp and cold, a final warning. The panic swallowed him whole, he said, and before he knew it, he was walking away from his family, convinced it was the only way to keep them safe.

"I-I . . . uh, wasn't thinking clearly," he admitted, his eyes fixed on the floor. "It all happened too fast . . . I started having an anxiety attack, and I had to get out of there. Not even time to warn Juliette."

Dana and Charlie sat on the edge of the bed, transfixed by Cyrus's story. Cyrus stood before them, arms crossed over his chest staring into space.

"But I kept walking, I couldn't control myself, and I couldn't think, so I kept walking. After a while I calmed down, but still I kept going. Day became night, and the next day, I convinced myself that I was protecting my family. I had tried everything else, and this was my last hope. I was scared, and I got rid of my wallet, credit cards and cell phone so I couldn't be traced. I decided to start hiking in the forest. I picked a direction and headed West."

Cyrus continued, voice quieter now, describing the lonely rhythm he'd fallen into after he left: the days of walking trails until he was near towns, finding a computer at a public library, picking up odd jobs that paid cash. He'd use the money to buy camping supplies, trail maps, and food.

He told them that after leaving the airport, he hadn't called Juliette. Fear held him back . . . if Mike ever found out, reaching out could provoke him further. But anger simmered too, raw and unresolved. Juliette hadn't believed him, hadn't trusted his instincts. In the end, she had forced his hand, leaving him to go alone as the only way he knew to protect them. The frustration cut deep, that she hadn't stood with him, hadn't helped him carry the weight.

Then, three weeks later, at a public library, he pulled up the local news. The headline stopped him cold: *Mike Painter Arrested for Mother's Murder*. It had turned out as Cyrus had worried, that Mike had used chlorine chemicals from his maintenance supplies to sabotage her breathing medicines. Relief surged through him, then came the thought that maybe, finally, he could go home.

He called Juliette, and when she picked up, her voice was tight with fury when she realized he was on the line. She told him how devastated she'd been after he left, how she'd thought he had abandoned them completely, or maybe even died. Now, she said, she was rethinking their entire relationship. In the meantime, the experience was so traumatic for her that she wanted a new start. She was moving with the kids to Portland to be near her parents and start over.

Cyrus's chest ached as he tried to explain that he just wanted to come back, be with his kids, put things right. But Juliette cut him off. She said she'd hired a lawyer and started divorce proceedings for abandonment. That was it.

Dana frowned. "Why didn't you drop everything and go back to Virginia and fight for your kids?"

"I was going to," he said. "I even called her a couple more times to talk. But something happened. I became more and more helpless . . . hopeless. Looking back, I think I became clinically depressed."

He rubbed his hands together. "You know, as a doctor I treated depression all the time. I knew, on paper, it's a disabling disease. But a part of me still thought people should be able to pull themselves up by their bootstraps. I'd had hard years, you know? I was small. I dealt with racism my whole life. I worked my way through college and med school. If I could do it, why couldn't they?"

He shook his head. "Then I realized I'd made a terrible mistake, and Juliette wouldn't even try to work things out. I went dark. I thought about suicide. Doing anything felt impossible. Depression bends reality. It makes normal things feel unreal."

He drew a breath, searching for the words. "Being depressed feels like a painful weight in your chest that never lifts. It doesn't matter what you do or say, nothing touches it, and after a while you start thinking the only thing that could stop it is death. It's a sickness that twists your brain and convinces you that you can't do anything. And the shame that comes with it tells you it's all your fault, that you're weak and that you don't deserve to feel happy ever again. I know those are lies the illness tells us, but knowing doesn't make them quieter."

Cyrus paused then continued after a breath. "I still feel like I was protecting my family leaving at first. I know I did it wrong, but all those things I should have done: gone back, fought for my kids, my marriage, stop running . . . clouded any sense of what I should have done."

Charlie's face fell. "I'm sure you know this, Doc, but there are medications for depression."

Cyrus rolled his eyes and managed a small smile. "Thanks, Dr. House." The smile faded. "I knew I needed treatment. But look where I was. Off grid, no money, no insurance. No doctor to prescribe anything, and no way to pay for meds even if I found one. That's when I really understood what a lot of my patients were living with. When you can't get care, the hopelessness multiplies."

He let out a breath. "I finally talked myself off that edge by deciding if I went far enough, I could outrun the darkness."

Cyrus looked down. "So, I kept going." He paused. "I had to get away from the dark, so I kept going."

Dana and Charlie looked at him with a mix of sympathy and surprise, and Dana opened her mouth as if to say something but closed it again. The three merely sat together, absorbing it all, letting the unspoken moment carry the weight of his confession.

After a long pause, Charlie shifted in his seat, clearly wanting to say something important but choosing his words carefully. "Look, Cyrus," he started gently, "I know you've been through a lot, and I'm really sorry for all you've had to handle. But . . . I've got to ask . . . is there any way you might know what's going on here? With everyone getting sick? And two people dying?" He paused, voice more urgent now. "It just seems strange that it all started when you arrived, you know? We want to trust you, man."

He gave Cyrus a hopeful look, waiting for reassurance.

An unexpected excitement filled Cyrus. It was as though a light had flickered on, illuminating a hidden corner of his mind.

"Yes," he said, leaning forward. "I think I know what's happening, or at least . . . I think I'm getting close."

22

The three of them agreed that the RV felt too cramped and cluttered after the heavy conversation they had shared. Cyrus led the way as they moved outside, the fresh air washing over them like a cleansing wave. They walked past the lush garden, with its vibrant green vegetables and neatly arranged herbs, the earthy scent mingling with the gentle breeze.

As they continued along the path, they eventually reached a meandering stream, it's clear water gliding over smooth stones, reflecting the dappled sunlight. They followed the stream's gentle curves, each step taking them further from the chaos of the RV and deeper into the tranquility of nature. The rustling leaves and distant bird songs enveloped them, offering a much-needed respite as they navigated their feelings and the uncertainty that lay ahead.

Cyrus breathed easier, his voice steady but urgent. "What happened to Brent is what first made me think something was wrong. Then Vlad, Cindy . . . and finally, what really pushed me over the edge was seeing James last night." He explained how in the middle of the night he had seen a car at Reckoning Grove, his heart racing at the recollection of James emptying something into the spring. The pieces of the puzzle were starting to come together in his mind, and he felt a mix of dread and determination.

"Then I remembered the rash Vlad and Calvin both had. That rash, Cindy's hair loss and nausea, that all matches with a couple of poisons that could contaminate the drinking water," Cyrus continued, his brow furrowed in concentration. "What makes the most sense to me is that those are signs of chronic poisoning, a slow accumulation of a substance over time. As if they weren't meant to kill at that amount. Then, when Cindy had a CHF exacerbation—"

Charlie interrupted him. "What the heck is CHF?"

Cyrus apologized for slipping into medical jargon. "Congestive heart failure is when the heart isn't pumping fluids and blood as efficiently as it should." He took a breath, gauging Charlie's understanding before continuing. "What's interesting is that Cindy had described drinking a lot more spring water because of her nausea. I remember Brent drinking a lot more too when I was taking him to the hospital. I think both Brent and Cindy drinking so much water caused them to go from chronic to an acute poisoning syndrome, leading to an arrhythmia."

He glanced between Charlie and Dana, realizing he should simplify his explanation. "Arrhythmia means their hearts started beating abnormally, and that's how they died."

When Charlie heard this, his eyes lit up with excitement. "Guys, this sounds like someone is after us! I wonder if it's the government. I know they hate that we're trying to make things work by ourselves."

Cyrus and Dana exchanged knowing glances, wordlessly acknowledging Charlie's penchant for conspiracy theories.

Cyrus explained to his companions that at first, he'd suspected contamination in the canned food, some infectious toxin spreading quietly through Reckoning Grove. "In fact, I was so convinced that I dropped off canned samples from here at the health department in Klamath Falls."

"Oh, with Justin?" Charlie cut in.

Cyrus looked up at him, eyes widening as the memory clicked.

Justin had mentioned someone from Reckoning Grove constantly pestering him.

Charlie caught the look and raised his brows in a silent *why so surprised?* "Yeah, I've been after him for months about the contrails," he said. "Those streaks the jets leave across the sky? Like I said that first night we met, chemicals fall down with them. I keep telling Justin he needs to test for it."

Cyrus rolled his eyes, exhaling hard. "Well, that explains it. No wonder they didn't take me seriously."

Cyrus continued, determined to keep the focus on the facts. "There are a few poisons that could cause symptoms like this in low doses but wouldn't immediately kill someone. Heavy metals do it, but I think arsenic makes the most sense; it fits in with all those symptoms." He paused, processing the implications.

"But" Cyrus said, leaning forward, "I do have a theory. When I first got here, Gus told me James used to be part of that church, the one that once tried to buy Reckoning Grove's land."

"Oh, the Church of the Sovereign Covenant," Charlie cut in.

"Yes," Cyrus nodded. "What if he's poisoning the people here so they could take over?"

Dana shook her head quickly. "No, I don't think so. James isn't part of that church anymore."

Cyrus hesitated, the certainty in his voice faltering. "Well, you may be right. But what if he only said he left to throw people off, to confuse them?"

After a moment's pause, Dana's eyes narrowed in thought. She reached up and tucked a loose strand of hair behind her ear, a small, familiar gesture that stirred a pang in Cyrus's chest; it was something his wife used to do when she was concentrating. Watching Dana, he felt a strange sense of déjà vu, a bittersweet reminder of his past life.

Dana took a breath. "Alright, let's put together what we know. We think someone might be trying to poison the people here. Cyrus, you saw James putting something, probably poison, into the water, and we know some of the symptoms fit with poisoning." She looked between Charlie and Cyrus, her face resolute but cautious. "But beyond that . . . we don't know much more. We're still in the dark on the why and if there's anyone behind it or if we're just jumping to conclusions."

Her voice trailed off as she glanced down at the stream, where water flowed slowly over rocks, oblivious to their fears and suspicions. The three of them stood there, each lost in thought, knowing they had uncovered only the beginning of a troubling mystery but unsure of where it would lead.

Charlie brushed his fingers thoughtfully over his handlebar mustache, a telltale sign he was gearing up to say something. "Alright, so here's what I'm thinking," he began. "Everyone's going to be at the bonfire tonight to talk about Cindy's ceremony." He leaned forward, practically buzzing. "That means we can keep an eye on James, watch for anything out of the ordinary. Cyrus you could even subtly ask about the church."

His voice dropped to a conspiratorial whisper, as if he couldn't contain his thrill. "This is huge, you guys. I'm thinking James is probably CIA or FBI, sent here to spy on us or something. Imagine if we could catch him in the act, right there in front of everyone. We'd finally have proof, could you imagine taking down someone like that?"

Cyrus and Dana exchanged glances, both concerned and a little amused. Charlie loved his theories, especially when it came to undercover operatives. But right now, any lead felt worth following. Charlie's enthusiasm, however offbeat, somehow added a strange comfort, a reminder that, despite the seriousness of their situation, they still had each other's quirks to rely on.

THAT NIGHT, Charlie, Cyrus, and Dana planned to arrive at the bonfire one-by-one after dinner, hoping not to draw attention to their suspicions. Dinner itself was unusually subdued; Cindy's absence weighed heavily on everyone, casting a shadow over the simple meal.

When they finally made their way to the bonfire, they found that Grady had already lit it, and the flames were crackling, casting warm light over the quiet circle of friends.

Cyrus scanned the people around the bonfire as he walked toward it. Off to one side, he spotted Calvin sitting alone, his broad shoulders slumped, hands clasped loosely in his lap.

Cyrus approached quietly and rested a hand on Calvin's shoulder. The older man looked up, his eyes rimmed with fatigue and sorrow. For a moment, they just held each other's gaze. Then Calvin placed his hand gently over Cyrus's, a gesture of thanks, solid, steady.

No words were exchanged. None were needed.

Cyrus gave a small nod, then moved on, weaving through the others until he reached James, who sat staring into the fire, the orange glow reflecting on his glasses. His usual energy was gone, replaced by a quiet, vacant stillness. Cyrus took a seat beside him, saying nothing, sensing the depth of the man's grief.

Charlie, who was standing nearby, glanced at Danny, James's roommate, the guy Cyrus recalled had introduced Brent to Reckoning Grove, and stepped closer to speak with him in hushed tones, perhaps hoping for some insight into how James was really holding up.

Meanwhile, Dana chose a spot on the edge of the circle, watching everyone carefully. She was keeping an eye on each member of the commune, looking for any signs of distress or suspicion.

After a while, Gus, Vlad's roommate, stood up from his seat near the fire, adjusting his glasses. His button-down shirt was neatly pressed, the sleeves rolled to his forearms. He cleared his throat, and the quiet murmur of conversation around the fire slowly faded.

"We're here tonight to talk about what we want to do for Cindy's ceremony," he said, his voice soft but clear. "Back when I was a hotshot city lawyer, I never understood the importance of true friendship. Cindy meant a lot to this place, to all of us. It feels right to take some time to figure out how to honor her in a way that fits who she was."

He paused, looking around at the gathered faces.

"We never really got around to doing a ceremony for Brent either," he added, his tone thoughtful. "It's been a hard couple week. Maybe . . . maybe we could find a way to honor them both together. Something that brings the whole community in."

He gave a small nod and stepped back, letting the idea settle into the space between them.

After a long pause, Calvin rose slowly to his feet. His eyes were damp, and when he spoke, his voice trembled.

"I just want to say thank you," he began. "To all of you, for the food, for checking in, for just being here. It means more than I can say."

He paused, swallowing hard. "Cindy and I . . . we've been through a lot over the years. You all know that. Folks look at us and see what they want to see, because of how we look, how we live." His voice cracked a little, but he went on. "We always said our bodies didn't define us. That's why we both chose cremation. She believed that's who we are . . . it's not this." He gestured loosely to his chest. "It's what we leave behind."

He looked down, gathering himself, then back up again. "Like Brent, she wanted her ashes here. This place mattered to her. You all mattered to her."

With that, Calvin sat back down. The fire popped softly, the hush that followed somber but respectful.

Gus gave a small nod. "Thank you, Calvin," he said quietly.

A few beats later, Grady stood. He cleared his throat, eyes on Calvin. "I'm real sorry for your loss," he said, voice low but sincere. "Cindy was . . . she was solid. We all knew that."

He shifted awkwardly, then added, "I called my cousin, he works over at the funeral home handling Brent's arrangements. He said Brent's ashes should be delivered in the next day or two. I'll call him again tomorrow. Let him know about Cindy."

Then he sat, and the group settled into quiet repose again, each person turning over their own memories.

Though sorrow hung heavy in the air, a quiet unity was forming, an agreement that Cindy would be remembered with the grace and love she had given so freely. They spoke softly of what would come next: a small ceremony on the grounds of Reckoning Grove, near the spot where their founder, Kevin Daugherty, was buried. It would be a time to celebrate the lives of both Cindy and Brent, honoring their devotion to the commune. Both would be cremated, their ashes released into the soil of Reckoning Grove, their presence carried forward in the land they had helped nurture.

Soon the conversation shifted, and people began talking in more relaxed tones. Cyrus turned to James, who had been sitting quietly the whole time. Noticing how upset James looked, Cyrus leaned in and gently asked, "You doing okay?"

James snapped out of his deep trance, looking at Cyrus with eyes brimming with unshed tears. He hesitated then said softly, "Things don't make sense anymore, you know? We all try to do our best, to make things right . . . but sometimes, all you can do is your best, right?"

His words hung in the air between them, weighted by a sorrow that felt all too familiar to Cyrus. For a moment, he wasn't sure how to respond. Then he thought this might be the right time to ask. "It must've been hard, starting a new life here," Cyrus said carefully. "Sometimes when people go through change like that, they get drawn to spiritual things."

To his surprise, James brightened, a laugh breaking through his grief. "Oh, yeah, when I first moved here, I got caught up with this strange church. The Church of the Sovereign Covenant." He shook his head, still half-laughing. "They were obsessed with these elaborate purification rituals, standing barefoot in freezing rivers to 'wash away the world's corruption.' Nearly froze my toes off. After that, I figured they were more interested in control than faith, so I cut ties."

Cyrus nodded slowly, masking his thoughts behind a faint smile. The depth of distress in James's eyes and his explanations seemed real. Maybe Dana was right, and there was no connection to the church. But James still seemed so distraught, and it held Cyrus back from pressing further. He decided he'd let it rest for now, maybe he'd find the right moment to talk with James again later.

Shifting his focus to the rest of the group, Cyrus noticed Grady and Vlad sharing a tense exchange across from him. Their voices were hushed but animated, and Grady's face was flushed, his hands gesturing sharply as he spoke. Vlad crossed his arms, his jaw clenched, giving a slight shake of his head as if resisting whatever point Grady was making.

Cyrus wasn't sure what to make of the disagreement but knew first-hand that Grady was hot headed.

Probably just annoyed with Vlad for coughing the wrong way, thought Cyrus.

After lingering a bit longer, Cyrus rose quietly from his seat and walked off into the night, making his way toward the RV under the cover of darkness. As they'd agreed beforehand, he, Charlie, and Dana left one by one, careful not to draw attention to their departure.

They gathered in the RV with an unspoken urgency as they prepared to piece together whatever clues they could about the strange events plaguing the commune.

Cyrus began tentatively, "When I was sitting next to James, he seemed so sad and upset." He trailed off, furrowing his brow as he tried to put his thoughts in order. "I can't figure out why James would be that upset if he was the one trying to poison everyone in the first place."

Dana and Charlie digested Cyrus's words. Dana crossed her arms, her gaze fixed somewhere beyond the RV window, while Charlie gazed off to one side, brushing his mustache. The possibility Cyrus suggested shifted something in the room, adding a new layer of unease.

Finally, Dana spoke up, her voice low. "So . . . if James was trying to make us sick, why? What would he gain from that?"

Charlie nodded, still pondering. "Right. I mean, if he's not trying to kill anyone outright, what's the endgame? Is it to scare people? Or is he testing the waters . . . literally?"

Cyrus looked from Dana to Charlie. "Exactly. It doesn't make sense to do this without a purpose, or to risk getting caught like that. But if he wanted to control or manipulate people in some way . . . that could explain it."

Dana paused for a moment, then said, "I didn't notice anything else out of the ordinary out there, except for how upset Grady got at the end."

Cyrus nodded, acknowledging he saw that too.

Charlie said, "I spoke with Danny for a while. He mentioned James has been acting weird for a while now. Recently, he's been leaving more trash around, and their room has been messier."

Cyrus raised an eyebrow at Charlie. "How in the world did you get that information from Danny?"

Charlie winked, a mischievous glint in his eye. "Let's just say I've read a lot of books on interrogation."

Cyrus and Dana laughed, and Cyrus teased, "Of course you would say that, Charlie!"

The group fell into a thoughtful hush. After a moment, Dana broke the stillness. "If Danny thinks James has been doing weird stuff in their room, maybe we should check it out ourselves."

Charlie nodded, his eyes brightening. "That's a solid idea, but we can't do it while James or Danny are around."

Dana agreed, adding, "And with so many people in the house, even if James and Danny aren't there, someone else might walk by and catch us."

A mischievous glint sparked in Cyrus's eyes as a plan formed. "Then we'll need a distraction."

23

They waited until the next morning after breakfast, when the kitchen was empty. With Charlie and Dana watching, Cyrus placed a large, wide bowl full of ice on the counter next to the sink. He gingerly stacked a tower of pots and pans as high as he could above the ice, carefully balancing them, like a game of Jenga on the edge of collapse, each piece teetering above the others as if daring gravity to intervene. Atop this precarious structure, he set an open bag of flour. Dana and Charlie looked on from the other side of the kitchen, their faces a mix of confusion and intrigue.

His brow furrowed, Cyrus carefully let go of the flour bag and raised his hands as if surrendering to the police. He took a few cautious steps back, satisfaction spreading across his face as he surveyed his creation. Next, he moved to the microwave, setting a damp towel inside and heating it up for several minutes.

As the microwave hummed, Cyrus explained his plan to Charlie and Dana. "When the ice melts, it will cause a loud clattering sound that anyone still in the house will hear. They'll rush in to check it out, and when they see all the flour everywhere, it'll take them a while to clean up. That gives us the perfect window to explore James' room."

Charlie and Dana exchanged impressed glances, clearly intrigued by the audacious scheme. Just then, the microwave beeped, signaling it was ready. Cyrus tentatively removed the steaming towel, wrapping it around the bowl at the bottom of the ice pile, ensuring the ice would melt slowly enough for them to make it away from the kitchen until the moment was right.

"Alright, let's all head to Dana's room," he instructed. "It's down the hall from James' room, and that way no one will see us involved. We'll have a clear path to get in and out quickly."

Once in Dana's room, they settled in, hearts racing with anticipation. The work schedule that morning confirmed that James would be busy in the garden while Danny was occupied cleaning the chicken coop and gathering eggs. The house felt quieter than usual, with only a few other Reckoning Grove members still lingering inside, leaving Cyrus, Dana, and Charlie with the perfect opportunity to execute their plan. They exchanged anxious glances, waiting for the sound of the impending distraction.

As they waited, Cyrus found himself glancing around, realizing he'd never been in Dana's room before. Being in her space felt like a personal intrusion, like snooping among the small details that revealed glimpses of her life outside Reckoning Grove.

Her bed, set against the wall, was neatly made with a colorful quilt in warm reds and oranges, and a blue pillow that looked soft and comfortable. On the dresser stood framed photos, one a middle-aged man and woman standing beside two teenagers. Cyrus squinted; the girl was likely Dana in her younger years, standing next to a boy who must be her brother. Beside the family photos were a couple of pictures of horses, likely from a time or place she'd loved.

His gaze moved to a small shelf lined with books. One spine caught his eye: *The Idiot* by Fyodor Dostoevsky. It surprised him somehow, seeing such heavy literature here in Dana's cozy, quiet space, yet he could see the parallels between her and the innocence of the character Aglaya. He felt a flicker of curiosity about the details of her life before Reckoning Grove, the ordinary rhythms and choices that had shaped her before her brother pushed her away from it.

Suddenly, a crescendo of crashing erupted from the kitchen, echoing up the stairs. The noise was quickly followed by hurried footsteps and panicked voices, though the words were muffled and indistinct from behind Dana's door.

They exchanged a quick glance, waited a beat, and then eased open the door. The hallway was clear, so they slipped out, moving quietly toward James and Danny's room. As they crept, yelling from the kitchen included the words "Damn it!" and "Flour on everything!" When they reached the door, Cyrus turned the knob, and the door opened easily. Dana let out a relieved breath.

As they filed into the room and quietly shut the door behind them, Cyrus took in the contrasting halves of the small space. Each side had a bed and a desk with cabinets beside it, but the differences were striking. One side was immaculate, with a bed made tightly, a few books stacked neatly on the desk, and an empty trashcan holding a single crumpled paper.

The other side, clearly James's, was a chaotic mess. Clothes lay strewn across the bed and floor, unmistakably his from the familiar, faded flannel shirts and worn jeans. His desk was cluttered with a random scattering of papers, curling at the edges and covered with hastily scrawled, barely legible notes. An overflowing trashcan sat by his bed, wrappers and crumpled tissues spilling onto the floor.

Dana and Charlie exchanged a look with Cyrus, their expressions a mix of curiosity and caution as they surveyed the clutter. They moved cautiously around the cramped space, careful not to make any unnecessary noise.

Cyrus quickly took charge, dividing their search with quiet efficiency. "Dana, check the trashcan. Charlie, see if there's anything under or around the bed," he instructed, his voice barely above a whisper. "I'll go through the desk."

Dana moved to the trashcan, carefully sifting through its contents. She nudged aside crumpled paper towels, snack wrappers, and a few scribbled notes, her expression intent as she looked for anything that might stand out.

Charlie knelt by the messy bed, patting down the blanket and reaching around the edges of the mattress. He leaned low to peer underneath, brushing aside stray socks and dust as he searched.

Meanwhile, Cyrus focused on the desk, taking in the books stacked and scattered across its surface. One book caught his eye; it lay open to a page filled with calculations, dense with technical equations. He closed it to read the title: *Fundamental Mass Transfer Concepts in Engineering Applications*. He recalled James had once been a chemical engineer. That fact seemed like an anchor point in the shifting puzzle they were trying to solve.

He moved the book aside, revealing a mess of papers beneath It. Most were scribbled with half-finished thoughts, disconnected words, and rough sketches hastily drawn. He carefully sifted through each page, searching for any patterns or unusual details that might hint at James's recent behavior. After a few moments, one page stopped him, a printed sheet with faint smudges on it listing six names. One name had been circled, a star drawn beside it. Cyrus frowned as he scanned the list, but then he continued sorting through the papers, hoping to find something more definitive.

Dana's voice cut through the rustle of movement. "What the heck?"

Cyrus and Charlie turned; she was holding up a dark glass bottle she'd retrieved from the bottom of the trashcan. They gathered around her, examining the label. It read *Dimercaptosuccinic acid (succimer; DMSA)*. The bottle looked similar in shape to what Cyrus had seen the previous night. *What was James up to?* He thought, knowing what DMSA was used for.

The three of them exchanged looks, each as baffled as the others. Dana's hand tightened around the bottle, her expression a mix of confusion and concern.

Loud footfalls clomped up the stairs. Dana looked sharply toward the door, her hand loosening. As if in slow motion, the bottle slipped from her grip and crashed onto the floor and broke, shards scattering across the wooden floor with a piercing sound that sent a jolt through all of them. All three froze, their eyes darting to the door in panic. Charlie reacted first, grabbing the empty trashcan from Danny's side of the room.

"Quick, put the pieces in here," he whispered, his voice low and urgent. On hands and knees, Dana and Cyrus scooped up the broken glass, trying to avoid cutting their fingers, and tossed the fragments into the trashcan. They worked quickly, barely daring to breathe, their ears straining for any sound of footsteps outside. Once all the shards were discarded, Dana swiftly picked up the can.

Cyrus immediately went to the door. He twisted the handle and peeked out into the hallway. It was empty, and he motioned for Dana and Charlie to follow. But as they slipped out and shut the door behind them, footsteps sounded closer.

Dana's grip tightened on the trashcan as they backed up, ducking into the hall closet just in time. They huddled together, pressing themselves against the walls of the cramped space. Dana's hands shook, and tiny clinking sounds escaped from the trashcan as the glass pieces rattled. Cyrus reached over, gently taking the can from her, holding it steady to silence the noise.

They watched through the narrow slits of the louvered door as Grady came down the hallway, his expression dark and suspicious. He stopped outside James's room but turned his head toward the closet door where Cyrus, Charlie, and Dana were hiding. He stepped slowly toward them and placed his hand on the closet doorknob; for a heart-stopping moment, he held it there as if he could sense their presence.

Cyrus's mind raced. Grady could be involved in this; but what in the world will they say if all three of us are found in a closet holding a trashcan with a shattered bottle of DMSA?

But Grady hesitated then shrugged, releasing the handle. With a sigh, he turned and continued down the hall, his footsteps fading.

They stayed still for a few more seconds before Cyrus opened the closet door. They hurried down the hallway to Dana's room, slipping inside and closing the door behind them. Dana wasted no time dumping the broken glass into her own trashcan.

"Be right back," she whispered, taking the trashcan and tiptoeing back down the hall to James's room and then restuffing all the garbage into it. She moved into the hallway as Grady came up the stairs.

Grady raised an eyebrow. "Dana? I already checked this floor, but then I heard noise up here again."

Dana kept her expression calm. "Oh, I was in the bathroom," she said with a casual shrug. "I just woke up." She quickly added, "Late night last night."

Grady, visibly irritated, shook his head. "I was downstairs helping Calvin, Danny, and Mags clean up a freakin' mess in the kitchen. Some idiot stacked all the pots and pans in a tower, and the whole thing came crashing down, knocking over a bag of flour, flour everywhere," he grumbled, crossing his arms. "You didn't hear any of that?"

Dana shrugged. "Guess not," she said, smiling a little. "I'm a deep sleeper, I suppose."

Grady sighed, glancing back down the hallway. "Well, some of us will be spending the rest of the day getting flour out of every crevice. Anyway, thought I'd check."

Dana slipped back into her room and collapsed onto her bed, letting out a deep, shaky breath. Cyrus and Charlie stood watching her, the three of them frozen in uncertainty, not knowing what to do.

Out of nowhere, Charlie chuckled, covering his mouth to muffle the sound. Dana shot him a look, but it was too late, the laughter was contagious. Cyrus, holding back at first, finally let go, and soon all three of them were laughing uncontrollably, the tension dissolving in waves of relief.

Charlie, catching his breath, mimed Dana's panicked look as she dropped the bottle, his eyes wide, hands flailing in slow motion. Dana clutched her sides, tears forming at the corners of her eyes as they laughed even harder, grateful for the release.

Finally, when they managed to calm down, they exchanged grins, each of them realizing how close they'd come to being caught.

After their laughter faded, the three exchanged serious looks, shifting back to the gravity of what they'd uncovered. Cyrus leaned forward, his voice barely above a whisper.

Alright, here's the thing," Cyrus said. "That bottle, DMSA, it's an antidote for heavy metal poisoning, arsenic especially. James was a chemical engineer. The book on his desk and those calculations weren't random. I think he realized what was happening and tried to counter it, figuring out how much water was leaving the commune and how to add just enough, a little at a time."

Dana raised her eyebrows, her expression thoughtful. "So . . . if he was putting DMSA in the water the night you saw him, maybe he knew the water was poisoned? Like, he was actually trying to help?"

Cyrus nodded. "That's what I'm guessing. But the thing is, I'm not even sure this approach would work. DMSA isn't something you put in water. I don't think it works that way, but maybe James did think so." He snapped his fingers. "I also saw a piece of paper with names on it. One of them was circled, but I couldn't make sense of it at the time."

Charlie frowned. "So James was trying to stop the poisoning without telling anyone? And what about that circled name? Could it be someone he suspects is responsible?"

Dana nodded, looking down thoughtfully before speaking up. "You know . . . if James really was trying to help by adding DMSA, that could explain why he's been so down lately. Maybe Cindy's death hit him hard because he'd been trying to protect everyone, and it still wasn't enough."

Cyrus hesitated, clucking his tongue. "There's another possibility we haven't considered. What if James was originally behind the arsenic poisoning but had a change of heart? Maybe he decided to try to undo the damage by adding the DMSA, hoping no one would notice."

They exchanged puzzled looks, trying to piece together the fragments of information. Finally, Dana broke the impasse. "I think we're past guessing. If James is at the center of this, then we need to confront him. We have to find out what he knows, and what he's hiding."

The weight of the situation settled over them, each knowing their next move would take them straight to James for answers.

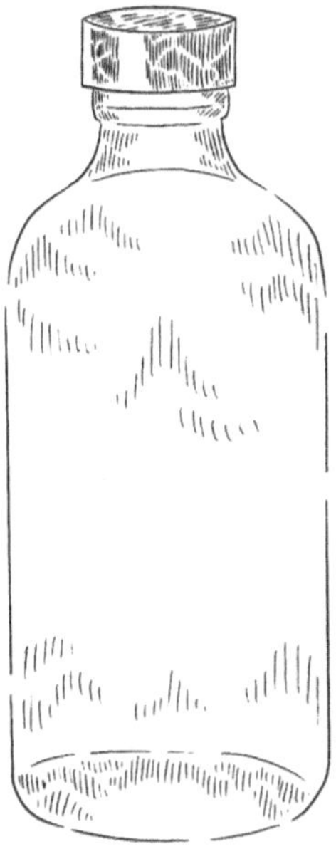

24

Cyrus, Dana, and Charlie gathered in the dining area at lunch, hoping James would come in after his morning chores in the garden. As the hour ticked by, people came and went, but James never appeared. Sharing uncertain glances, the three decided to head to the garden in hopes of finding someone who had seen him. They soon spotted Vlad, large and burly, wearing muddy overalls, his hands rough and thick with soil. The knees of his overalls were caked with earth, showing the hours he'd spent crouched and working the rows. He was in the middle of digging up potatoes, each hefty shovelful landing with a solid thud.

Vlad straightened up when he saw them approach, wiping his brow. When they asked about James, Vlad shrugged. "He was here with me earlier," he said in his deep, gruff voice. "We worked together most of the morning, but I haven't seen him since before lunch." Without another word, he returned to his digging, focused and unbothered.

Cyrus, Dana, and Charlie shared uneasy looks, unsure of what to do next. They decided to regroup at dinner, hoping James would show up then. But dinner came and went, still with no sign of him.

Growing more worried, they made their way to Danny's room after dinner. Danny greeted them with a puzzled expression when they asked if he'd seen James. Danny shook his head. "Not since this morning. But James . . . sometimes, when he's upset, he'll just sleep outside. He's done it before. Says he loves the stars."

Unsettled, the three exchanged glances, wondering why they were having such a hard time finding him. They finally agreed they'd start looking for him at first light tomorrow, hoping he'd simply wandered off for time alone and would be back by then.

The next morning, Dana and Charlie met up with Cyrus by the RV, both looking anxious but ready for the search. Dana handed Cyrus a steaming cup of coffee she'd brought from the house. "I made it with bottled water," she said with a tight smile. Cyrus chuckled softly and accepted the cup, nodding in appreciation.

They chatted quietly as he sipped, the warmth of the coffee providing a small comfort.

While Cyrus finished his coffee, the conversation turned to their plan for finding James. "Maybe we should go back to the garden," Charlie suggested. "That's where Vlad saw him last, right?"

With a nod of agreement, the three made their way to the fenced-in space. Still no James, so they decided it would be best to split up to cover more ground. Dana volunteered to search by the spring, there was a quiet area nearby where James sometimes liked to go. Charlie took the path leading farther into the fields, hoping he might catch sight of him there. Cyrus, meanwhile, set off in the direction of the stream past the spring and solar panels, his steps determined as he scanned the surrounding woods and underbrush.

As Cyrus neared the stream, the soft rush of water over rocks filled the air, stirring an unexpected memory. A week after he'd left the airport, he'd found himself by a similar stream, this time with a cheap fishing pole he'd picked up from the local department store. The gear was flimsy, the line tangled easily, and he felt ridiculous fumbling over a task that seemed so simple to everyone else. But after endless attempts, he finally hooked a small trout.

The surge of excitement when he pulled it out of the water, the fish twisting in his hand, was the most exhilarated he'd felt in a long time. The thrill of doing something new and self-reliant, even if it was just a humble catch. For that brief moment, he felt alive in a way he hadn't realized he'd been missing.

The stream's rush tore through his memory, snapping him back to the present. Cyrus walked along the bank a few more steps, scanning the shifting light through the trees, then he saw it: the outline of a body lying near the water's edge. Heart pounding, he carefully stepped closer, half-convinced it might be James sleeping beside the stream, as Danny had mentioned. But as he drew nearer, dread crept in, the body lay half on the bank, half submerged, with water rushing over the submerged head and torso as though they were nothing more than a rock in the current. It was definitely James.

Cyrus broke into a run, closing the distance in seconds. He dropped down beside the body, taking in the grim details in a frantic blur. One foot was wedged awkwardly in a hole at the edge of the stream, as if James had stumbled and gotten caught. A large rock nearby carried a dark smear of dried blood, showing where his head must have struck in the fall. From there, it looked like he had pitched forward, unconscious, and landed face-first in the water. Briefly Cyrus thought he shouldn't disturb the crime scene, but survival instincts took over. He grabbed James's ankles, trying to pull him out of the stream.

The body was heavy, the clothing sodden with water, and Cyrus's grip slipped, sending him sprawling backward onto the ground. With no other choice, he waded into the ice-cold water to get better leverage. Shivering, he grasped James by the arm, and with a desperate pull, dragged him fully onto the bank. But as soon as he took in the cold, bluish pallor of James's face, with a large gash on the forehead, his stomach sank. James was dead. There was no fixing this; it was too late given the cold, stiff rigidity of the body and the unnatural pallor of the skin. James's lifeless gaze fixed on him, as if in great effort, as though his whole being was concentrating on the gash on his forehead.

Cyrus froze, his hands shaking as the grim realization settled over him. The body was stiff and cold, too long gone for CPR, too still for anything but a futile hope.

Cyrus, Dana, and Charlie stood next to the county sheriff as the ambulance crew carefully loaded James's lifeless body onto a stretcher. The scene felt surreal, the commotion around them fading into a muffled backdrop of whispers and gasps.

Behind them, members of Reckoning Grove stood in various states of disbelief. Danny had his hand clasped tightly over his mouth, tears brimming in his eyes, while Grady stood with arms crossed, fixated on the unfolding scene, his expression a mixture of horror and resignation. Next to him, Vlad stood in his dirty overalls, hands at his sides, a sad look etched on his face as he took in the tragic sight.

Cyrus turned to the sheriff, who loomed next to him with a confident stance, a stout man, his uniform crisp and neatly pressed, contrasting sharply with the overgrown surroundings. A wide-brimmed hat cast a shadow over his rugged face, where a well-trimmed mustache framed his upper lip. His eyes, dark and scrutinizing, flicked between the scene and the gathered crowd, radiating an air of authority that felt patronizing rather than reassuring. His name badge read "Christensen."

Cyrus turned to the sheriff, desperation creeping into his voice as he asked, "What do you think happened here?"

Sheriff Christensen responded with a condescending tone, "It's clear this guy tripped when his foot got stuck in that hole." He gestured dismissively toward the hole by the stream. "Then he hit his head on that rock." He pointed to the large stone stained with blood, as if it were an obvious conclusion. "Passed out face-down in the water. Just an unfortunate accident, that's all."

Cyrus's frustration swelled at the sheriff's nonchalance, the words sinking like a weight in his stomach. To him, it didn't feel like an accident, it felt like a cover-up.

Cyrus pointed to the blood-stained rock, trying to keep his voice steady. "Sheriff Christensen, with all due respect, it doesn't look like the mark of someone who simply hit their head on it." He paused, letting that fact sink in. "And why would I have found his foot still in the hole? It should have slipped out with his fall. This doesn't add up."

The sheriff rolled his eyes. "Listen, I appreciate your concern, but we've done our job here. The scene's been secured, photographs and notes taken, and we've got initial statements from everyone present, including you." His voice carried the practiced weight of authority. "There were no signs of a struggle, no defensive wounds, nothing that can't be explained by an accident. The position of the body, exactly as you found it, fits the mechanism of injury. Nobody saw anything suspicious. No witnesses."

He tipped his head toward a man standing nearby in blue slacks and a white button-down shirt. "That's our coroner. He's trained in forensic pathology, and he's just evaluated the situation. He agrees, it's an accident. The body's being sent to the state Medical Examiner's office. They'll run the autopsy and toxicology. That'll take a couple weeks, maybe longer, and if anything comes back showing this wasn't a mishap, then I'll be back. Until then, this is closed."

Cyrus bit back the retort rising in his throat. He glanced at Dana and Charlie, both wearing the same look of disbelief he felt. The sheriff's dismissal burned, but what lingered deeper was the gnawing sense that something was being overlooked.

Once the ambulance and sheriff's department staff packed up and left, yet another heavy stillness settled over the group. Cyrus, Dana, and Charlie sat on the grassy bank beside the stream, the gentle flow of water providing a stark contrast to the turmoil swirling in their minds. Charlie ran a hand through his disheveled hair, staring blankly at the stream.

"Ever since that article came out in the local paper," he began, his voice bitter, "about the commune being a bunch of outsiders with 'loose morals' and 'communist ideology' . . . people around here stopped taking us seriously. It's like they've decided we don't even deserve the courtesy of listening."

Dana picked at the blades of grass, her jaw tight. "It's not just about not listening. They consider us outsiders. They've made us . . . invisible."

Charlie nodded, his frustration simmering beneath the surface. "It was clear the sheriff didn't care about any of the details. All he wanted was to do the bare minimum and get out of here as fast as he could."

Cyrus sighed, staring at the water as it flowed past. "He didn't seem interested in listening to any of us. The toxicology report probably won't even show arsenic because James only drank Diet Cokes. They'd definitely never believe us then. Even if there is a sign of wrongdoing on the autopsy, I really don't think we have two or more weeks to wait. I think we're on our own, guys."

The three of them lapsed into quiet once more. Finally, Dana broke the stillness, her voice tinged with urgency. "You know, I think I agree with you, Cyrus. This wasn't an accident. But if someone killed James, then who did it?"

Charlie shifted, considering her words carefully. "Do you guys remember how quickly Grady jumped to help arrange Brent's cremation? How eager he was to check on James's room the other day? He was too interested in the whole situation."

A chill ran through Cyrus as he processed Charlie's suggestion. "Are you saying you think Grady is the one who killed James? That he's the one poisoning everyone?"

"It's possible," Charlie continued, his voice lowering to a conspiratorial whisper. "What if he needed to cover his tracks? James could have found out something, or maybe he was getting too close to figuring it out. Grady might've felt threatened."

The three pondered Charlie's comment.

Dana added, "If someone killed James, then they must've known he was onto something. But . . . how did James even figure out something was wrong in the first place?"

As Cyrus wracked his brain for answers, a memory flickered to life. "Wait," he said, his voice gaining intensity. "I saw that piece of paper in James's room the other day. There were names on it, about six of them, I think, with one circled in red and a star next to it."

Dana's eyes widened. "That's right! We need to look at that again."

Charlie nodded, his enthusiasm reignited. "We don't have any other real clues, and it's worth a shot to go back to it."

"Let's head back to James's room," Cyrus suggested, urgency creeping into his voice. "We need to see if we can find that paper and figure out what it means."

Dana paused, her eyes narrowing as she glanced at Cyrus. "I don't think I can handle the stress of being in James's room again. The last time was . . . too much."

Charlie spoke with a determined grin. "Don't worry, Dana. I have a better idea. Follow me."

25

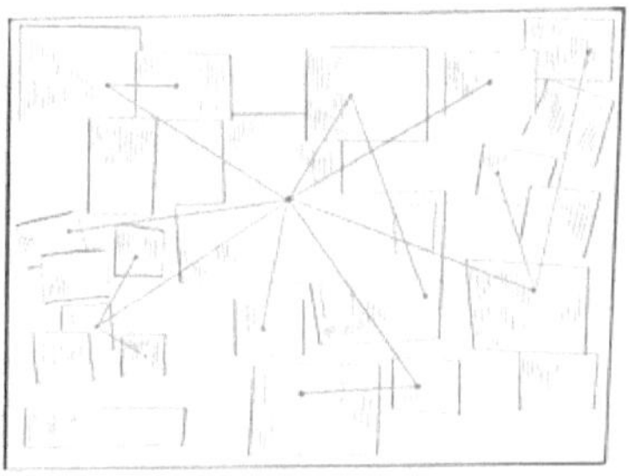

The three of them gathered at James's door. Charlie took a breath and knocked softly. A moment later, Danny opened the door, revealing a somber expression that tugged at their hearts. His eyes were bloodshot, the remnants of tears fresh on his cheeks. His usually neat button-down shirt hung loosely, untucked and carelessly hanging over his chinos, a testament to his grief.

Charlie said solemnly, "I'm sorry about what happened to James. You must have been close, since you were roommates."

"Thank you," Danny replied, his voice thick with emotion. "It means a lot."

Charlie nodded, his gaze compassionate. "We'd like to add a few personal belongings of James's for a service in conjunction with Brent's. We were hoping to grab a picture of him from the room, if that's okay."

"Of course," Danny said, stepping aside to let them in.

As they entered, Charlie turned to Danny, guiding him toward his side of the room. "So what kind of pictures do you think we can find?" he asked, keeping his tone light, distracting Danny as Cyrus quickly moved to James's desk.

Danny led Charlie to the wall of photographs. He pointed to a framed photo of James standing proudly beside a massive mountain, its snow-dusted peak rising sharply behind him.

"That one," Danny said, tapping the glass. "That was up near Mount McLoughlin."

Charlie leaned in with a grin. "Oh, man, I remember that trip. James was all fired up about climbing McLoughlin, kept going on about reconnecting with nature or finding his mountain legs or something." He laughed. "But about thirty minutes in, the guy looked like he'd just run a marathon in a sauna. Turns out, coming straight from sea level in San Diego doesn't prep you for switchbacks at six thousand feet."

Danny chuckled.

"Anyway," Charlie went on, "he bailed on the climb, declared victory over altitude sickness, and dragged us all back down to that little bar in K-Falls with the taxidermy raccoon wearing sunglasses."

As Charlie continued to distract Danny, Cyrus's heart raced as he rifled through the clutter, searching for the piece of paper he had seen the day before. He found it wedged between random papers, its surface smudged but still readable. Quickly, he folded it and tucked it into his pocket, glancing back at Charlie and Danny to ensure they were still engaged in their conversation.

With a wink to Charlie, Cyrus signaled he was ready. Once the memory-sharing came to a natural pause, Dana approached Danny and wrapped her arms around him in a comforting hug. Danny stiffened at first, surprised by the gesture, but then melted into her embrace, grateful for the warmth and sympathy she offered.

"It's going to be okay," Dana whispered, pulling back to meet his gaze. "We're all here for you."

Danny nodded, his expression softening, even if only for a moment. "Thanks, Dana. I appreciate it."

With that, the three conspirators exchanged solemn glances, each aware of the stakes. They quietly left the room and moved into the hallway, the task ahead pressing down on them.

They gathered in Charlie's room, each settling into their places: Cyrus perched on the bed, leaning forward with his elbows on his knees, and Dana sitting to Charlie's right on an old desk chair.

Charlie's room was as quirky as Cyrus expected. On one wall, newspaper clippings and magazine headlines tacked up haphazardly formed a chaotic collage of conspiracy theories and eccentric ideas. One faded printout shouted, "Chemtrails Are Destroying Our Future," while another featured a poorly-edited headline: "Obamacare: What the Media Won't Tell You!"

"Not exactly designer decor," Cyrus remarked.

Charlie shrugged, his smirk widening. "I like to keep an open mind." He glanced at his wall with a gleam of pride.

Cyrus's gaze drifted to the opposite wall, equally cluttered, displaying a map of the United States with colored pins marking key cities connected by red string in a chaotic web. Next to it hung a corkboard holding a collage of other clippings with headlines such as "Moon Landing or Manure Landing, NASA Tricked Us All" and "The Government Killed JFK."

Dana cut through the quiet. "Hey, where's the paper?"

Cyrus blinked, his focus snapping back to the task at hand. "Right," he said, reaching into his back pocket. He pulled out the folded sheet and smoothed it flat on the table between them.

All three leaned in.

Six names were typed neatly on the page. At first glance, they seemed completely unremarkable:

Kim M Satterlee
Lawrence Pettit
Marek Kovacs
Scott Pressner
Shannon Puckett
Courtney Weber

The name Marek Kovacs had been circled and marked with a small star.

They contemplated in quiet for a moment, scanning the list.

"Do any of these ring a bell?" Dana asked.

Charlie shook his head. "Not a one."

"Same," Dana added. "I've never heard of any of them."

"We need to look them up." Cyrus turned to Charlie. "Hey, what was the website you said you looked me up on?"

Charlie grinned like he'd been waiting to be asked. "Searchbug. It's the kind they don't want you knowing about. Like I said before, when Dana and I were looking up your name, it's built for tracking all kinds of records, property, court stuff, even sealed stuff, if you dig right." He winked conspiratorially. "I've got a buddy who's a PI back in Shasta. He lets me use his login so I don't have to pay or get tracked myself."

Dana smirked, but her eyes stayed on the list. "That's how we found the first info about you. We went to the Lakeview Library and pulled up everything we could."

Cyrus looked at the paper again, the names blurring as his mind started racing. "Then that's where we need to go. The library. See what we can dig up on these people."

Charlie was already packing to go. "Let's Searchbug the hell out of 'em."

Dana rolled her eyes. "Let's get moving."

26

The small white Toyota pickup rattled down the gravel road, its tires kicking up dust in pale spirals behind it. Charlie sat behind the wheel, one tanned arm slung casually out the open window, the other resting lightly on the steering wheel. He wore his wide-brimmed cowboy hat tilted back, and his thick handlebar mustache twitched as he hummed along to a tune only he could hear.

Squeezed shoulder-to-shoulder on the bench seat, Dana and Cyrus jostled with each bump in the road. Dana, petite with a mess of brown hair pulled into a loose braid, had her elbows tucked in tight, avoiding both the door and Cyrus. Cyrus, short and wiry, his olive-toned skin catching the glint of sunlight through the windshield, sat stiffly in the center, knees angled to avoid the stick shift. He tried to take up less space than physically possible.

Charlie pulled his arm in and twisted the ends of his mustache, eyes still on the road ahead. "Y'know," he said after a moment, "driving Mystique makes me miss Brent."

Dana glanced at him kindly but said nothing.

Charlie went on, softer now. "You think I could have that old T-shirt of his? The one that said, *My wife still misses me . . . but her aim is getting better.*"

Dana smiled, and even Cyrus cracked a grin. The image of Brent in that ridiculous shirt, grinning like a man who loved getting in trouble, floated briefly between them, warm and bittersweet.

Charlie gave a small nod to himself, like the thought had settled something, and the truck rolled on.

They coasted to a stop along the front pavement of the library. Dust settled slowly in the air behind them. Cyrus stared up at the building, its facade worn but formal, the pale concrete pillars at the entrance somehow more imposing than he remembered. They stood like sentinels, unmoved by the years. Tightness rose in his chest, a familiar weight, part memory, part instinct.

Charlie leaned forward, eyeing the mostly empty parking lot. "Looks quiet."

Cyrus didn't answer. He kept his eyes on the pillars, jaw set tight. Being back here made the air feel heavier.

The three of them climbed out of the truck, the doors creaking in protest, and made their way up the library steps. The sun-warmed concrete radiated heat through their shoes, and Cyrus stayed a few steps behind Dana and Charlie, his hands tucked in the pockets of his jacket.

As they passed through the doors into the cool, still air of the library, Cyrus immediately spotted the man at the front desk, the same one from the other day. His neck still looked too thin for his head. He sat upright behind the desk, fingers poised over the keyboard, eyes scanning the room with ferret-like suspicion.

Charlie strode up to the desk like he owned the place and slapped a hand down with a grin. "Hey, Garrett, we'd like your finest computer, please."

Garrett cracked a smile. "Hey, Charlie, sure. You can have number eight."

But when Garrett's eyes shifted past Charlie and landed on Cyrus, a flicker of recognition crossed his face. It was the look of someone certain they had seen him before, but unable to place where.

The moment passed, and the group moved on, gathering around computer number eight, tucked against the far wall beneath a flickering fluorescent light. Charlie took the center seat, cracking his knuckles with exaggerated flair before placing his fingers on the keyboard like a concert pianist preparing for a grand performance.

"Time to do a little digital snooping," he muttered.

Cyrus and Dana pulled up the free chairs from the neighboring desks, sliding in close on either side of him. The screen was ominous and dark as Charlie typed with surprising speed, navigating through a couple layers of login prompts before the Searchbug homepage loaded, a plain, no-frills interface that hinted at how much it wasn't supposed to exist.

"Okay," Charlie said, glancing at the folded paper Cyrus passed to him. "Let's meet our mystery crew."

Cyrus leaned in closer, looking over Charlie's shoulder. The website interface had a stark, ominous design, a dark background with bold, white letters. Beneath the site title "Searchbug" and its provocative tagline—*Want to know the real truth?*—blank fields were lined up for details such as *Full Name*, *Date of Birth*, and *Last Known Location*.

Cyrus took the folded paper from his back pocket, then flattened it on Charlie's desk, the edges of the paper curling just a little.

"Let's start with the circled name," Cyrus said. He spelled out the name for Charlie to type into the website.

Moments later, the site's output listed result options. Hundreds of people named Marek Kovacs—too many to sort through.

"Don't sweat it, guys," Charlie said. "This baby can cross reference up to four names to make this easier. Let's see if there's anything linking these names." He typed them in carefully, Marek Kovacs first. With a final tap, the database began to process.

Seconds later, a result flashed up on the screen.

"It says they're all linked to Nevada," Charlie murmured, leaning forward. He glanced at the others, whose wide eyes reflected both curiosity and dread. "Now let's narrow the search down . . . to Marek Kovacs, Nevada."

Three profiles appeared.

Charlie pulled up the first: a man in his sixties, nowhere close to who they were looking for. He clicked to the second: a young man in his twenties, unfamiliar as well. He clicked to the third, and all three froze.

The familiar face filled the screen, Vlad's face, yes, but his cold, calculating eyes stared back at them even through the flat, grainy driver's license photo.

A chill ran down Cyrus's spine. "That's him . . . isn't it?"

Dana nodded, her voice barely above a whisper. "Vlad is Marek Kovacs?"

They exchanged uneasy glances, the weight of the discovery pressing on them like lead. They had stumbled into something dark involving someone they thought they knew.

Cyrus spoke, his voice cracking faintly. "He is the nicest guy ever. What the heck?"

Dana leaned forward, glancing at Charlie. "Can we look up more information about him? There has to be something else on this site. Maybe it'll tell us why he was even here."

Charlie scrolled down the page, and they all squinted at the results. Charlie frowned. "That's . . . weird. There's nothing here other than his name, date of birth, and employment info. Says he works for a company called KIP Development."

Cyrus raised an eyebrow. "KIP Development? Never heard of it."

Charlie opened a new browser tab and typed in "KIP Development." They all leaned in, eyes fixed on the screen and found a simple, nondescript website with a bland design with only a few tabs and a contact form. A small emblem caught their attention: a minimalist, industrial-looking logo featuring blocky letters and a faded design.

Charlie leaned closer. "Is that . . . ?"

Dana's eyes widened as she recognized it. "Charlie, is that what I think it is?"

Charlie nodded. "Yeah, it's the same company that sent that sales rep a couple of years back. He tried to buy out the commune land, said they were planning 'upscale developments for billionaires' or something."

Cyrus blinked, trying to connect the dots. "So Vlad, Marek, might've been working for them this whole time?"

Charlie frowned. "Something's funny about their website though. I've only seen something like this with shell companies," he muttered, shaking his head. "When there isn't much info on a company website or the address is some weird PO box, like this one, those are clues. But if it is, I have no idea how we'd track that down."

Dana's face lit up. "Wait, I might know how! Back in college, in summer I worked for a lawyer's office. I handled all kinds of public records searches. Let me take over."

She nudged Charlie aside, her fingers flying over the keyboard as she pulled up local and state databases, digging through obscure records. After about a half hour of intense searching, Cyrus and Charlie had moved to a desk behind her, eyes narrowed with anxiety.

At last, her voice broke through. "*Aha!*" She glanced back at them, her eyes gleaming. "I traced KIP Development to a supposed owner listed in their documentation. But when I did a basic search, it was like the person didn't even exist, no records, no history, nothing. The only thing I could find was an address, and even that led nowhere."

She gestured to the screen, frustration creeping into her voice. "It's like the name is a ghost."

Charlie's eyes lit up too, a spark of excitement replacing the tension in his face. "Alright, my turn!" he declared, grinning as he gently nudged Dana aside.

He took control of the keyboard again. "Time to work Searchbug magic," he said. His fingers flew across the keys as the others watched intently. After a few moments, Charlie froze, his grin widening. "Got it!" he exclaimed triumphantly.

"What?" Dana and Cyrus asked in unison, leaning over his shoulder.

Charlie pointed to the screen. "The address listed for the so-called owner? It's bogus. But what's interesting is the address is linked to a completely different entity: BGI Incorporated. And guess what? One of the owners of BGI is listed as a shareholder in KIP Development."

"Well, what are you waiting for?" Cyrus said. "Look up BGI Incorporated."

"Alright, alright, hold your horses." Charlie opened up a new tab and searched for the name.

The first link connected to the company's official website. A slick page opened with the tagline in bold letters: "Bringing Rare Earth to the U.S." Below, images of pristine landscapes next to shots of massive mining equipment flashed across the screen, with a description detailing BGI's mission to extract rare earth metals essential for modern technology:

Rare earth minerals are essential components in the production of semiconductors used in everyday technology, from cell phones and computers to electric vehicles and self-driving cars. As global demand continues to rise, developing domestic sources helps ensure long-term economic stability and keeps the U.S. competitive in an increasingly international market.

As they scrolled, a chill settled over them, each piecing together the implications of this discovery. Then Charlie shot up from his chair, his face a mix of anger and realization. "Holy crap," he said. "The freaking *mine* on our land!"

Dana and Cyrus exchanged glances, wide-eyed as the truth sank in. Reckoning Grove, the corporate land offers, and now the tragedies, it was all coming together in a picture more sinister than any of them could have imagined.

Cyrus took a deep breath, trying to connect the pieces out loud. "Okay, so several years ago, a land development company came around offering to buy Reckoning Grove's land. That company turns out to be tied to a rare earth mining corporation, who must have had their scientists checking this area for these minerals. And I guess they found some. So we have to assume that Vlad, or whatever his name is, works for them. Now we've got people getting poisoned, and it all seems connected." Cyrus paused to think. "And what about James? Was he killed? Was it an accident? Did Vlad find out he knew something?"

Charlie shook his head, letting out a nervous chuckle. "I can't believe I'm saying this, but we might actually have to call the FBI."

Dana gave him a skeptical look. "They'd laugh us out of the room, Charlie. It's all circumstantial, a couple names, a hidden company connection, and our suspicions. There's no hard evidence."

Cyrus nodded, resigned. "Well, all this seems to point to the mine out there. We may have to check out the mine ourselves."

Charlie's expression turned pensive. "You know . . . I told James the other day I'd seen people out by the mine, but he brushed it off."

Cyrus nodded. "Yeah, I was here that day. I thought he didn't believe you, but maybe he was trying to protect you by changing the subject."

Charlie sighed and frowned. "If we'd gone out there the day we were planning on it . . . the day Vlad had that breathing problem, we could have saved two innocent lives."

No one responded. The words sat heavy between them.

They left the library in a subdued mood, and the doors shut behind them with a hollow whoosh. The late afternoon sun had dropped lower, casting long shadows across the sidewalk as they walked back to Mystique. No jokes from Charlie this time. No casual small talk. Only the sounds of their footsteps and the low groan of the truck's doors as they climbed in.

The drive back was quiet, the desert road stretching out before them in soft, golden light. Charlie kept one hand on the wheel, the other resting on the windowsill, his face unreadable beneath the brim of his hat. Dana stared out at the passing landscape, her thoughts elsewhere. Cyrus sat still between them, the list of names folded tightly in his hand.

Each of them was thinking the same thing.

Tomorrow, they would hike to the mine.

27

The commune's land stretched a mile across and a little more than a mile long, enough to make up roughly eight hundred and fifty acres. The terrain was rugged enough that walking from one end to the other took close to forty minutes, and the old mine lay at the far edge.

They began in the fertile heart of Reckoning Grove, where a winding stream supported patches of grass and the garden. But once Cyrus, Charlie, and Dana crossed the stream, the greenery gave way to the high desert of south-central Oregon, arid ground dotted with sagebrush and wiry shrubs, a vast sky of deep blue overhead, and the rise of rugged hills waiting in the distance.

The air was still, thick with the faint smell of baked earth and sage. A distant turkey vulture circled lazily in the sky, the only movement breaking the vast stillness. As they walked toward the high hills, their footsteps stirred small clouds of dust, the sound of gravel crunching beneath their boots amplified in the otherwise quiet landscape.

As they walked, they did not speak at first, letting only the sound of their footsteps break the stillness of the high desert.

Eventually, Charlie glanced over at Cyrus and asked, "So, where are you originally from?"

Cyrus smiled. "My parents are from Iran, but I was born here in the U.S. Grew up in Indiana."

Dana asked, "Then why'd you tell Grady you were from Persia?"

Cyrus gave a wry grin, shaking his head. "When I'm talking to someone I'm not sure I can trust, or if they might not know much about Iran, I use the former name, Persia. It makes people think of Persian carpets and ancient palaces instead of whatever negative news headlines they have in mind."

Dana chuckled. "Yeah, I get that. Iran has a pretty bad reputation in the news. But everyone loves Persian carpets!"

Charlie grinned, nudging him. "Well, I'm glad I got to know you first. Otherwise, I might've made up all sorts of theories about you."

As they walked, Cyrus's gaze fell on Dana's small daypack. A tiny compass dangled from a clip on the back, alongside a tiny mirror catching faint glimmers of sunlight. In one sporting goods store in Colorado, a salesperson had eagerly pointed out to him the importance of a mirror, how it could save a life by signaling for help if someone ever got lost.

As they crossed a particularly parched area, where even fewer scrub plants grew, Cyrus spoke up. "I always thought Oregon was supposed to be all rain."

Charlie shook his head. "That's only west of the Cascade mountain range," he said. He gestured toward the arid landscape around them. "Out here, it's all sun and rock and dry air."

Cyrus looked out over the wide expanse stretching into the foothills, taking in the muted browns and dusty greens of the desert. They were nearing the base of a small, rugged range of hills, their path leading straight toward where, according to Charlie, the mine lay hidden in its rugged folds.

After a pause, Dana spoke up, "When I was in college studying agriculture and animal science, I took an elective class that covered mining history in Oregon. I remember some of the stuff we learned."

She glanced at Cyrus and Charlie. "The gold rush in California started in the 1840s, but it wasn't until the late 1850s that they found gold here in Oregon. That set off a small gold rush of its own, and mines popped up all over, people were digging for gold, and what they called quicksilver, which is mercury."

She looked out toward the distant hills. "By the late 1860s, most of it was over. The mines were played out, abandoned, like the one we're heading to."

Cyrus followed her gaze. "You think BGI's interested because they think there's more than abandoned mine shafts out here?"

Dana nodded thoughtfully. "It wouldn't surprise me. Rare earth metals are valuable for tech, and isn't that the whole point of BGI based on the website we saw?"

The three eventually reached the base of a steep, rocky slope, about forty feet high, with no clear trail through a scattering of jagged stones and loose scree. The incline was sharp enough to require the use of both hands and feet, and each step sent pebbles skittering downhill, making the climb more of a scramble than a hike. As the three trudged up the steep incline, the rough terrain forced them to watch each step closely. Dana led the way, looking back every so often to check on Charlie and Cyrus as loose rocks slid beneath their feet.

As Cyrus reached for a handhold on rock, his boot slipped on loose gravel. He slid ten feet down the incline before catching himself on a jagged rock. The edge tore into his palm, and he hissed at the sting. Above him, Charlie and Dana called his name, fear flashing across their faces until he steadied and climbed back up.

"Crap!" Cyrus cried with relief. "That would have sucked!"

Catching his breath, Cyrus traded a quick glance with the others before they pressed on. They climbed cautiously, the slope steepening with each step, Cyrus's palm stinging at every hold.

At last, they crested the peak, pulling themselves onto the narrow ridge. The view opened up below them, revealing the secluded valley nestled between steep, hilly slopes. They stood side by side, catching their breath in the eerie stillness, broken only by the sound of their own breathing. Behind them lay Reckoning Grove, and as they regained their breath they stared down at the desolate spot where the old mine entrance lay hidden in the shadows below.

The descent was shorter and much less steep, but still tricky, loose rocks shifting underfoot as Cyrus, Charlie, and Dana moved carefully down into the valley.

At the bottom of the hill lay a flat stretch about the length of a football field, its dusty ground scattered with rocks. At the far end rose a sheer wall of stone, where a natural opening yawned dark and wide, its mouth reinforced with heavy wooden beams that looked old and strained, barely holding together. On either side, steep hills hemmed them in, their slopes so severe they looked impossible to climb.

Dana's voice broke the silence. "That must be the adit." She pointed toward the dark opening framed by the old wooden beams. "The entrance to the mine."

As they drew closer to the mine, Cyrus stumbled, his boot catching against a large stone half-buried in the ground. The rock shifted under the impact, rolling just enough to uncover what lay beneath. A cylindrical hole gaped below, dark and narrow, plunging straight into the earth.

Charlie frowned, scanning the ground. "That's weird. There's another stone over here, set the same way." He pushed it aside with his boot, revealing a second hole nearly identical to the first.

Dana crouched, running her hand along the rim. The edges were too clean, too even to have formed naturally.

Only then did they notice the pattern: the valley floor in front of the mine adit was scattered with such stones, each concealing a deep, hidden shaft beneath. Not erosion, not chance, something deliberate. The whole stretch of earth was riddled with these covered holes, an unsettling design buried just beneath the surface.

Dana, crouched down, studied the pattern, her eyes narrowing. "I think these are from core drilling samples. This has got to be proof that BGI was down here poking around without our permission." She stood up. "In mining, when companies are scoping out a new site, they drill holes like these to take core samples. They analyze the samples for minerals, so they can see if the area's worth mining. These holes are practically a signature move; BGI was definitely testing for something here." She squinted at the holes, her brow furrowed as she pieced it together. "I'm guessing BGI Inc. must have snuck in with equipment, probably from one of the neighboring properties. It would've been easier to get in that way without raising suspicion. The people at Reckoning Grove couldn't have seen anything, because even though it's technically part of our land, as you can see, this mine is tucked away, hidden from view."

Once they reached the adit, the three sat on the rocky ground, backs leaning against the weathered beams of the mine entrance.

Dana slipped off her backpack and unzipped it, pulling out a bottle of water. As she moved, the sun caught the tiny mirror on her pack, sending a quick flash of light into Cyrus's eyes, making him squint. She held out the bottle to the others with a small smile. "Don't worry, it's not from the spring."

The three took turns drinking, the cool water soothing their parched throats as they passed the bottle around. Each sip brought a brief reprieve from the dry heat, their breathing steadying as they quenched their thirst in the shadow of the mine entrance.

After a while Dana spoke. "We know BGI has an interest in the land. With what we dug up on Vlad, it's clear he's tied to them. If we could get someone to look into this, we might be able to show that Vlad, or BGI, is responsible for the poisonings too. I think this even links them to James's death."

Cyrus nodded thoughtfully. "The local police are never going to take us seriously, though. They see the commune as a bunch of fringe cultists. That was obvious when they came to *investigate* James's death. They weren't listening."

Charlie took a deep breath, a wry smile crossing his face. "Fuckin' FBI guys. I can't believe we're really getting them involved."

28

Marek shadowed the trio at a distance, careful not to close the gap. James had been right about them acting strange, and now they were onto him. Poor James. He shook his head. It hadn't needed to end that way.

The trail narrowed into a rise of loose stone and jagged rock. The hill cut sharp against the pale sky, its face tilted and broken like a collapsed wall. Looking up at the climb ahead, he flexed his fingers, testing them, then began the ascent, each movement deliberate and unrelenting. The task was nothing compared to the tangle of thoughts in his mind.

As he climbed, his hands found the next rock with practiced ease, his broad fingers wrapping around it like iron clamps. He hauled himself up the steep incline without hesitation, the weight of his towering frame no hindrance to his steady climb. Loose dirt and small stones crumbled beneath him, skittering down below him. His movements were precise, mechanical, but his mind churned with frustration.

Not anger, frustration.

Cyrus had saved his life not a week ago. Marek hadn't forgotten.

He *couldn't* forget. And Dana and Charlie, he had come to admire their quick thinking, their loyalty to one another. He didn't want to think of them as enemies. He didn't *want* to think of them at all right now.

But his job was clear.

He didn't want to hurt them, not really. Hurting people wasn't his way, not unless he had no choice.

Reaching the summit, Marek stood and dusted himself off, glancing back at the incline with a shake of his head. His broad chest heaved with a sigh. He swept his gaze across the terrain, searching for signs of the trio. The ache in his chest wasn't from the climb; it was from the weight of what came next. Marek rolled his shoulders and exhaled slowly, his clean-shaven jaw tightening as he forced the emotion from his mind. He had no room for doubt, no time to dwell on what *should* be.

Without a second glance at the incline, he started toward the mine, his powerful strides fueled by a singular purpose: to find Cyrus, Dana, and Charlie and make things right.

Still, Marek hoped, deep down, there might be another way. Something, *anything*, that would let him repay the life Cyrus had saved without ending it. But hope was a fragile thing, and Marek wasn't a man who dealt in fragility.

From the top of the slope, Marek spotted them, Cyrus, Dana, and Charlie, sitting in front of the mine's adit. A little over a year earlier he had arranged for the samples to be analyzed there, the choice of the site a symbol of what the mine itself held. The place was familiar; he knew every rise and cut of this ground from his time with BGI, back when they'd first explored it. Steep slopes hemmed in the little valley on both sides. There was no way the three could escape.

He exhaled, a long, resigned sigh, then started down toward them, each step bringing the confrontation closer.

As he moved, a thought wormed its way into his mind: *How in the world did I end up here?* The question wasn't new, but it carried extra weight now, pressing down on him with every step. Life had twisted in ways Marek hadn't foreseen, turning loyalty and survival into a cruel paradox.

Marek's path to this moment, hiking toward the old mine in pursuit of Cyrus, Dana, and Charlie—his commune friends—had been anything but simple.

He had been born in Romania, the only child of Andrei and Lidia, but his life changed irrevocably when his mother died giving birth to him. Grief-stricken but determined to give his son a better future, Andrei brought Marek to the United States when he was still a boy. They settled in Nevada, where Andrei's cousin worked in a mine and helped Andrei secure a job.

Their early years in the United States were harsh. Marek and his father shared a cramped, one-bedroom apartment with Andrei's cousin's family, seven people crammed into a space meant for two. Privacy was non-existent, and luxuries out of reach, but Andrei worked tirelessly, determined to make the best of their circumstances.

Fate intervened one day when the owner of the mine, Phil Bueker, was visiting on a routine tour. An unexpected rockfall sent workers scattering, but Andrei leaped into action, shielding Phil with his own body. Andrei suffered severe injuries, spinal fractures and broken ribs, and spent weeks in the ICU. When he finally regained consciousness, Phil was at his bedside. Grateful for Andrei's sacrifice, Phil made him his right-hand man, a position that transformed their lives.

Over the years, Phil treated Marek like family. He took him fishing and on vacations with his own son, Ben, and even paid for Marek to attend college. Phil saw potential in Marek, something solid and dependable, and it was clear he valued Marek far beyond what he owed to Andrei. After graduating from high school, Marek returned to BGI to work alongside his father, assisting in managing operations and earning the respect of the workforce through his competence and calm resilience.

But three years ago, the dynamic shifted. Phil's son, Ben, finally graduated from UNLV after six long years, a milestone Phil openly admitted had required significant financial persuasion to achieve. Ben was spoiled, reckless, and unfit for responsibility, but Phil, ever the doting father, made him vice president of BGI and asked Marek to be his right-hand man. The request wasn't a favor, it was a demand. Marek's role became less about managing operations and more about managing Ben, keeping the company afloat despite Ben's ineptitude and frequent missteps.

Now, as Marek hiked toward the mine, the weight of those years pressed against him. BGI wasn't just a company, it was his entire history, his family's legacy, tied to Phil's generosity and Andrei's sacrifice. He his gaze shifted from the past to the harsh sunlight and barren slope before him. The trio, Cyrus, Dana, and Charlie, emerged as he drew closer.

He was back in Ben's office, the faint smell of polished wood and leather filling the air. The room was lavish, every detail designed to exude wealth and power, from the deep, dark wood of the desk to the floor-to-ceiling windows that bathed the space in natural light. Ben was sitting behind the desk, late-twenties, face smooth and boyish, fine features sharp and framed by jet-black hair. His expensive button-down shirt was crisp, and when he looked up at Marek, his expression was self-assured, smug.

"Thanks for coming in, Marek," Ben said, leaning back in his chair. His voice carried a tone of command that came naturally to someone who had never been told "no." He gestured to the center of the desk, where a large rock sat, dull gray and unassuming.

Marek sat down across from him, glancing briefly at the rock before looking back at Ben.

"This," Ben said, tapping the rock with a manicured finger, "is lanthanum. You know what that is?"

Marek shook his head, though he could already sense where the conversation was going.

Ben grinned, clearly relishing the explanation. "Lanthanum is the future of BGI. My dad built this company on silver and gold. Made us famous. Made us rich." He leaned forward, his hand still resting on the rock. "But it's time to branch out. Time to start thinking bigger."

Marek remained silent, letting Ben continue. It was a skill he'd mastered over the years, listening without reacting, even when he wanted to.

"Rare earth metals, like this one, are used in semiconductors for microchips," Ben went on, his voice picking up momentum. "And those chips? They're in everything. Cell phones, computers, and now, the future, self-driving cars. If we don't start exploring the U.S. for these metals, China and Russia will keep ruling the market, and we'll be left in the dust." Ben leaned back again, folding his hands behind his head, his grin widening. "It's my turn to move BGI Inc. into the future," he declared. "And this is how we're going to do it."

The memory faded as Marek's gaze drifted back to the mine entrance. He started walking again, the crunch of his boots on the dry ground steady and deliberate. He thought about the lanthanum, about Ben's vision, about how much of his own life had been shaped by decisions made in rooms like that.

As he made his way across the valley floor, another memory came forward, sharp and sudden, anchored to the mine's entrance ahead.

He was back in Ben's office, the air heavy with tension despite Ben's overt excitement. The setting was the same, but now the confidence Ben had exhibited before was tinged with nervous energy. He paced behind the desk, running a hand through his jet-black hair, his crisp shirt wrinkled for once.

"Marek, this is it," Ben said, his voice trembling with anticipation. "The prelim results from the flyovers and core samples at that abandoned mine in Central Oregon, they're better than I could've hoped. This will make BGI *very* rich."

Marek, seated across from him, crossed his arms. "You've been saying that for months," he said evenly. "Your dad's getting nervous. All these explorations, flyovers, drills, new tech, it's pushing BGI's finances to the edge."

Ben waved a dismissive hand, his grin faltering but not disappearing. "I know, I know. But this is different. If I can lock this down, it'll all be worth it."

Marek leaned forward, his gaze steady. "And if you can't?"

Ben hesitated for a fraction of a second then shook his head as if to clear the thought. "It's not an 'if.' It's a 'when.'" He sat abruptly, his excitement shifting into something more conspiratorial. "But there's a problem. That mine? It's on the property of some commune. A bunch of idiot hippies living off the grid, thinking they can save the world or whatever."

Marek raised an eyebrow, waiting for the inevitable twist.

"I had my lawyers set up a shell company, KIP Incorporated. It's a real estate development front," Ben explained. "Named it after my best friend from my fraternity at UNLV. Anyway, we tried to get the commune to sell. Made them a *very* generous offer. But they won't budge."

He leaned back, his chair creaking, and stared at Marek with a calculating expression. "I need you to infiltrate the commune," he said, his voice low. "Get close to them. Figure out what'll make them crack. Either get them to sell the land, or find a way to make them lose it. Once they're out of the picture, we'll snap it up through KIP Incorporated, and it'll never point back to BGI."

Ben took a breath and added, "I also took the liberty of switching your employment documentation from BGI Inc. to KIP Inc. so you won't have any ties to us."

Marek hesitated, the request sitting uneasily with him. Ben's expression darkened, and he leaned forward, his voice low and sharp. "Marek, you're part of this family. You know Dad . . . after everything he's done for you, and for your father. This isn't just about the company; it's about the future. *Our* future."

Ben straightened, his tone softening but still laced with urgency. "This could make you rich beyond anything you've imagined. Don't overthink it. Just get it done."

Marek nodded reluctantly, the weight of guilt and obligation heavier than the words he could muster. "I'm in," he said quietly.

The memory dissolved as Marek moved closer to his confrontation with the three. As he did, the faces of the other members of Reckoning Grove flashed through his mind, their warmth, their kindness, the way they'd treated him like family. A pang of guilt twisted in his chest, but the pull of loyalty to his father and Phil was just as strong, an unshakable weight tethering him to his past.

29

A faint sound of gravel tumbling echoed through the clearing. The three explorers froze, their attention snapping up to the path they had taken from the summit to where they sat. Walking towards them from about eighty yards away was Vlad, his hulking figure showcased against the rugged backdrop of the landscape. His broad shoulders and thick arms bulged beneath the tight-fitting T-shirt, the fabric straining. He looked like part of the wild terrain around him, his imposing stature mirroring the stark, unforgiving land.

"Vlad," Dana muttered.

"Marek," Charlie said under his breath. "Or whatever name he's using this week."

They watched in surprise as the man walked slowly toward them. He moved like someone with purpose, not aggression.

Cyrus narrowed his eyes. If Marek had figured out what they knew, would he really come alone?

Dana leaned in and whispered. "Does he know?"

"I don't think so," Cyrus murmured. "But he suspects something. Otherwise he wouldn't be out here."

Charlie squinted into the distance, then bent down and picked up a small rock, tossing it from hand to hand.

"We play dumb," Dana said. "Just hikers. A picnic."

"Agreed," Cyrus said. "No reason to give him anything he doesn't already have."

They stood as Marek approached, casual but unreadable. Dust clung to the front of his shirt, and his sunglasses caught slivers of sky, masking his eyes completely. He stopped ten feet away, hands resting loosely at his sides.

"Didn't expect to run into anyone out here," he said, glancing past them toward the mine adit. "New lunchtime hangout?"

Cyrus gave a tight smile. "Just out for some fresh air. Stretching our legs. I wanted to see some more of the property that makes up the commune."

Dana pointed off toward the southern hills. "And someone said there were wildflowers."

Marek's mouth twitched at the corner, maybe amusement, maybe suspicion. "Sure," he said. "And I hear abandoned mine sites make excellent picnic spots."

Charlie chuckled, trying to lean into his usual half-mocking tone. "Figured we'd check out where the corporate vampires are drilling next."

The words landed too heavily. Cyrus felt it like a punch to the air.

Dana's head turned sharply. Charlie froze, as if just realizing what he'd said.

Marek didn't move. But something behind his expression shifted. A flicker of recognition, or calculation.

"Drilling?" he repeated, voice low. "That's an interesting word choice."

Charlie scratched the back of his neck. "Yeah, well, I listen to a lot of podcasts."

Marek stepped forward, slow and steady, gaze fixed on Cyrus now.

"You've been doing more than listening."

No one answered. The only sound was the wind moving over the ridge.

Cyrus took a breath, slow and controlled. The pretense was gone. No more bluffing.

"We know who you are," he said. "We know your real name is Marek. And we know BGI is behind this, whatever this is. Poisoning the water. Driving people out. Drilling into land that doesn't belong to you."

For a moment, Vlad Marek stared at them without a word, his expression unreadable. Then his shoulders sagged by a fraction, and his face softened into something unexpected: sadness.

"I was sent to Reckoning Grove by BGI," he admitted, his tone tinged with regret. "At first, it was just a job. But then . . . I started to love the place. You people. I didn't want to leave."

Dana's voice trembled as she asked, "Then how did James know you were working for them?"

Marek's gaze shifted to the ground. "James was a chemical engineer. We became friends, and I told him about how BGI wanted to pay Reckoning Grove enough money for the members to start a new commune on other land completely free of debt. I told him BGI even had politicians ready to help us get the mineral rights once we got the land. James was stressed about the loan too, so I told him about my plan to put just a little arsenic in the spring water, enough to make people sick, not to kill them. Once enough people became sick I was going to arrange for us to test the spring. Once the tests showed contamination, the members of Reckoning Grove would have no choice but to sell the land and move somewhere else. It was supposed to be painless."

Dana shook her head, disbelief in her voice. "No way. James would never agree to something like that. He would never want to harm anyone."

Marek's expression darkened, and he shifted his weight, eyes flicking to the ground before meeting Dana's gaze again. "He was hesitant at first," he admitted, his voice low. "But when I explained it, when I told him the symptoms were harmless, just a little nausea or a headache, nothing serious, and that it could all be reversed with a simple treatment, he came around. He realized it was the only way out. The only way to help Reckoning Grove."

Cyrus's heart raced, his mind struggling to reconcile the man he'd met with the version of him Marek was describing. "You made him believe it was for the greater good?"

Marek let out a sigh, his hands clasped tightly in front of him. "James believed me. At least, he convinced himself it was the only way forward."

Dana clenched her fists, her voice sharp. "And you thought no one would trace the arsenic back to BGI?"

Marek let out a short, humorless laugh, his massive shoulders shaking. "Look around. Ranches, farms, so many herbicides and pesticides being used in the area. There are some herbicides that have arsenic; you should know that, Cyrus. It's the perfect cover. Officials would say it seeped into the aquifer naturally. No one would suspect me. After all, I was drinking the same water and getting sick, too."

"But that doesn't add up," Cyrus shot back. "James was putting an antidote in the spring."

Marek's expression crumbled, his sadness apparent. "He got cold feet when Brent died. He had an old work buddy of his bring the antidote. Cindy's death broke him. After that, James told me he was going to the authorities."

Dana's face went pale. "So, you killed him?"

Marek nodded slowly, the weight of his actions etched on his face. "It was the only way. If James talked, Reckoning Grove would be ruined and so would the plan. Made it look like an accident."

The midday sun beat down mercilessly, but the enormity of Marek's confession pressed down on them more than the heat.

Just then, something clicked for Cyrus. "Marek," he said, "were you the one who left the notes on Brent's RV door, and broke the steps?"

Marek stared at the dust a moment, then nodded. "Yes. I wanted you looking the wrong way. If you chased the canning angle, you could play hero, tell folks to do it right, and then leave." He swallowed. "After I wrote the note telling you to leave in the morning, I was going to push harder, scare you off if I had to. But then you saved my life." He glanced up at Cyrus, ashamed. "I felt bad. I hoped you would just give up and leave on your own."

Marek's face turned serious. "But this changes everything," he said. "I meant it when I said you shouldn't have come here."

The finality in his tone sent a jolt through Cyrus, Dana, and Charlie. Marek's broad shoulders tensed as he took a step forward, blocking their path back to Reckoning Grove.

Cyrus glanced at Dana and Charlie, his heart pounding. "We're leaving," he said firmly, trying to edge forward.

Marek's lips twisted into a grim smile, but he didn't move. "No. You're not."

Cyrus's heart pounded in his chest, the adrenaline surging through his veins. They had no choice but to face Marek together, to act as a unit. His voice shook as he whispered to Charlie and Dana, "We can't run, we'll get caught. We have to do this all at once."

The three of them moved slowly, their feet shifting carefully on the gravel, circling around Marek. He stood still, a slight smirk tugging at the corner of his mouth, clearly entertained by their hesitant movements.

In a burst of motion, Dana lunged forward, jumping and grabbing onto Marek's thick neck from behind, her arms locking around him in a vise and screaming in his ear.

Cyrus dove at Marek's legs, hoping to take him off balance. His hands grabbed at the massive limbs, but the strength of Marek's legs resembled steel as Cyrus struggled to lift one. He tried to shift his weight, but it was like trying to move a mountain.

Meanwhile, Charlie was scrambling for something, anything, to hit Marek with. His hand closed around a jagged rock, which he hurled at Marek's chest. It connected with a dull thud, but Marek didn't flinch.

With terrifying speed and force, Marek spun around, throwing Dana off his back like a rag doll. She crashed into the dirt, gasping for air. Cyrus barely had time to react before Marek's leg shot out, kicking him across the ground as if he were no more than a piece of trash.

Charlie barely had time to brace himself before Marek's massive hand slammed into the other side of his head, sending him sprawling across the rocky earth.

The three of them lay scattered, breathless, staring up at the towering figure of Marek. He didn't look angry. He looked . . . annoyed.

A sharp, pulsing pain developed in Cyrus's head, an ache that throbbed with every beat of his heart. His shoulder was sore from where he'd been kicked, and his body felt like it had been pummeled by a freight train. Charlie groaned, clutching his head as though trying to hold his skull together, the slap from Marek thundering in his ears. Dana wasn't faring much better, she clutched her side where she'd landed hard.

Struggling to sit up, her face twisted with pain, she gritted her teeth and said, "We've got to get back to Reckoning Grove, *now*." Her voice was strained but determined. Without needing to speak, they all understood: their only option was to retreat toward Reckoning Grove, retracing their path up to the ridge then somehow navigating down the steep slope with their injuries. All the while, they'd have to stay one step ahead of Marek, an unstoppable behemoth who refused to give up the chase.

Charlie's eyes darted around, stopping at a thick, old piece of wood half-buried in the dirt. He grabbed it with both hands, the rough edges digging into his palms as he hefted the makeshift club. Beside him, Dana found a jagged rock, sharp as a knife, and clenched it with her good hand.

Cyrus did something else.

Without a word, he dropped to one knee and yanked off his boot, then peeled off his sock. The others stared as he began scooping handfuls of dry, powdery rock dust and dirt into the fabric, tying it off in a quick knot.

Charlie blinked at him. "What the hell are you doing?"

Cyrus held up the lumpy sock. "Improvising." He pulled his boot back on over his bare foot.

They turned and ran across the flat valley towards the incline, boots kicking dust as they crossed the open ground. Cyrus risked a glance back. Marek was still near the base, moving now but unhurried, his pace almost casual. He wasn't chasing them. He was following, letting the distance stretch, letting them think they had time.

Cyrus's pulse spiked as the slope loomed closer. Something about it felt wrong.

Why?

He shoved the thought aside. There was no time for doubt. Not now.

As they surged upward, Cyrus caught sight of a slender stick lying half-buried in the dust, a two-foot length of dry, sturdy wood. He snatched it up without breaking stride, his mind already turning it over for possibilities.

Behind them, Marek followed, climbing steadily, without urgency.

Finally, they scrambled over the crest of the ridge, lungs heaving, muscles trembling with exhaustion. But there was no time to rest.

Cyrus spun toward Dana's backpack and unclipped the small mirror that dangled from one of the exterior loops. His fingers moved quickly, desperately, he grabbed the stick he'd picked up earlier, then bent over to unlace his boot. Dirt caked his knuckles as he worked the lace free.

"What are you doing?" Dana asked, still doubled over in pain.

"Just buy me a second," he muttered, looping the lace around the mirror's handle and lashing it to the end of the slender stick. It wasn't perfect, but it held.

He turned to Charlie. "Stand near the edge, just to the side, look casual."

Charlie blinked, still winded, but nodded and limped over to the spot where the slope began its steep drop.

Cyrus jammed the base of the stick into a crack between two rocks, angling it so the mirror faced up. He adjusted it again and again, squinting at the sun, tilting the mirror with micro-movements until the reflected light shimmered just above where Charlie's head was. He backed up, checked the angle again, then made one last adjustment.

He exhaled.

Then they heard the crunch of gravel.

Marek crested the incline a moment later, rising over the edge like he'd just returned from a casual afternoon stroll. Not even breathing hard.

"You did my work for me, guys," he called, his voice eerily calm. "You made it to the top."

They froze, confused.

"It would have been annoying for me to carry you guys up here." Marek's Eastern European accent carried a direct, no-nonsense rhythm. "This is where it ends for you."

A chill ran down Cyrus's spine, his heart thudding in his chest as Marek's words sank in. No wonder he walked so slowly as they frantically ran up the slope.

Marek continued, his tone chillingly casual. "It'll look like you all fell. And you died by accident."

"Just a little closer," Cyrus whispered, barely audible over the wind.

The towering man took another step up the slope, then another, drawn in, unaware. With his last step, the sun caught the mirror at just the right angle and a sudden flash of light exploded across his eyes.

Marek jerked back, snarling, one arm rising to shield his face. "What the—"

Cyrus didn't wait. He sprang forward, opening the dirt-filled sock, and spraying the dirt outwards. The cloud of fine rock dust and dirt hit Marek square in the face.

Marek roared in pain, clutching at his eyes as the gritty powder filled them. He staggered backward, blinking wildly, hands clawing at his face.

"*Fuck!*" he bellowed, stumbling near the edge.

Without hesitation, Charlie swung the thick beam of wood, aiming for Marek's midsection. There was a thud and the massive man doubled over, lurching forward.

Seizing the moment, Dana's arm shot out, and she hurled a jagged rock with everything she had. It sailed through the air, hitting Marek squarely in the face with a sickening *smack*.

Cyrus didn't waste a moment. His heart pounding, he darted forward, his legs burning with the effort. He grabbed Marek's leg from behind, yanking it with all his strength. Marek let out a startled grunt.

At that moment, Marek lost his balance, his massive frame tipping dangerously to the side. Time slowed as the giant man teetered, unable to catch himself. Marek toppled backward, in the direction of Reckoning Grove, disappearing down the steep hill as if the earth had swallowed him whole.

Marek's scream reverberated through the air as his body hurtled down the cliff, crashing into rocks and scattering debris in all directions. The sound of his body hitting the rough terrain was sickening, a series of thuds and groans that dragged on forever. For a brief moment, Cyrus, Charlie, and Dana stood frozen, staring in disbelief at the place from where he had fallen. They could hardly believe it.

They peered down at him. He lay still at first. Then, to their horror, he moved. Through the haze of dust and debris, Marek's hulking figure slowly rose from the chaos of rocks below. His eyes were wild with rage, his face twisted in fury as he stumbled to his feet, ignoring the pain and the blood. With a guttural shout, he started climbing back up the cliff, his movements inhumanly determined.

"Jesus," Charlie muttered. "What is he, made of concrete?"

Cyrus's heart hammered in his chest. "No way," he muttered, shaking his head in disbelief. "How is he—?"

But they had no time to process anything. Marek's massive form was scrambling up toward them with dogged intent. The three of them backed up instinctively, eyes wide. They couldn't outrun him, not now. Their chance to escape was slipping away.

Cyrus's voice trembled with urgency as he looked at Charlie and Dana. "There's no way we can make it back to Reckoning Grove with him coming after us from that direction," he said, his chest heaving with each breath.

Cyrus could hardly think. His gaze darted around, scanning for a way out, but the steep incline and the vast openness left them exposed. "We can't even go around the mine with those steep slopes on either side. We won't make it out of this valley before Marek gets up here, and he'll see where we've gone. Our best choice is to try to hide in the mine."

They sprinted down the slope and headed toward the mine, skidding to a halt at the gaping adit. For a moment, they stared into its shadowy mouth, catching their breath. Dana dropped her backpack to the ground, her hands fumbling as she pulled out a small flashlight. She clicked it on, casting a thin, jittery beam that barely pierced the darkness ahead.

Exchanging a glance between them, they reluctantly took their first steps inside, the cavern swallowing them whole. Ten feet in, the daylight faded completely, and the mine's interior took on an eerie, unnatural stillness.

The flashlight beam, thin and unsteady, barely cut through the darkness ahead. Shadows slid along the irregular rock walls, their surfaces flashing briefly as the light wavered in her hand. Every few steps, the beam caught on a wooden support frame set into the passage, old and splintered, the beams bowed and strained under the weight of the hill above.

30

Cyrus, Dana, and Charlie crept through the stifling mine tunnel, hunched low as the mine's suffocating walls pressed in. They shuffled slowly, nerves frayed, listening with their breath held, straining for any sound that might signal Marek's approach from behind. Eventually, they entered a small chamber where the tunnel split into two narrow passages.

They paused, whispering in a hurried debate. Cyrus suggested the left tunnel, which sloped downward.

Dana aimed her flashlight at the right tunnel. "This one's wider," she murmured. "Maybe that gives us better odds."

Charlie, eager to break the tension, said, "Well, as my teenage niece says, L is for losers, so . . . right it is."

Dana and Cyrus smiled, appreciating the tiny bit of levity.

They headed into the right tunnel. As they moved farther in, the passage narrowed, forcing them to hunch down and squeeze between jutting rocks. Soon, they reached a spot where part of the tunnel had collapsed, splintered wood framing a tight gap barely wide enough to crawl through.

They whispered, debating what to do next, but froze at the unmistakable sound of Marek's heavy footsteps growing louder behind them. With a silent, urgent glance at each other, they agreed there was no turning back. Without a word, Dana went first, gripping the flashlight as she squeezed through the narrow gap left by the cave-in.

A heartbeat later she shrieked, sharp and close, and at first Cyrus had no idea why, the tunnel was so dark it felt solid. Then a mass rushed at him, like a black blanket sweeping down the passage, only it wasn't cloth at all, it was a thousand separate bodies. The swarm broke over him, bats pouring past like shredded fabric come alive, wings brushing his cheeks and ears, thudding into his shoulders, skittering through his hair. The sound was all wingbeat and rush, a dry, papery flutter, and a sharp ammoniac tang that hit his nose as the cloud boiled by.

Through the blur he saw them swarm Dana. One clipped her cheek. Her flashlight spun out of her hand. The beam skittered over rock, jumping and stuttering, then winked out. Total darkness swallowed the tunnel.

The bats eventually streamed away. Silence fell hard. In it, Marek's footsteps began to carry toward them again.

All three dropped to their knees, palms sweeping cold stone. "I can't find it," Dana whispered. "I'm sorry."

"Don't worry," Cyrus said, keeping his voice low and steady. "Keep crawling forward. We have to lose him."

He found her ankle and held on so he wouldn't lose her in the dark. Behind him, Charlie's fingers closed around Cyrus's heel. They moved as a chain, inch by inch into the crawl, guided by touch and breath.

Cyrus shifted to his knees. The space was still dark, but it no longer pressed on his ribs. For a moment he let the relief settle, then he listened. Marek's steps were softer now, somewhere back in the tunnel.

Just then Cyrus's heart sank as he heard footsteps behind him grow louder, then Marek's voice, low and chilling in the dark.

"Sorry, guys," he called, sounding almost regretful. "I can't leave you to ruin this for me. I'm pulling out the main beam, you'll never get out once this comes down."

A guttural groan followed. Marek must have been straining with effort somewhere behind them. Then came the splintering crack of timber torn from its brace.

An instant later, an ear-splitting roar tore through the shaft as the ground shuddered beneath them. Dust exploded into the air, thick and choking, while the wooden supports overhead cracked and failed in rapid succession. Rocks fell hard and close, slamming into the ground and skidding past them as the walls shifted and pressed in. In the darkness, Cyrus heard Dana scream, the sound nearly lost beneath the crash of stone and splintering wood. He stumbled forward, hands out, lungs burning as the passage behind them collapsed in on itself, sealing shut with a final, crushing rumble.

Now cut off, they stood in absolute blackness. The air was thick and stale, as if every ounce of oxygen were being swallowed by the weight of the mountain around them. The silence was so complete that even their panicked breaths felt muffled. The darkness was impenetrable, leaving them no sense of where they were, where to turn, or how deep this mine truly went.

31

The space they occupied was completely, utterly black, like being inside the belly of a great, yawning void, and the longer they sat in it, the more it felt like it was closing in on them. There was nothing else. No other sensation. Just the weight of the dark pressing down, suffocating them. No escape. No light.

No one spoke for a long time. The only sound that existed in that space was the rapid, shaky breaths of the three prisoners of the mine, shallow and erratic.

Just then, Cyrus felt a slight shift in the air, a barely perceptible chill. But it was enough to make him pause. A breeze. Barely noticeable, but unmistakable.

"Do you feel that?" he asked.

Dana whispered, her voice hoarse, barely above a breath. "People who constructed mines sometimes created ventilation shafts to let air through. God, I hope that's what that was; we have to try to move that way."

The words gave them something to cling to, thin, uncertain, but hope all the same. Slowly, cautiously, they edged forward, hands sweeping against stone, knees dragging over the rough ground, following the faint promise of air. Cyrus took point, sliding his hand along the jagged walls. Then something pale flickered ahead, so faint he almost missed it.

At first, Cyrus thought the light was a trick of his eyes, a lingering ghost of darkness giving way. Then it steadied. Shapes began to form. Stone. Space. The tunnel widened ahead, and the air felt cooler, easier to breathe. They moved faster now, no longer scraping the walls, until they stepped into a larger chamber. Pale light spilled across uneven ground and scattered rock, revealing a broad, natural space, more cave than tunnel. Cyrus lifted his head, tracking the source of the light upward. That's when he saw it.

In front of them, an old wooden ladder leaned against the vertical stone wall. At the top of the ladder, they saw a sliver of blue sky where the opening in the cave breached the surface. The ladder's rungs were splintered, some broken or missing entirely, leaving only half of its original structure intact. It didn't look safe, but it was their only way out.

"Alright, this is it," Cyrus said, his voice steady but tinged with the weight of their situation. "We have to climb. I'll go first, and when I get to the top, I'll call down to you."

After a pause Dana nodded, though neither she nor Charlie looked entirely convinced.

Cyrus stepped forward and climbed onto the first rung. It creaked under his weight but held. He took another step up, his boots finding purchase as he slowly ascended. But when he reached for the third rung, it snapped. Cyrus sagged but held onto the side rails with his hands.

"Well, don't use that one," Cyrus called down with a grim laugh, his voice barely masking the anxiety in it.

"Great, thanks, Einstein," Charlie muttered under his breath, his voice still holding a thread of sarcasm.

Cyrus kept climbing, the ladder trembling with each movement. Rungs creaked and cracked, but he pushed on, his heart pounding in his chest. His muscles burned, the exhaustion of the tunnel still lingering in his limbs. Finally, after what felt like an eternity, he reached the top, gripping the final rung tightly before hauling himself over the edge of an opening only a yard in diameter.

He squinted into the bright sunlight, blinking to adjust his vision. It was so quiet, too quiet, and the bright blue sky above him seemed like a cruel reminder of how close they had been to the surface, yet still so far from safety. The rugged mountains stretched out before him, dry dirt and sparse brush dotting the landscape in every direction.

As Cyrus stood on the edge of the hidden cave opening, taking in the stark mountains and the endless expanse of dry brush, his heart sank. A sharp, unnerving sound cut through the still air, the unmistakable crunch of footsteps on gravel. His gaze shot to the right, and his blood ran cold.

A silhouette emerged from behind a hill, barely visible against the bright sky, but unmistakably human. Marek.

32

At first, only Marek's head appeared over the rise of the hill, broad, shaved, unmistakable. Then, slowly, the rest of him emerged, massive shoulders rising like a mountain cresting the earth. He moved with a deliberate, unhurried pace, each step measured as he descended toward the base of the cliff, his hulking form growing clearer with every stride. A cold shiver ran down Cyrus's spine. Marek was like some unstoppable machine from a science fiction movie.

Cyrus looked down at his friends, his heart pounding, then up at Marek. The sight of the hulking figure made his stomach drop, a cold wave of dread crashing over him. The tunnel, the darkness, the constant threat of death, it was too much; everything was working against him.

He was trapped. Cornered.

A wave crashed over him, a sensation he'd felt before, so vivid it took his breath away. He was back at the airport gateway with the overwhelming sense that the world was closing in, pressing down on him from all sides. One directive flashed into his mind, simple and clear: RUN. The urge was primal, a desperate pull in his chest. The only way out of this, the only way to escape the suffocating weight of everything around him, was to run. Run and leave it all behind.

How easy it would be to leave this trouble behind. If it were only him, he would pick a direction and outrun Marek. He could vanish into the mountains, slip away into the rough terrain, and back to the solitude of hiking alone. Back to the life he had before, before Brent, before this mess. Just him and the trails.

But as he stood frozen between the pull of escape and the weight of responsibility for the others still below, a darker thought cut through the fear. He shouldn't have left his family the way he did. At the time, he told himself that he had left to protect them. Then, disappearing, wandering the country with nothing but a backpack, was a kind of penance, a way to atone for the mistakes that had torn their lives apart.

Now, staring at Marek in the open air above the mine, he saw it differently. The real trial had never been about the miles he walked or the nights he spent alone. It was about facing fear without running, about proving he wasn't the coward he had once been. That was the lesson he had been chasing all along.

Charlie and Dana had become like family to him in ways he hadn't expected. They had stood by him, even when they had no reason to. To abandon them now, to slip back into the habit of running, would undo everything he had fought to learn.

Cyrus clenched his jaw, the weight of his past pressing hard against the resolve forming in his chest. No. He wasn't going to run. Not now. Not when he finally had a chance to do something right.

Cyrus crouched at the lip of the shaft, the cool breath of the mine rising against his back. His lungs burned, but his mind stayed sharp, cataloguing options the way he once had as a doctor. He had no weapon, no leverage but his own body. Against Marek's sheer size, that meant nothing.

But speed, speed and quick thinking, that had saved him before. It would have to save him now.

He scrambled up the slope, boots slipping on loose gravel, heart hammering in his chest. At the crest he spotted it: a block of basalt the size of a kitchen chair, jagged and sun-baked, easily eighty pounds or more. If he could push it down the far side, away from the mine shaft, it might sound like the three of them had bolted in that direction. It could draw Marek off, just long enough for Dana and Charlie to escape.

He set his shoulder against the rock, muscles screaming as he shoved with everything he had left. The block shifted, teetered, and then thundered down the far slope. The crash echoed like a landslide, the sound rolling across the high desert. Perfect. To Marek it would sound like prey fleeing fast and heavy-footed, away from the shaft.

Cyrus staggered back, chest heaving, sweat dripping into his eyes. For a moment, time stretched. The echoes of the falling boulder faded into silence. He squinted down the bottom of the slope he had just come up, toward the shaft's dark mouth, waiting for a glimpse of Dana or Charlie emerging. Nothing. No movement.

Then, footsteps. Not one, but steady, deliberate thuds crunching on stone. Marek was climbing towards him. The rhythm carried up the steep slope, closer with each strike.

Cyrus clenched his fists, jaw tight. *Come on. Run. If I keep him here, you'll have the time you need.* But the shaft below stayed empty. *Where are they? I need to buy them more time.*

He spun, searching for anything, a weapon, a tool. His hands closed on a shard of basalt no longer than his forearm, sharp-edged and rough. He gripped it like a club, knuckles white, and planted his feet against the sliding gravel.

The shadow rose over him before he was ready. Cyrus swung, the shard cracking against Marek's arm with a hollow thud. It barely slowed him.

A hand like an iron trap seized his shoulder and yanked him around. Marek's face loomed inches from his own, pitiless, unmoved.

"You think you can trick me?" Marek's voice was low, almost bored. "BGI scouted the mine long before you ever came down here.

We logged the shafts, the breaks, all of it. The air shaft wasn't exactly a secret."

Cyrus twisted, swinging again, desperate, but Marek batted the stone away with casual force. Cyrus's chest heaved as he gasped, "Marek, listen to me. I saved your life. Nothing's more important than that. The people at Reckoning Grove love you. You're part of a family there. You don't have to do this."

For a fraction of a second, something flickered behind Marek's eyes, regret, maybe, or only the shadow of it. Then his jaw tightened.

"I'm sorry, Cyrus," he rumbled. "But life's more complicated than that. I have other . . . obligations."

His grip clamped tighter, and with terrifying ease he hurled Cyrus down the slope.

The world flipped into a blur of sky and rock. Cyrus's body skidded and bounced, pain tearing through his ribs and arms. He slammed hard against the earth, rolling to a stop in the dirt just yards from the ventilation shaft's entrance.

Dust stung his eyes. He tried to crawl, but Marek was already descending after him, massive and relentless. In an instant, Marek's hands clamped around him, hauling him up like a rag doll. With a brutal heave, he flung Cyrus back into the narrow ventilation shaft he had just climbed.

Cyrus plunged into darkness, the walls of the shaft rushing past in a blur. Air tore at his clothes, his stomach dropped, his arms flailed wildly for something, anything, to hold. His fingers scraped stone, then wood,

Suddenly, his elbow caught a rung of the ladder. The impact exploded through him, the crook of his arm crushed against the hard edge. Pain shot up into his shoulder, white-hot and blinding. His body swung, jerking to a halt, tendons screaming, his breath ripped from his chest.

The rung groaned but held.

His body screamed in pain, but he forced himself to hang on, gasping against the ache in his arm. Above, the light from the shaft was cut off by Marek's looming silhouette, his shadow blotting out everything.

Cyrus twisted his head, blinking into the gloom below. Dana and Charlie were still there, pressed close to the wall, their faces pale in the half-light.

"Why are you still here?" he rasped, his voice raw.

Charlie shook his head. "Dana started climbing out, but then she saw Marek come past the shaft. We couldn't run then. He would've seen us."

The truth sank in like a stone. They were all cornered now, nowhere left to go.

33

Marek's voice echoed into the darkness, low and cold. "Cyrus, I'm sorry. You saved my life, and I am grateful," he said, his tone reluctant. "But this is how it has to end."

He stepped closer to the shaft entrance, his looming figure casting a shadow over Cyrus, Dana, and Charlie.

"I don't want to do this," he muttered, more to himself than to them. He exhaled sharply, as though the weight of what he was about to do was sinking in. "But I have to close off this entrance," he continued, his words carrying the burden of inevitability. He sounded apologetic, as if he were explaining a painful duty rather than a deliberate act of malice.

The threat hung in the air before he added, his voice still tinged with reluctance, "Don't worry. The oxygen will run out quickly. It will be . . . painless."

Marek glanced up at the sky as if searching for something, before looking back down at the three of them. "The sheriff won't bother looking for you," he said, his voice harder now, as if to convince himself. "He thinks you're a bunch of . . . idiots, some wacky cult. They won't even know where to start."

Cyrus's heart pounded as Marek went on, his voice steady, almost matter of fact. "I've already told BGI that the symptoms are showing up. Once the people here find out there's arsenic in the water, once they understand that's what's been making them sick, they won't have a choice. They'll have to leave. Someone from BGI is already on their way right now to notify them and buy the land cheap."

The realization hit Cyrus like a punch to the gut. They weren't collateral damage. They were obstacles.

Marek didn't pause. "After that, BGI moves in and starts mining."

The three looked up helplessly at Marek, the weight of their fate settling on their shoulders. Their breaths came in shallow, panicked gasps; with the tunnel they'd come through collapsed behind them, there was no way out, no escape.

Thud!

The dull sound of impact rang out through the still air. Marek's head jerked forward, his body buckling under some force. He then collapsed to the ground out of view. For a moment, the world held its breath.

Cyrus, Dana, and Charlie stared at the empty circle of sky in shock, unable to process what had just happened. Then, from above, a familiar face appeared. Grady's head poked over the edge, his eyes wide.

"Well, well, well," he muttered with a grin. He gazed at Cyrus six feet below him, still grasping the ladder. "What's up, Doc? Guess you guys didn't expect to see me here."

Disbelief gave way to manic relief. Their laughter bubbled up uncontrollably, a mixture of exhaustion, and joy. Cyrus, still clutching the ladder with one hand, nearly lost his grip as a fit of laughter made him wobble dangerously. It felt as though every tense, unbearable moment that had led up to this was finally bursting out of him.

Dana wiped tears from her eyes, still snickering, and even Charlie let out a few breathless chuckles. It felt unreal. After everything, after the mine, the danger, Marek, they were alive. They made it.

After a few moments, they managed to regain their composure, still grinning like fools. One by one, they climbed carefully to the top of the rickety ladder, shaking with fatigue and stress. When Cyrus reached the top, his heart skipped a beat. Marek lay motionless on the ground nearby, a deep gash on the back of his head where the blow had struck. His body was still, the weight of his unconsciousness a relief.

Grady looked out of place as a hero in his dirty jeans and a faded *Neil Young* T-shirt, the fabric torn and smudged with grime. He had an old green military backpack slung over his shoulder and a large shotgun cradled in his arms, the barrel aimed at the ground as he watched them climb from the hole.

For a moment, Cyrus stood unmoving, his breath caught in his chest. He never imagined seeing Grady in this situation, especially after everything that happened. He wasn't sure if it was relief or something else entirely that rushed over him, but seeing Grady standing there brought a sensation of exhilaration.

"Nice to see you again," Grady said, his voice low but with a hint of a grin tugging at the corner of his mouth.

"How in God's name did you get here?" Cyrus asked.

Grady shifted the shotgun in his hands, drawing in a breath as he looked down at them. "I've always gone with my gut. First time you showed up, Doc, I figured you were trouble. Turns out I was dead wrong about you." He gave a short, humorless huff. "But Vlad . . . my gut never stopped itching about him. The way he looked at people, the way he kept slipping off. I couldn't pin it down, but I knew he was hiding something. That's why I lit into him at the bonfire. You probably remember me shouting."

Cyrus nodded faintly, the firelight argument flashing back.

"After that," Grady went on, "I started watching him closer. He kept tailing you three, and it didn't sit right. So, I figured I'd tag along, see what he was up to. Honestly, I didn't know if I was being smart or just stubborn." He gave a dry, crooked grin. "At least I'm glad I took along some insurance." He patted the stock of the shotgun.

His expression sobered. "And then, when I heard him, heard him admit what he'd done to the water, what he planned for this place . . . that's when it clicked."

He glanced at Cyrus, awkward but earnest. "Guess I should've seen it sooner. But I'm glad I was here when it counted."

Cyrus winced, shifting against the rock, but managed a faint smile. "Timing's what matters. And you were right on time."

Grady tipped his head toward the way out. "Let's get out of here, for real this time. Let me ask you though, why do you all keep calling him Marek?"

"It's a long story," Cyrus said. "I'll explain as we hike out of here."

As Marek stirred, groaning and blinking groggily, Grady pulled out a length of rope from his pack. Cyrus, Charlie, and Dana didn't hesitate, working together to bind Marek's hands securely behind his back before he could fully regain his strength.

Grady kept his shotgun trained on Marek, his jaw set and eyes watchful as they walked back to Reckoning Grove. The group moved without a word, the silence broken only by the crunch of boots on pebbles and dirt and the occasional muttered grumble from Marek.

34

They finally reached Reckoning Grove in the late afternoon. As they neared the farmhouse, people slowly gathered, their eyes widening as they took in the sight: Marek, disheveled and defeated, with his hands tied and face still streaked with blood and grime from his fall down the slope and the ensuing scuffle; Grady, looming behind him with a shotgun aimed squarely at Marek's back; and, behind them, the battered trio who looked both exhausted and vindicated.

A growing noise in the distance interrupted the low hum of conversation, a helicopter. Heads turned as the sound grew louder, the blades slicing through the air toward them. Moments later, the helicopter came into view, descending into the open field behind the farmhouse. Dust swirled as it landed, its blades slowly winding down.

A man stepped out, dressed in a tailored suit that looked out of place against the rugged backdrop. His jet-black hair was perfectly styled, his features composed, controlled. As he strode toward them and the helicopter's noise faded, it clicked into place for Cyrus. This had to be the BGI representative Marek said was already on his way.

The gathered crowd fell silent as the man approached. He

paused for a moment, his gaze flickering over Marek, his expression briefly shifting from confusion to realization. But just as quickly, he composed himself, his face smoothing into polite detachment. He stepped past Marek as though he were not there, addressing the members of Reckoning Grove.

"Ben Bueker," he introduced himself with a polished smile. "I'm the head of a mining company, BGI Inc. I heard about the unfortunate situation here, some of you falling ill, some even maybe dying . . . and I came to offer my assistance. I suspect there might be an issue with the water supply. I'd like to help by purchasing this property for a generous price and supporting your relocation to a place better suited for your wonderful commune."

The group stared, the tension thick in the air.

Charlie stepped forward, his jaw tight with anger. "You can go to hell," he spat. "We know everything Marek was doing. Everything *you're* doing."

Ben blinked, his expression shifting to one of mild surprise. "I'm sorry," he said, his tone measured and calm. "I don't understand. Who's Marek?" He gestured vaguely toward the bound man, a polite, dismissive smile on his lips. "I've never met him in my life."

Marek's jaw tightened, his frustration boiling over. He took a step forward despite the shotgun at his back, his voice low and dangerous. "Cut the crap, Ben. You think you can walk in here, flash that fake smile, and make all this disappear? You'd better go back to where you came from and get ready. They know about us poisoning the water. The shit's about to hit the fan at BGI, and it'll land right in your face."

Ben's polished demeanor faltered as Marek's words hung in the air. His smile faded, replaced by a strained expression. He suddenly realized that Marek was tied up, with an armed man standing guard. His gaze shifted to the crowd gathering around them. The murmur of the members of Reckoning Grove grew louder, their unease and suspicion palpable.

Before anyone could respond, Calvin stepped forward, calm and deliberate. Without a word, he drew back and punched Ben square in the face.

Ben staggered backward and hit the ground hard, stunned. For a moment, no one moved. Then he scrambled upright, blood pouring from his nose, already staining the collar of his pristine shirt. He fumbled a handkerchief from his coat pocket and clutched it over his face, eyes wild, composure gone.

"My wife *died.*" Calvin's voice was harsh with contempt. "She died because you poisoned our water."

Without another word, Ben turned on his heel and strode quickly back toward the field, his movements now hurried. The murmurs turned into shouts, but he ignored them, his pace quickening as the blades of the helicopter began to spin again.

The crowd watched as the helicopter lifted off, the roar of its blades drowning out the rising voices of the commune members. Dust swirled through the air, obscuring Ben's retreating profile as the chopper carried him higher and higher. Within moments it was gone, leaving behind a tense hush.

35

Two nights later, the dining area was filled with the clatter of dishes and the easy rhythm of conversation. Sunlight slanted through the windows, catching motes of dust and the soft steam rising from mismatched mugs.

Grady leaned back in his chair, patting his belly. "I'm just sayin', if this whole commune thing doesn't work out, Dana's lasagna could get her a Michelin star, assuming the inspectors don't mind ducking under barbed wire and dodging conspiracy theorists."

Everyone laughed, and Dana shook her head. "You're welcome for the lasagna, Grady. Don't push your luck."

She turned toward Charlie, grinning. "You should've seen the look on your face when we walked into the FBI field office with Marek. You never mentioned that was the first time you'd actually interacted with an FBI agent."

Charlie flushed, glancing down at his plate. "Yeah, well," he muttered, "we couldn't exactly take him to the sheriff, could we? Half the time those guys just brush us off like we're crazy."

Grady raised an eyebrow. "Half the time?"

The table erupted into laughter again, the warmth of the moment briefly pushing aside the weight of everything they'd just been through.

Charlie leaned forward, a sly grin on his face. "Still not sure where you disappeared to, Cyrus. One minute we're walking into the FBI office, next minute you're gone like smoke."

Cyrus smiled, unbothered. "Leave no trace," he said, reaching for his mug.

Dana laughed. "Seriously, though, I couldn't believe how fast those agents sat up when they realized we figured out Vlad was Marek and how BGI was involved."

Grady let out a low whistle. "Man, I wish I could've been there to see it. My cousin works over at the sheriff's office, he told me the sheriff was up in arms, swearing it was his jurisdiction. But the FBI agent in charge just spelled it out: Marek had come from Nevada on orders from BGI. Crossing state lines, corporate conspiracy, poisoning a water supply, that put it squarely in federal hands. Sheriff didn't have much left to argue after that."

Dana nodded. "Yeah. And Vlad . . . as soon as he knew they were onto him, he cracked. Cut a deal within the hour. Spilled everything —BGI's plan to poison the water, force us off the land, make it look like a bunch of us just got sick and vanished."

The table fell briefly quiet, the weight of the charges settling in. Then Charlie shook his head.

"Unbelievable," he muttered. "And here I thought he was just a quiet guy who liked to haul firewood."

Grady leaned forward, his voice dropping a notch. "Yeah, I read in the news that after Marek spilled the beans, they raided BGI headquarters. Found all kinds of documents, stuff about sneaking into the old mine, taking samples without permits, testing things they had no business touching."

He shook his head slowly. "They even had detailed notes about the plan to poison us. Actual memos. I mean, who writes that stuff down?"

Charlie let out a low whistle.

"I still feel a little sick from that arsenic stuff," Grady added, rubbing his chest. "Doc Bronson's supposed to stop by here later. Said he's bringing the real antidote; the one James was trying to get into the water supply before everything blew up."

A hush settled over the table for a beat, the gravity of what they'd survived pulling their thoughts inward.

Dana grinned. "The best part was watching the FBI agents try to deal with Charlie when they came to Reckoning Grove to go through Marek's stuff. He swore up and down they were here to plant surveillance devices."

She shook her head. "Made them let him watch every second while they searched. Like he was some kind of homegrown inspector general."

Cyrus raised one hand. "No, the funniest part was when he asked them, completely serious, if he could see their 'directed energy weapons.' Said he knew they had 'em. Devices that could sap your life force. *Psychic vampire tech.*"

Charlie blinked, then sat up straighter, clearly unashamed. "They do have them," he said defensively. "They just didn't admit it."

The table burst into laughter again, even Dana covering her face with one hand, trying not to spill her tea.

The laughter eventually faded, trailing off into soft smiles and the clink of dishes. A stillness settled over the table, the kind that comes when people have said what they needed to say.

Dana looked down at her hands for a moment, then lifted her gaze. "Everything's set for the ceremony tomorrow," she said quietly. "For Brent. For Cindy. For James."

The weight of those names hung in the air for a long moment.

"It won't fix everything," she went on, "but it'll help us start putting this nightmare behind us. And maybe . . . start building again. Stronger this time."

No one said anything right away, but there was a shared understanding in the silence, something solid, something healing.

Outside, the wind rustled through the trees like a gentle reminder: the worst had passed, and a new day was coming.

36

At the far edge of Reckoning Grove, a group of slender aspen trees stood, their golden leaves trembling like coins catching the last warmth of the season. Among them, a few tall pines held their place in stillness, dark and steady. In front of the aspens, the grass had faded to a muted ochre, soft and dry underfoot like a well-worn blanket. At the edge of the clearing lay a simple bronze marker, flush with the ground and inscribed with the words: "In memory of Kevin Daugherty, Let Reckoning Grove Thrive." Beside it, a fresh mound marked a new burial site, still unmarked but heavy with meaning.

The members of Reckoning Grove gathered chairs from the main house and arranged them in a loose semicircle near the gravesite. They sat quietly, some with heads bowed, others staring ahead, waiting. The main house stood in the background, unchanged, its windows dark and still.

Calvin rose from his chair, the ceramic urn steady in his hands. He stepped forward and paused, facing the group, taking a moment before he spoke.

"I spent most of my life," he began, his voice low and steady, "wondering if I truly belonged anywhere. Always aware of my skin color. Of how I stood out. Of where I didn't fit."

He glanced down at the urn, his fingers tightening around its curve.

"Then I met Cindy." His lips twitched with the shadow of a smile. "It was like . . . something clicked into place. Like a piece of me I didn't know was missing just, found its home."

He looked out at the faces around him, eyes shining.

"And when we came here, to Reckoning Grove, we both felt it, that the puzzle was finally complete."

His gaze dropped to the urn once more.

"We will always miss you. Always love you. Cindy Ellingson."

With slow, reverent hands, he opened the lid. The ashes lifted into the breeze in a silvery plume. Calvin watched until the last of them faded, then turned and made his way back to his seat.

As Calvin sat down, the group fell quiet again. After a brief pause, Dana stood. She moved to the front, her steps slow and deliberate, eyes down as she gathered herself. When she reached the graves, she stopped and looked out at the others, then back down. She took a steady breath before speaking.

"James left behind a world that always seemed like a storm to him. Before he came to us, he said he was in a space that never quite felt like home, one where he struggled to find his place. But when he came to Reckoning Grove, he found something different. Here, he was part of something good, something new and wonderful. He became part of our family."

She paused, her eyes misting. "James will be remembered not for the struggles he brought with him, but for the way he helped protect our community when it mattered most. He chose to stand with us, to defend what he believed in, even when it was hard. I hope that brings him the peace he was looking for."

When Dana finished, Cyrus and Charlie then rose slowly from their seats to join Dana at the front. Charlie, with his graying hair pulled back into a ponytail, had dressed up for the occasion in his own way, wearing a dark, worn sports jacket over a faded plaid button-down, and old jeans that were dusty around the knees. The jacket was rough around the edges, but Charlie wore it like it was the finest thing he owned.

Beside him, Cyrus stood holding a small container with a fitted lid. He wore simple jeans and a borrowed sport coat a touch too big in the shoulders, giving him an air of youthful formality both modest and sincere. Though he was shorter than both Dana and Charlie, his grounded stance revealed a quiet resolve that made him feel taller; he now believed his presence deserved to fill more space than his frame took up.

Cyrus considered the small container in his hands, thoughtful. "I only knew Brent for a short time," he said, "but it feels like I knew him my whole life. I miss his laid-back way of seeing things, his curiosity about the world, like he was a child learning it all for the first time."

He looked out at the other members of Reckoning Grove. "I think we all miss his humor and the way he was always there to help, no questions asked. Most of all, we miss him as a friend."

He passed the container gently to Charlie, who took it with both hands, looking down at it for a long moment. "I appreciated Brent for a lot of things, but mostly because he listened." He glanced up with a small, wry smile. "And, well, I was thinking these ashes could help with, you know, cleaning up the chemtrails that HAARP keeps spreading, "

Dana nudged him with her elbow, a firm but gentle reminder. Charlie blinked, catching himself. "Oh . . . right. Sorry." Sheepishly, he cleared his throat, returning his focus to the purpose of the moment.

He lifted the urn and started to turn the lid. Cyrus reached out and caught his wrist, gentle but firm. Charlie looked up, surprised.

Cyrus leaned in and whispered urgently, "Dude, if you open it like that, we'll all get Brent's ashes in our faces."

Charlie froze. "Oh. Right," he said, then shifted a few steps so the breeze was at his back. He unscrewed the lid and tipped the urn. The ashes lifted and drifted away, carried cleanly toward the shimmering leaves of the aspens.

Later, they all gathered outside, tables and chairs from the dining area carried out under the open sky, forming a makeshift dining space in front of the house. They piled their plates high with spaghetti and meatballs, and passed around Dana's fresh bread, its warm, yeasty scent mingling with the fresh high desert air.

Laughter and voices filled the air, the somberness of the ceremony lifting as people leaned close, sharing stories and memories over the hearty meal. It was a scene of joy and closeness, a simple, shared meal turning into an unspoken celebration of resilience and community.

Cyrus and Charlie draped their jackets over the backs of their chairs while they settled into the relaxed comfort of shirtsleeves before tucking into their plates of spaghetti and Dana's fresh bread. Grady, in his plaid button-down, sat with a napkin tied around his neck like a bib, the front stained with bright red smudges of marinara.

As the hum of conversation flowed around him, Cyrus found himself scanning the room, quietly counting. Eighteen. *It had been twenty-one before Brent died,* he thought. *Before everything unraveled and the roller coaster began.*

Then his eyes landed on Gus, who sat animated and beaming, surrounded by Danny, and some others. The small group leaned in eagerly, peppering him with questions as he gestured enthusiastically.

Curious, Cyrus turned to the others. "What's going on over there?"

Grady chuckled, setting down his bottled water. "Before Gus moved here, he was some big-shot lawyer. Used to sue corporations into the ground. He says he made more money than God before he realized he hated the work."

Cyrus's eyebrows shot up. "Really? So why's everyone so interested now?"

"Well," Grady said, a sly grin spreading across his face, "now that BGI's being prosecuted for poisoning our water, and for what happened to James and Brent, Reckoning Grove's gonna sue the pants off them. Gus figures he can squeeze enough out of BGI to pay off the whole loan on this place. Could be enough to keep us debt-free and independent for years."

Charlie let out a low whistle. "If Gus pulls this off, Reckoning Grove will be sittin' pretty. The tables have turned. I love it when the little guy wins."

They all nodded, satisfaction settling over them. Across the way, Gus met Cyrus's gaze and gave him a small, confident nod before diving back into the flurry of questions.

After dinner, everyone pitched in to help carry the dishes, tables, and chairs back to the house. The evening air grew cool, and the lingering sounds of laughter and conversation slowly faded as the group dispersed. Dana and Cyrus, feeling the need for quiet time, slipped away from the bustle.

They walked side by side, their footsteps soft on the earth, as they made their way past the water reservoir. The evening light cast long shadows across the still water, its surface reflecting the deepening blue of the sky. They walked in comfortable silence, the sounds of nature surrounding them, the chirping of crickets, the rustle of leaves in the breeze, and the distant call of an owl.

When they reached the creek, the sound of running water filled the air, a calming, rhythmic flow that washed away the weight of the day. The creek bubbled and splashed over the rocks, its coolness inviting. Dana stopped for a moment, crouching to dip her fingers into the water. Cyrus stood beside her, watching the water flow, both of them lost in the peace of the moment.

His mind drifted back, unprompted, to a warm summer afternoon years earlier in Ithaca, New York. He could feel the sun again, how it poured down gently through the trees, casting shifting shadows across the grass. The sound of rushing water echoed softly in the distance, constant and calming.

It had been his first real date with Juliette. They were both off for the summer during grad school, Cyrus had enrolled in a biochemistry course before deciding to pursue medicine, and Juliette had been in the same class. One conversation turned into two, and then a study session, and then this, an impromptu picnic beneath the towering cliffs of Taughannock Falls.

They sat side by side on a blanket spread over the grass, the mist of the falls occasionally drifting their way, cool and refreshing in the summer heat. They'd brought sandwiches and too much fruit, most of which remained untouched, the conversation having taken over everything else.

At one point, Cyrus glanced over at her, and the moment burned itself into his memory.

Her brown hair hung past her shoulders, shifting faintly in the breeze stirred up by the waterfall. Strands danced lazily in the sunlight, catching little flecks of gold. Her skin glowed warm under the sun, highlighting the freckles scattered across her cheeks, the elegant line of her neck, and the way her eyes, those deep, intense brown eyes, looked straight through him. Not in a way that made him feel exposed but understood. Like she could see past everything he said and everything he tried not to say.

She smiled at him, easy and open, and something expanded in his chest, a quiet certainty he didn't need to explain.

In that moment, sitting under a perfect blue sky beside a waterfall and a woman who cut through every defense he had, Cyrus realized he wanted to spend the rest of his life with her.

At the time, he truly believed he would.

Dana turned to Cyrus, her face soft in the twilight, her voice gentle but firm. "The remaining members . . . we've all agreed you should stay," she said, her words carrying a weight that settled between them. "If you want to."

Cyrus paused, gratitude blending with something heavier in his chest. "Thank you," he said, his voice low. "You all . . . you're like family to me." He took a breath, feeling the familiar pull of something unspoken, something that had lingered in him for weeks. He looked down at the ground; his thoughts scattered for a moment before he gathered them again. "But I've got something I need to make amends for, unfinished business I can't ignore anymore. I need to face it."

Dana's gaze faltered, a shadow crossing her features, but she nodded slowly, as if she had been preparing for this moment, even though it hurt. "I understand," she murmured, her voice thick with emotion. Sadness filled her eyes, but also a quiet acceptance.

Cyrus looked at her one last time, the weight of his decision pressing against his chest, but leaving now was something he had to do. "Maybe . . . maybe I'll be able to come back later," he added, perhaps to reassure himself more than her.

Dana didn't answer right away, but the soft smile she gave him spoke volumes. "We'll be here," she said, her words simple but filled with meaning.

Epilogue

Cyrus stood by the trailhead, a large, worn backpack slung over his shoulders. Because of his small frame, the pack seemed oversized, its straps pulling tightly across his chest as it hung low on his back.

He reached into his pocket and drew out a creased photograph, the one he had carried since the beginning. The paper was soft at the edges from being folded and unfolded so many times. In it, he and

Juliette stood side by side, her long dark hair catching the light, her smile steady, unguarded. Beside them was their son, Feridoon, or Freddie, as everyone called him, grinning wide at six years old, while Samira, still a toddler then, leaned against Cyrus's leg as if the world were safe as long as he was there.

For a long moment, he studied their faces. At the start of his journey, the photo had been a wound, a reminder of all he had abandoned. Now it felt different. He no longer saw a man defined by fear or shame, but one who had learned to stand his ground, to face threats he once would have run from. The image marked more than loss. It showed who they were, who they still were. And it forced him to admit the truth he'd been circling for months. He had left them when they needed him most. But for the first time, he felt capable of standing in front of them, saying what needed to be said, and accepting whatever came next.

After a moment, he folded the photograph with deliberate care and slid it back into his pocket, close against his chest.

His gaze lifted to the sign ahead of him, a simple, weathered marker that read *Pacific Crest Trail.* He had already walked more than a thousand miles to get here. All that remained was to follow the trail north to Mount Hood, then turn west toward Portland, Oregon.

He adjusted the straps of his pack, the weight settling against his shoulders. Without looking back, he stepped forward, the crunch of his boots on the path carrying him into the waiting day.

THE END

Thank you for reading The Doctor's Reckoning. We hope you enjoyed spending time in this world as much as we enjoyed creating it.

As independent authors, reader support makes an enormous

difference. If you found this story meaningful, entertaining, or thought-provoking, we would be incredibly grateful if you took a moment to leave a review on Amazon or Goodreads. Even a few words helps more than you might realize.

Thank you for reading, and for supporting independent storytellers.

— Arsheeya & Ari Mashaw

Acknowledgments

To Danielle and Aliya: thank you for putting up with the two of us while we debated every sentence, rewrote whole chapters, and requested at all hours: "what do you think about this rewrite" countless times. Your patience, humor, and love kept us going.

We are also deeply grateful to our colleagues and friends who generously shared their time and expertise to help ensure the technical accuracy of Cyrus's story. In particular, we would like to thank Kian Banks, MD and Matthew S. McCoy, MD (Without you Brent would never have made it out of the forest), Jessie Fan, MD (If it weren't for you I may have chosen a #3 Miller blade), and Laura Ryan (for helping figure out the *how* behind the crime). Your thoughtful guidance helped shape some of the book's most important details. Any remaining errors are entirely our own.

About the Authors

Arsheeya Mashaw is a physician and author who began his career in the Shenandoah Valley of Virginia and now practices in Portland, Oregon. He has published short medical memoirs in scientific journals and in the literary magazine *Hippocampus*. His fiction draws on his medical background and his love of suspense, rural settings, and human connection.

Ari Mashaw, his son and co-author, is an artist and writer. Their partnership began unexpectedly during a car ride when a conversation about storytelling turned into a shared creative project. That moment grew into *The Doctor's Reckoning* and a creative journey they continue together.

Outside of writing, Arsheeya and Ari love spending time with their family skiing, mountain biking, surfing, and exploring the Pacific Northwest.

Find us on www.doubleApress.com

Also by Arsheeya Mashaw and Ari Mashaw

Cyrus's Story Continues

A new chapter in the series is coming soon and we'd love for you to be the first to read it.

Join our newsletter at:

www.doubleApress.com

and get a free early chapter from the upcoming book.

You'll also receive bonus content from The Doctor's Reckoning, including deleted scenes and behind-the-scenes material just for readers.

www.ingramcontent.com/pod-product-compliance
Lightning Source LLC
LaVergne TN
LVHW041906070526
838199LV00051BA/2523